LOVE,
HEATHER

ALSO AVAILABLE BY LAURIE PETROU

Sister of Mine

Between

LOVE, HEATHER

A Novel

Laurie Petrou

CROOKED
LANE

NEW YORK

Copyright © 2019 by Laurie Petrou.

Published in the United States by Crooked Lane Books, an imprint of The Quick Brown Fox & Company LLC.

Crooked Lane Books and its logo are trademarks of The Quick Brown Fox & Company LLC.

Library of Congress Catalog-in-Publication data available upon request.

ISBN (hardcover): 978-1-64385-116-7
ISBN (ePub): 978-1-64385-117-4

Cover design by Melanie Sun
Book design by Jennifer Canzone

Printed in the United States.

www.crookedlanebooks.com

Crooked Lane Books
34 West 27th St., 10th Floor
New York, NY 10001

First Edition: October 2019

10 9 8 7 6 5 4 3 2 1

For all the kids hiding in stairwells.
I see you.

*I*t sits at the bottom of her bag like an anchor and a parachute, this thing that will hold her steady and set her free. Over and over, she reaches in and touches it, weighs it in her hand, feels its cool potential, its power. She withdraws, Not now. Not yet. The school buzzes around her. Laughing, joking, pushing, shouting. No one knows what she can do. No one has ever known.

MARCH

1

Episode 65 00:00
Hello, cinephiles, FlickChick subscribers old and new!
I'm back, bringing you the best in rants and raves about
classic and contemporary films, basically anything that
strikes my fancy. In this episode, we talk high school
films. That melting pot of cool and cruel, that place that
will change you for the better and worse. It's where mem-
ories are made, right? In my mind, the very best high
school movies are from the eighties and nineties. Of
course, that might just be because of the clothes and
music. Let's dig in.

Lottie and I are in her room, listening to records. She is sitting on the floor with her eyes closed, and I am flopped on
her red-and-blue-checkered bedspread, looking through a
pile of albums. I look around me at the assorted piles of crap.

"God, your room is a disaster," I say.

She doesn't move, but chuckles. "I like to think of it more
like a statement of self-expression. It's like an art installation."

"Uh-huh. And what's that cup of juice on the dresser, a science experiment?"

You could chart my life from the things in this house like rings on a tree. Lottie lives on a nice street, just one over from mine but prettier, happier. Huge trees, houses from the eighties. She has a great tree house that her dad built when we were kids, I think to make up for the fact that neither of us has siblings.

Lottie is not some hipster who just got a record player. It was in this room before she was, like a dinosaur bone found in a cave. The room still has some of the relics of their life before they had Lottie: an embroidered wall hanging of a bright-yellow bird, a small painting of a little creek and some shadowy trees, and a big poster for Pink Floyd's "Dark Side of the Moon."

Over the years, Lottie and I have combed through all of her parents' old records, laughing at the covers and playing songs from unheard bands. Now she buys new vinyl, too, and she spent her birthday money on decent headphones—not wireless, but still good. I'll come over sometimes and she'll be sitting in the room hidden behind a pile of crap, and I have to follow the cord to locate her.

I flip through a book from a stack on her night table. She looks over.

"You can borrow that if you want. It's really good."

"Okay, maybe," I say, knowing I won't, tossing it back on the pile. Lottie's into books the way I'm into movies—these have always been our "things." "Stevie and her movies," my mom proudly tells anyone who will listen, "and her best friend is a reader. Go figure."

Sometimes Lottie will start reading a book while I'm there, and I'll just go hang out with her mom. Half the dinners we have together I have helped prepare. I know where they keep their peeler and their measuring cups. My dreams take place in this house. I know its nooks and crannies, the scary basement that still has drawings on the unfinished drywall that Lottie and I did as kids, and the cupboard where all the board games are kept. I know the smell of her room like it's part of me, and until she got taller than me, I used to see her closet as an extension of my own.

"Are you going to Paige's Saturday night?" she asks me now, turning around.

"Yeah, for sure," I say quickly, then pause, picking at a thread on her comforter. I have been nervously looking forward to it all week. I've never been to Paige's before, but the way she says it, I kind of wonder if Lottie has been there already. The hierarchy of the high school status system is always shifting on me lately, and Paige is definitely higher on the ladder than either of us. I try to make up some ground. "I didn't know you were, too," I say. "That's cool."

"Yeah, she asked me ages ago," Lottie says, turning back. "She told me to make sure to invite you."

I nod and look at an old Dolly Parton album. "Yeah, no, she already told me. A while ago, actually." Tit. Tat.

We don't say anything for a bit, just listen to the record reach its end, the needle skipping over and over with a *tic tic tic* until Lottie gets up and presses the return button. The needle moves sleepily to its start position and I wonder when they were hanging out without me, what they were doing. I picture Paige telling Lottie to invite me, and wonder if it really was ages ago, and how long exactly.

We just started hanging out with Paige and her friends a few weeks ago. At one of the school dances, Lottie and I were standing like ninth-grade nerds off to the side, near the exit, when Paige walked in from outside and kind of lurched into us, spilling some Coke from a bottle she was carrying.

"Oops!" She laughed, while I shook out my sleeve. She smelled like booze, so I figured it wasn't actually Coke. Breanne Davis called her over from a few feet away, where she was standing with a bunch of guys. Paige ignored her and came up really close to me with a pained look on her pretty face. "I am *so* sorry," she said, her voice solemn. Lottie laughed, but not meanly, and Paige looked at her shyly and said, "Do you guys want some?"

"What the hell," I said, and Lottie stared at me, surprised. I shrugged, taking a pull of the bottle. She grabbed it from me and did the same.

Woepine High is like every other school: there's a hierarchy. The cool, the pretty, the athletic, the slim, and sometimes, if all else fails, the kids with hustle and brains and chutzpah—they rise to the top. If they are cruel, they punish people for what they wear and how they talk and who they hang out with. They troll kids behind the curtain, throw shade grenades in the backstage life of their little handheld war zones: on social. And if they are displeased, they will drop you, ghost you, and swipe you into nonexistence; they do things that no one can really put their fingers on, because they are slippery. But when they are nice, they bless you with a smile, a dazzling sparkle of glitter that you find later in the cuffs of your pants, pick out of your teeth, and choke on if you're not careful. I know all this. I knew the risks of falling from a height if I tried to climb the ladder. And yet.

By the end of the night, we were dancing with Paige, Breanne, Aidan, and a bunch of other popular kids I'd only ever watched from a distance. It was the best time I'd had so far in high school. We shared the drinks, hid from the teachers, stumbled into the bathroom laughing, danced until we were gasping and holding each other up.

"I like this girl!" Paige announced, holding my hand up to the others like a boxer who'd won a match. "She is *so* funny!"

And I preened in the spotlight in spite of myself, hamming it up, being a goof, being funny and fun and up for anything. I winked at Lottie, who rolled her eyes and laughed at me. She knows how insufferable I am. Our whole lives, it's been me looking for a spotlight and Lottie calming me down. Lottie danced with her hair in her eyes, her long body bending and swaying; she was careless and happy and drunk. We walked home that night, the two of us, laughing at how funny life was. I mean, what were the chances that Paige would crash into us in the first place?

"They aren't that bad," I said, looking at Lottie's flushed face. "I always thought they'd be total bitches, because . . . I dunno . . ."

"Yeah, they were cool. Who knew?"

And we grinned our rummy grins, the darkness of the night pouring out in front of us.

I woke up with my first hangover, and thought it had been a one-time thing, spending the evening with those people, but then I got some texts from Paige. I guess I'd given her my number. She sent a lot of barfing emojis that made me smile to myself like I'd gotten a gift. That one night turned into others, and they're my friends now, and Lottie's too. And yes, I know that it could be short-lived, that it could be pulled out from under us, but so far, so good, although it feels like Lottie has more leverage with them than I do.

Maybe it was a fluke that they happened to be together without me. Still, I hate being left out, and I have to remind myself to keep it in check. I think back on whether there were times when they asked me to do something and I couldn't. There is a yawning space between me and Lottie. She hasn't seemed totally herself lately. She's quieter, distracted, and every time I ask, she says she's fine. I dunno. Things seem different. I can't get a read on her, and I feel a creeping uneasiness.

Lottie stretches her long arms over her head. She is tall and lanky, and she would make a great model or high jumper, not that she wants to be either. Her features are a bit weird, some people say: her nose is very long and straight, her eyes wide apart and kind of big, her lips unintentionally pouty. But people are noticing her, whenever we're out together, and usually they look like they can't quite make up their minds if she's pretty or not. She has this exotic look about her, like a doll made of buttons and string, nothing exactly where it should be. My mom says she will grow into her face eventually and be a real looker. She also says using a brush wouldn't kill her. Even now her hair is a pattern of knots running down her back like angel-hair pasta that's been sitting on the stove too long.

She presses her hands on her lower back and lets out a groan. "I have a ton of homework." She sticks out her tongue and rolls her eyes, and I smile.

"Yeah, me too. I should get going." I remember when we would have begged her parents to let me stay later. I look at her, her face relaxed into something distracted and a bit sad. "You okay?" I ask.

"Hmm? Oh, totally, yeah." A weak smile. Not totally okay. I know her enough to know this, but not why she's not telling me.

"Okay . . . well, talk to you later," I say.

She nods, grabbing her phone, already lost in whatever is on there—Paige?—as I leave her room. I catch my reflection in her mirror as I leave and see a girl, anxious and worried. I run a hand over my hair and shake off the feeling that a door is closing on me.

On my way out, I pass Lottie's parents, who are sitting at the kitchen table, drinking wine and talking about something in low voices. Her mom, Mrs. Sherman—or, when we're not at school, Rhonda— waves to me. Her short messy hair is sticking up all over, and her shirt is unbuttoned at the top. This is what it looks like when you unwind after teaching at a high school all day, I guess. None of the other kids get to see this version of her, and I like that. Except Lottie, of course. But I know Rhonda personally; they only know who they see in the classroom. She's my homeroom teacher. Maybe most kids wouldn't want their best friend's mom as their teacher, but she's more like my favorite aunt, or like a mom I sometimes wish my mom was like.

"You leaving, kid?" she asks.

"Yeah," I say, looking at them both. Usually they invite me for dinner at this point, but there is an awkward moment when no one says anything and then Rhonda pushes her chair out and says, "I'll walk you out." She's never "walked me out" before, and this weird formality seems like one more person just trying to get rid of me, like she doesn't want to risk me overstaying my welcome.

Jacob smiles vaguely. "Bye, Stevie," he says, his voice quiet. "Sorry, we're just . . ." He doesn't finish his sentence, but shrugs, and rubs his face.

I've never seen them like this; they are usually pretty cheerful and happy, at least for the most part. I mean, they're not perfect. I've known them my whole life, so I've seen them grouchy and irritable with me and Lottie and each other. Sometimes Rhonda hangs out in the garage by herself late at night, the smell of weed and the sounds of Van Morrison wafting through the vents. Jacob says she has an artist's temperament, which I guess means she sometimes gets really down and needs to hang out alone. Occasionally she goes on weekend "retreats," whatever that means. But she always comes back smiling and refreshed, her old chipper self. As a couple, they are happier than most people I know. They laugh, they spend time all together as a family, they seem to actually enjoy each other.

But right now, there's something in the air between them. Jacob gets up and leaves the kitchen. Rhonda watches him go, then looks back at me with a tight smile.

"Sorry, having kind of a serious talk here." I don't know what to say, but then she changes tack quickly, taking a big breath and blowing out her cheeks. "So!" she says brightly, "Everything good? Other classes at school treating you all right?" She follows me down a few stairs to the front door. What is going on?

"Oh yeah. A-okay."

"You been hanging out with that Paige and her girl-boss Breanne, too?" Rhonda looks back toward the kitchen distractedly.

"What? Oh, ha. Yeah, a little, I guess."

"Yeah, they've been coming around here to see Lottie. Well, Paige comes, mostly."

"Oh yeah?" I put on my shoes and feel my face flush with jealousy, but I'm not even sure of whom. My house is so close, but Paige has never come by, and I am surprised that Lottie's been having Paige over without me. My thoughts are interrupted by Rhonda's chatter.

"Are they good people? I mean—are they 'our people,' Stevie?" She laughs. "I don't want you or Lottie running with a bad crew."

Rhonda has always treated me like one of the family, so of course she's looking out for me. These parents are like better versions of my own, and Lottie has always been like my sister. For good or bad, up and down, we've just always been together. Our parents are friendly, if not friends, and for our whole lives they've driven or walked us together to sleepovers and dentist appointments, to movies and parks. I have gone stretches of having dinner at Lottie's house more than my own, and when my dad left two years ago, Rhonda and Lottie doted on me like I'd lost a limb.

A couple of months ago we were all playing a semiregular round of Settlers of Catan—Rhonda, Jacob, Lottie, and me—and Lottie and I teamed up to beat them, using whispered strategies and hard-won tactics. Rhonda threw up her cards in defeat and said, "You beat us again! God, you're thick as thieves! Jacob, hide the valuables, I think they're old enough to perform a coup."

Lottie fist-bumped me and said, "Slinky."

"Rex," I said, both of us referring to our nicknames that had originated after our first viewing of *Toy Story* as kids.

Jacob started to disassemble the board and said, "I have seen our future, Rhonda, and it is bleak and involves us working for these two."

That feels like a long time ago now.

Are they good people? Rhonda just asked.

I look up and say, "Yeah, they're cool."

"Yeah," she says, almost to herself, "that's what I'm afraid of." She looks at me closely and cocks her head. "You okay, short stuff?"

Rhonda and her goddamn sixth sense.

"Yep, for sure." I grin moronically, trying to reassure her. "I'm just a little tired." I watch her taking in this excuse I've been trotting out to parents for years. I expect that she'll push me on this, but then Jacob calls out to her in a flat voice:

"Rhonda? Are you coming back?"

She looks back up into the house and bites her lip. "Sorry, yep, I'm coming," she calls, and turns to me, and looks like she's forgotten what we were talking about.

"Well," she says, hands on her hips. "Have a good night, Stevie. Don't forget you can go your own way," she says, quoting a Fleetwood Mac song that she never tires of singing to me. I look back toward the kitchen and see Jacob with his head in his hands. I don't like the looks of this.

I smile at Rhonda. "Ha. Yes. Well," I say, opening the door. "See ya tomorrow."

"All right, kiddo. See you. Bright and early!"

2

Episode 65 1:25
Friendships in the high school film arena are some of my
favorites. You've got your jocks, your nerds, your goths
and art freaks. Best friends are the glue that holds our
heroes together and helps them navigate the social lad-
ders, like Tai and Cher in Clueless *and Cady, Janis, and*
Damian in Mean Girls. *People always say that these will*
be the best time of our lives, and that the friends we
make now will last a lifetime. Well, here's hoping, right?

I love old films—the ones between 1975 and 1995 are the best.
They are my passion. My raison d'être, but also the reason for
my YouTube channel, FlickChick.

"Hiii, Stevie's fans!" My mom waves into my computer
screen every time she knows I'm working on a video. She
doesn't seem to get that I edit her out later or that no one knows
my actual name on there. I don't really tell anyone about my
channel. It's like I have my own little YouTube secret identity,
where I can live out all the movie obsessions I have.

Sometimes Mom rifles through my movies, which used to be hers, holding them up and offering her nonexpert opinions. "Oh, this one is soooo good," she might say, and then yell, "'Give my daughter the shot!'" in her best Sally Field voice, shaking the *Terms of Endearment* cover. My mom and dad and I used to watch movies all the time—tons of them from every genre, starting with their own pretty substantial stash, then moving beyond that. We had movie marathon nights where we binged on everything from well-known rom-coms to cult classics to more contemporary stuff. Mom's favorites were always the cheesy romances and tearjerkers, but she also loved a good *Friday the 13th* sequel. She would dig her nails into my arm and scream at every predictable scary part. She grew to love *Carrie* after many screenings.

I'll never forget her saying the last time we watched it, "Poor girl. She had no choice. They forced her hand." She even helped me transform an old white dress we found at the Woepine Benevolent Fund into Carrie's blood-stained gown for Halloween one year. Our bathroom floor still has red in the grout between the tiles.

It felt weird at first, having a "family movie night" without my dad, but Mom tried so hard to make it fun. She went all out. Bought so many kinds of popcorn that we both felt sick halfway through the movie.

Once, she got a "Detention Pack" of DVDs for cheap, featuring *Ferris Bueller's Day Off*, *Some Kind of Wonderful*, *Heathers*, and *The Breakfast Club*. We laughed at it but watched them all the time, quoting the movies at each other, singing the songs in snippets, making references that no one else got. Mom's a hairdresser, with a salon in our basement, so sometimes she and I would get right into it: she'd crimp and style our hair like

16

the eighties, hair-spraying it so much we could hardly breathe. During that time, whenever one of us wanted in the bathroom, the other would shout, "Keep your tits on!"—our fav line from Carrie.

Sometimes, in those early days, I felt guilty that Dad was missing out, but I figured I could stay at his place and have a movie night there whenever he wanted.

"Eleanor's dying to get to know you better," he told me, about his girlfriend, "and there's a pull-out couch for you if you want to stay over."

It's never really worked out for me to do that yet. They're busy running a coffee shop together a bus ride away from here, in his new place in Hamilton. But Eleanor's nice, from what I remember. She'll probably make a great mom when they decide they want to start a family together, which Mom has been preparing me for from the get-go: "Trust me, that child bride of his will want to have a baby," she says, and I remind her that they're not married, and she says, darkly, "Yet."

When he left, he made a big speech about how he and Mom never went anywhere, never traveled, never went to Europe or museums or art shows. He didn't ever strike me as the kind of person who liked art, especially if you took his clothes into account, although he does wear a slouchy toque pretty often now. Mom said the gig was up later when it was discovered that he had a "lady friend" who happened to work with him. I don't know if they go to a lot of art galleries; when he comes to visit every few months, we mostly just go to Boston Pizza. I kind of feel sorry for him, but I miss him, too. I liked having him around, liked how he always joked with me, and tickle-tackled me as a kid. He was like having a much older brother, and then he was gone, having his own life. He texts me though and calls sometimes, and it's like hearing from an old friend from camp. He'll ask about Mom and tell me that Eleanor says hi. It always makes me smile, and we talk about how we should see each other, but then it fizzles out. He never seemed to mind that we did family stuff without him. If he called when we were watching a movie, he'd laugh and tell me he missed me and to call him when it was over.

Still, it was good when it just was us at home, before I started high school, before she started dating, before everything changed. Mom works from home, cutting hair in our basement in a room she's outfitted with all her hairdressing gear. I could always count on her to be at home for me when I wasn't at school or Lottie's. It felt like it was the two of us against the world, hanging out and having movie nights. Sometimes Mom says we should do it again, but it never happens anymore. She's hardly ever home. I started my own channel a couple of years ago so I can talk about films with other people like me out there. It fills up the time when there's no one else around. It's not totally the same, but it's something.

I send the latest episode of FlickChick out into the world and get dressed for Paige's.

I text Mom, who is on a date with a guy she's been seeing.

Hey mom. Going out. Won't be too late

Kk hun. Think u will like this guy!!!!!! U can meet him soon! Where r u going?

W lottie to a friends house

Have fun. Can't wait for u to meet new guy. He's amazing

I don't have high hopes for whoever my mom is dating this time. Ever since she put herself "back out there," she has sent so many versions of that text—YOU'RE GOING TO LOVE HIM! HE CAN'T WAIT TO MEET YOU!—telling me the guy is a real winner and maybe the one, but they've all turned out to be douche-bags. I feel bad for her. Her taste in men is shit, but mostly because she doesn't have high enough standards. Even my dad, who I have to have some loyalty to, is honestly a bit of a loser sometimes. This new guy's name is Reg, like in *Riverdale*, and that's how I picture him, as the kind of guy no girl with a brain would like. I mean, maybe I'll end up being wrong, but I bet I'm not.

I ride my bike over to Lottie's house so we can go to Paige's together. I ring the doorbell and wait, scrolling through Insta-gram until I hear the door opening.

"Hey kid," Rhonda says, smiling. "Lottie's already left for Paige's."

"Oh . . ." I say, dumbly. I just assumed we'd head over at the same time and now feel stupid.

"You guys get your signals crossed? Hard to imagine," she laughs, gesturing at my phone, "since that thing is like another appendage." Her voice softens. "Sorry, hon. Did Lottie say she'd be here?"

"No, no. It's okay. I'll just meet her there." I smile and turn around, grabbing my bike by the handlebars.

I've never been to Paige's house before, but she pinned it on a map in the text, so I study it on my phone before hop-ping on my bike and heading in the direction of the newer developments in the suburban maze of our town. The wind is whipping through my jean jacket, and my hands are getting cold, so I'm relieved when I find that it's not that far. But her neighborhood feels like a different planet. Even the streetlights are stylish—they stand up straight like skinny supermodels with their noses in the air. The houses are big and the lawns have short green grass without any crap lying around on them. I pull my bike into her driveway and lean it carefully against the brick of the house.

"Fancy . . ." I murmur under my breath as I push the doorbell and a series of chimes ring out.

Paige opens the door while yelling and laughing at something over her shoulder. She glances at me, smiles, and gives me a singsongy "He-ay." She turns around, disappearing into the house, her hair swinging at her back. I quickly kick my shoes off and follow her into the basement, which is huge and loud with music.

There are a bunch of kids there from school; I recognize a few of them, including this new girl, Dee, who I've been seeing around. She's leafing through a paperback from a bookshelf behind her, ignoring everyone else. She doesn't say much, like she's too cool or something, but always seems to be watching, judging. She looks at me now and holds my gaze until I look away.

People are sprawled on chairs and sofas, arms and legs all over each other, hanging on and off one another's words and bodies. Lottie is there, sitting on a couch and talking to some blond jock, laughing. I try to shake off the hurt feeling of her coming without me, but it's got teeth and won't go so easily. She looks so comfortable, and I wonder again if she's been here before, and when, and what she and Paige did together, and why they didn't ask me. God, why do we do this? I consider leaving, cutting my losses and bolting, but then I look at Lottie again, and a spurt of competitive juice surges in me. She waves briefly, happily, when she sees me, and then turns back to the guy.

If she can do this, I can. I get a couple of nods and some blank faces, and I sit on the floor and try to act normal. Maybe this is my chance to branch out a little, to reinvent myself, or at least experience a taste of what all those eighties movies were getting at. I look bored and bob my head to the music.

I am nothing if not an overachiever. I have always gotten top marks, excelled at everything I decided I wanted, even if it elicited eye rolls and exchanged looks. Me, Stevie, holding up an award with a shit-eating grin: that is the essence of every photo in our house. Lottie, on the other hand, has some kind of genetically blessed blasé, an effortless ease that has only ever made me look like I am trying too hard. You can't really overachieve while being cool, which is the terrible paradox for people like me, but I'll be damned if I won't give it a go. I'm here, aren't I?

Nothing really seems to be happening, but everything matters. We watch YouTube on the gigantic TV, one video leading to the next, from silly to gross, unpredictable to funny and back again. People call out vids, take over, type in their favorites. I laugh loudly and throw out a couple of corny jokes. I relax, sort of. I drink a beer handed to me and try not to worry that they'll find my channel, which I keep pretty secret from my real life. I wonder if Lottie has ever mentioned it, or if she will. I mean, not that I'm hiding it, but I don't publicize it to anyone else in my real life. What would they say if they learned I have a super-geeky cinephile channel that I've been operating since I was twelve? I sip my beer and keep my eye on the exit. People scream and laugh. Someone spills a beer on a rug, and Paige freaks out, and there is momentary drama. I catch Lottie's eye and she laughs and shrugs, and so do I. Easy peasy.

Breanne is there. She's Paige's best friend, I guess, but sometimes it's hard to tell. She is the unspoken grand pooh-bah of this gang. Paige is more like her second in command than her friend, it seems.

"You look different," I hear her say to Paige, who kind of freezes.

"What do you mean?"

Breanne purses her lips and cocks her head. "I don't know. Maybe you're just tired."

Paige's hand goes to her face. She is pale and delicate and looks like you could blow her over.

"Or maybe it's just me!" Breanne laughs. "God, I have been up for practice like every morning at five."

Breanne is on the rowing team. Her toned arms, sun-kissed hair, and freckled face—she's like Athlete Barbie. Sometimes she arrives in the cafeteria with her teammates after a competition, laughing loudly and cheering. They're celebrities.

Paige smiles weakly and asks if anyone wants anything. Lottie swallows the end of her beer and raises the can, shaking it back and forth. She is so comfortable here. Not like—

"Stevie?" I hear someone say, and I look around and it's Breanne, smiling, and everyone is laughing. I didn't hear what she said, but I laugh, too, taking a sip of beer, feeling my face go red to my ears.

Paige scoots back into an oversized chair and snuggles up under the arm of her boyfriend, Aidan. She keeps swatting away his hand when he grabs her boob. He laughs at her and does it over and over again. He looks over and winks at me. I grin like we're friends in on the joke, but then kind of hate myself for it, because he seems like that kind of likable asshole who can get away with anything. But I'm working so hard here, determined to fit in. Anything goes.

And then, in a moment straight out of a movie, someone suggests we play truth or dare. There is *ooh*ing and *ah*ing and giggling, and I say, maybe a little too loudly, "Oh yeah!" and everyone laughs.

I catch Breanne's eye and she stonewalls me, then switches gears and says, all bubbly, flipping her hair, "Okay, let me go first!" She points a hand at Aidan, who hams it up, pretending to choke on his beer, and she demands, in a booming voice like some evil queen, "Truth or dare?"

"Truth, always truth," he laughs, shrugging at this no-brainer.

Breanne strokes her chin, appraising him. Someone tells her to bust his balls, and another says, "Go get 'im, Bree!" She looks around the room now, sizing everyone up. I squirm a little when her eyes rest on me but hold her gaze, smiling. She nods now, arriving at a question.

"Okay, okay, Aidan," she says, and there is nervous giggling. "Do you vow to tell the truth, the whole truth, and nothing but the truth, so help you God?"

He puts one hand on his heart and another on his crotch. "I swear," he deadpans.

"Okay." She leers at him, then darts a glance at Paige. "Where is the most public place you've had sex?"

A whoop blows up in the room, and I notice that Paige looks uncomfortable, like she is actually shrinking. He looks at her with a scamp's smile before saying, "Sorry, baby, but this is for research purposes. Gotta be honest." There is a long pause, then, "And I can *honestly* say that the supply closet in the art room is *very small* but does the job. Or . . . has enough room so someone *can* do the job."

Everyone is howling, except Paige, who has stood up and left the room, which just provokes more laughing, and Aidan shrugs, his hair falling in his eyes. Breanne nods her approval, sitting down with her long legs open, her elbows resting on her knees. She lazily gestures to him, a queen on a throne; it's his turn. He surveys the room, hardly noticing when Paige returns and sits somewhere else. His eyes rove around, and I see them rest on Lottie, and he smiles wickedly. She throws her head back in acceptance, defeat, groaning. He lifts a finger and points at her. "You know the drill, blondie. Truth or dare."

Lottie sighs and sits up, ready. "Okay, fine. Fine, you know what? Dare. Let's go," she laughs, making a *come at me, bro* gesture with her arms.

Without missing a beat, Aidan says, "Kiss that girl." He jerks his thumb at me over his shoulder without looking at me. Unmistakably me. Lottie's eyes bug out and then close in exaggerated agony. I feel the sound of the room, the wild booming commotion surge in my ears and then quiet.

"You are such a pervert, McFear," I hear someone say, as from a distance. It is Aidan's nickname version of his last name, McPhearson.

I am suddenly standing. An opportunity, a stage, a chance, held out to me like a bright thing. Lottie is still on the couch, looking horrified, when I raise a beer bottle to my lips and take a long haul while the room cheers. I cock my head at her, challenging, waiting. I've won already, before she knew it was a contest.

Lottie drags her feet, her eyebrows up up up, moving slowly toward me.

"Come on, I won't bite," I say, swaggering like a cowgirl, bravado making my cheeks sweat with the glow of the perfect spectacle.

I catch the eye of Dee, still in the corner, sitting up now, paying attention, her eyes full of a kind of lusty fire you only get from these charged moments. She tips her head, a smirk of approval on her face.

When she's in front of me, a foot away, Lottie, my oldest friend, my sister from another mister, closes her eyes and purses her lips in a grimace. I seize my opportunity by robbing her of her own. Grabbing her face, taking my cues from all my favorite movies, I plant a passionate, juicy kiss on her, making her arms fling out in surprise. With a smacking sound, I pull back, and over the riot in the room, I look at Aidan and shout, "My name. Is Stevie."

3

Episode 65 2:10
The thing about female friendships is the intimacy. It's not all chummy-chummy-back-slapping bro culture. It's deep. It's real. Intense. They go from 0 to 100 in no time and can fall apart just as fast. They are allies and competitors, each other's biggest fans and liabilities. And, at least in the movies, friends urge the heroes on, push them to do things they maybe wouldn't have done otherwise.

Sunday: It's probably too cold to be at the skate park, but Lottie and I go anyway, pushing our skateboards along the sidewalks on our way, making that rhythmic and satisfying *kajunk* over the cracks as we go. We've been going there since we were old enough to explore the town beyond our streets.

We don't say much for a while, and I need to break the silence.

"Dude, I had to do something! It was just a joke."

"No, I know." She laughs. "I know." We exchange looks and she smiles. "You freak."

I laugh, relieved.

I wish I'd worn gloves. I stick my hands in my hoodie pockets. Lottie sniffs a few times, then wipes her nose on her sleeve.

"Who was that guy you were talking to last night?" I ask.

"Oh. Um, Luke. He's a junior. He's cool."

"Nice." I know who he is, and that he's got a sister in our grade, but not much more. He's one of those hockey guys. Part of a gang of goons I never thought Lottie would be into. I wonder if she likes him but feel I can't ask for some reason. Some kind of wall went up when we started hanging out with all of them, and I'm not sure where the door is.

Kajunk kajunk.

"What's the deal with Breanne?" I ask, feeling my way around for an opening, fumbling for a key.

"What d'you mean?"

"Like, don't you think she's mean to Paige?"

Lottie shrugs, flipping her board up into her hand as we arrive at the park. "Not really. She's all right."

"No, I know. But I guess she seems kind of bitchy sometimes."

"Nah, that's just how she is. She takes some getting used to. You'll see."

She gets back on her board and sails down a ramp. I wonder if she's been getting used to Breanne when I'm not there, and what happens without me.

The park is empty, which is a relief, because we don't really like showing off how bad we are on the ramps while other kids are doing tricks. Lottie does a couple of easy runs, then comes up to sit with me on the bench at the top of the bowl.

"What'd you do after Paige's?" I ask her.

"Just went home, why?"

"I dunno," I say, at a loss.

But the truth is that I do know. We had all been standing around under the streetlamps outside. I had my hands on my handlebars, my legs straddling the bike frame. I was watching Lottie, looking to catch her eye so we could head back into our neighborhood together. She was talking to that Luke guy, and when she finally turned and saw me, she said, "You going?" and I said, "Yeah, you coming?"

"I'll catch up with you later, K?" she said.

"Okay. Bye!" I called out to everyone, and turned my bike around and rode away alone, because what else could I do?

But at home, I wondered if they had all done something afterward, if I had missed out on something.

Lottie looks out past the park where the highway rumbles.

"What's going on with you?" I ask, finally.

"Nothing!" she snaps, then softens and sighs. "Sorry. I just have some stuff going on."

I put my arm around her shoulder, and she leans into me. "What is it?" I ask. "Did something happen at the party? Is it me? Did I do something?"

She chuckles and shakes her head, then takes a deep breath. "No. No, Stevie, it's not about you. Not any of that." She sits back and looks at me, her eyes welling up. "My mom came out. As in, 'out of the closet.'" She uses air quotes.

I suck the air through my teeth. "What?"

"Yup."

"Holy shit." I look at her, testing the waters, thinking of Rhonda, her short hair and button-downs and wondering if I could have guessed at this, and why I didn't know, why she didn't tell us together. I think of how she puts on a smiling face for the world but then retreats to her own spaces. I realize I don't know anything about anything. "Are you okay? Like, how do you feel?"

She shrugs. "I dunno. Like she's been keeping a secret. And that makes me mad, and then I feel like I'm not being understanding enough. It fucking sucks, actually."

"Yeah . . . I get that." I'm kind of feeling the same thing, and it's not even my family. But they might as well be. I feel hurt, too. Part of me wishes Rhonda had told me, and then I realize how stupid that is. They are not actually my family, no matter how many board games we've played together. "What'd your dad do?"

"He cried and then laughed because he said he had his suspicions, and it was kind of a relief. Things have been tense lately. Anyway, he told her he wants her to be happy, but I dunno if he means it. I mean, I think he's in shock. They opened a bottle of wine they'd been saving and let me have some. Then my dad went out by himself and got wasted. I heard him knocking things over when he came home."

"Are they splitting up?"

"They're both staying here for now. But, I mean, it's not exactly sustainable."

I give her shoulder a squeeze, then loop my arm through hers, and it feels like when we were little. I have missed that connection, the warmth of her. "That's hard, babe. No matter what happens."

"Thanks. I'm sorry I didn't tell you sooner. Things have just been . . . weird."

I wonder if she means weird at home or weird with me, but before I can ask, she stands up and gets on her board and flies down the bowl like a pro, like it's nothing. Up the other side, too, her face a mask, like she's bored. I laugh and clap my hands together, and then she hams it up with a big grin, wiggling her hips. I get on my board and try to do the same, but I'm shorter and less coordinated. I bail almost immediately, sprawling out at the bottom, but I'm good at playing dead, too. I stick my tongue out. I lay there while Lottie rolls past me, and I stare up at the sky. The clouds are gathering, pulling together in a big mass. I think about skies in all my favorite movies. Poetic fallacy. Doom. Foreboding. What are these skies telling me? The clouds dart about, avoiding my eyes like shifty assholes who owe you money and have no loyalty. I have that urge, that terrible panicky impotent wish to stop time. To stop growing up and older, to not worry about my friends or my family, to not have to keep up and be strong. Just for things to stop. Stay.

Her third time past me, Lottie mutters, loud enough for me to hear, "Get up, ya loser," and I can't help but laugh, the sound of my voice echoing in the cement bowl.

4

Episode 66 2:30
A note on Mean Girls. *Not just the movie, but the genre.*
Girls just seem to know how deep a small cut can be.
So much can be gained or lost by a tiny faux pas, the
wrong look, an oversight. We watch as our heroes and
villains move around social minefields. Look at Heathers, *for example. I mean, it's hard to know who to root*
for, isn't it?

Lottie and I meet to walk to school together the next day. She smiles and starts walking.

I keep in step and look over at her. "How are you feeling?"

"Hmm? Oh, fine."

"Like, I mean, with your mom."

She smirks at me, then says, "Yes, I know, Stevie."

"Any updates?"

"Updates? Sorry, no." She stops and turns to me. "Look, thank you for being so understanding, but it's cool. I'm fine."

She gives me a little smile, almost like she feels sorry for me, then says, "Let's just . . . We don't have to talk about it all the time, okay?" and keeps walking.

"Um, okay." I hurry to keep up with her. "It's just that, like, I get it. My parents split up, so I know what this can be like."

"My parents aren't splitting up," Lottie says, still staring ahead.

"Well, not yet, but—"

"I'm fine, Stevie," she says, and that is that, even if I don't believe her, and even if she's being a bitch about it.

"Okay, you're fine," I say, and we walk the rest of the way making awkward small talk.

* * *

In homeroom I watch Rhonda and wonder if she knows that I know. She acts no differently to me, but I can't help feeling a little stung. I mean, aren't I like a daughter to her? She's always said so. I wait after class to see if maybe she wants to talk to me, but she just looks up from her desk and asks if I need anything.

"No, no, I'm good," I say.

"You sure are, kid," she says, smiling and getting up as the next class files in. In the hallway, I see Paige giving Lottie a hug.

"Hey guys," I say, joining them as they separate.

"Hey," says Paige. Then she looks at Lottie and says in a low voice, "You good?" Lottie nods, smiling gratefully. "Cool. I gotta get to class. See you guys!" She rushes off down the hallway.

"What's up?" I ask Lottie. Then, "Does Paige know about"—I drop my voice to a whisper—"you know?"

Lottie nods. "Oh yeah, she's been awesome." But before I can register if this is a dig, she says, "Oh shit! I forgot my bag in homeroom!" And she dashes off, leaving me standing there.

* * *

I walk home with Paige and Lottie, who seem to have developed their own rhythm. They are laughing about something Luke said to Paige about Lottie.

"I mean, he is *into* you," Paige says, nudging Lottie, who pushes back, clearly pleased.

"Whatever. He's kind of a player, so . . ."

"So what? Who says you can't be, too? You should totally hit that."

"Totally," I say, a beat late, and the words sound completely fake. Lottie is as big a virgin as me.

Lottie glances at me and says, "Maybe . . ."

Paige looks from Lottie to me. There is silence for a couple of minutes.

"There is, like, no one I want at that school," I say, as if they asked.

"No?" Paige asks. "Why? What are you into?"

"Um. It's not that I'm *into* anything, but I mean, there's no one I like . . ." I finish lamely.

"Right," Paige says, her head bobbing in vague agreement. Soon she peels off to go toward her street, and Lottie and I continue together.

"So . . ." I venture, "Luke, hey?"

"What?" Lottie says. "Something wrong with him?"

"No, not at all."

"I know. He's one of those guys," she says, shrugging, "I dunno. It's just flattering."

"Oh, for sure. I think it's great!" I say, enthusiastically. Ugh. It feels so forced. I'm almost relieved when we get to her house and she waves good-bye. I cut through someone's backyard to get to my street, startled when a little dog jumps against a window, barking furiously.

*   *   *

Later, at home, I take the garbage out, grumbling as I drag the big bin out to the curb. I feel like something is getting away from me. I bite at my thumbnail, which has become irritated and red. I look out toward Lottie's street. The sun is setting, and the tops of all the houses are a pretty red. I pull out my phone. I text her.

Hey hey

Nothing. I walk back to the house and nudge her again.

What r u doing. I'm so bored

No response, which is bullshit. It's not like she didn't see it. We all have our phones with us all the time.

I think of Paige, and then on a whim text her to see if she wants to go to the movies together.

To see what

isle of dogs is playing at the old theater

Yea ok. Want to ask Lottie too

I think about this, and how Lottie would probably say yes to Paige, and then I'd end up feeling like the third wheel.

I feel a little bad, but say, *I think she's got something tonight.*

* * *

I'm nervous, like it's a date or something. I get to the theater and see her standing there, alone. She's tapping away on her phone but looks up and smiles when I jump in front of her and say "Boo!" like an idiot. *Oh God.* I calm down and put my hands in my pockets.

We get the movie tickets and line up to get popcorn.

"Are you a fan?" I ask her.

"Of what?" Paige says. She is so pretty: dark-blonde hair hanging in perfect beachy waves, her face kind of pale and delicate, finely carved cheekbones and thick dark eyebrows that show every expression. "Of Wes Anderson. I've been a fan since I saw *Bottle Rocket.* Love that one. It's so unpolished, you know, like you can see what he'll become?"

"Right," she says, dipping her head to look at her phone. I remind myself to dial it back on the film nerd talk.

I take a large popcorn from the concession stand kid and pop a handful in my mouth, offering some to Paige, who bought nothing. She stares at the popcorn and shakes her head.

"Aren't you hungry?" I ask as we walk into the dark theater.

She looks up at me and smiles. "Hmm? No, I'm fine. Full, actually."

After the movie, we walk through town in the dark, talking. It's cool and fresh out; spring is here. I take some deep breaths. It feels like a treat, being here with Paige, to not be home, scrolling through my phone, making a video, listening to my mom ramble on, or worse, if she's not there at all. I wonder about Lottie and feel a bit bad, but I deserve friends outside of her, too, and it's not like she and Paige include me in everything.

"I mean," I continue, "I can totally see what everyone is saying about the appropriation issue."

"Uh-huh," Paige says, agreeing vaguely.

"But—and I know this is not an excuse—but you can tell that he was trying to do it respectfully. More like an homage, you know?"

"I can't believe they can make that stuff, like the puppets or whatever," she says.

"Right? So amazing! *Fantastic Mr. Fox* took *years* but was so worth it."

Paige looks at me and smiles kindly. "You really know a lot about this shit."

I try to look modest, but it's not my strong suit. "Well, my mom and I used to watch a lot of movies together. Mostly old movies, like from when she was young. She used to love movies. She got me hooked."

"Oh no—" Paige covers her mouth and raises her eyebrows. "Did she die?"

"What?" I laugh. "No, no. Tiffany is *very* much alive. We just don't really hang out together anymore. She's—" I look up, searching for the words. "I dunno. Dating, I guess. Busy. She's just kind of not around anymore."

"Oh. Yeah, I get it. Phew! I thought she was dead!"

I laugh with her, and then we are quiet for a while. We walk behind the main street, the backs of all the shops to us. I have the urge to do something goofy, change the subject. There's a grocery cart outside the Giant Tiger that catches my eye.

"Hey!" I turn to Paige and then run, grabbing it. "Get in!"

She laughs, "Really?"

I wheel it over. "Get. In."

And she does, and I start pushing her around the parking lot, and it's fun. She is laughing and screaming like I'm going to tip her over any second, and I half want to. I do a couple of loops, then stop, gasping. The parking lot is so lonely and quiet, but in a nice way.

And then I remember that I have my Polaroid camera down in the bottom of my bag. I root around for it, finally pulling it out triumphantly.

"But I'm in a shopping cart!" Paige screeches. I get in front of her, and she puts one arm around my neck, and I hold the camera out in front of us. It makes a whirring and spits out the picture, and we laugh and grab it back and forth, shaking it, while the image of the two of us slowly reveals itself. I'm barely perceptible in the darkness, but Paige's pale face glows menacingly, her white teeth like fangs

* * *

When I get home, I'm feeling happy and light. I flop on my bed, but then feel a small guilty twinge. I text Lottie.

Hey girl you good?

There are a few ellipses that start and stop while she responds, then reconsiders.

Finally:

Fine. How was movie.

I jump, my cheeks flushing. Now the whole night feels slightly pathetic, like something they talked about together.

Lottie knows I went out without her and didn't invite her even though I could have, normally would have.

Good. Sorry was last minute

np.

Oh, the period. Never in the history of time has one tiny dot of punctuation been charged with so much passive aggression.

* * *

The next day, our geography class is in the library to work on some research assignment we were given. No one really takes any books out at the library anymore. Everyone works on laptops, pretending to research, but they're really trying to see if they can look up porn and checking which sites are blocked.

There's a table of girls, including Paige and Breanne, sitting in a circle blowing gossip rings up into the low ceiling, their giggles making the pages of the books shiver. I see the way other kids try to step out of their range, but some of them are caught by a snarky once-over or a low comment. Matthew, a freckle-faced, redheaded kid I've known since elementary school, who is heartbreakingly gangly and nerdy, gives them a wide berth as he passes the table, his head dipping. Their eyes follow him with the bored looks of well-fed lionesses. I wander between the stacks, too nervous to invite myself to sit with them.

I find myself in the fiction section, far from the gossiping crowd, and pull out a few well-worn copies of the books I loved when I was a kid. *The Babysitters Club* covers, in their fuzzy worn-and-faded beauty, give me that happy-sad feeling I hate but can't seem to dodge, like some heat-seeking missile in old cartoons. I thumb through one, wishing I was in the tub or on the toilet at my house, with nothing to worry about except whether or not the characters will solve their fairly simple problem by the end of the book. I put it back and lean against the shelves. So much has changed since then. Sadness takes me completely by surprise, and I find myself swallowing against a lump in my throat, wondering what is wrong with me.

"What are you doing?"

It's Matthew.

"Nothing. Just standing here."

"Yeah. I can see why. This is a good place to stand." He leans against the stacks beside me and pretends to enjoy the view of the bookcase directly across from us.

"What are you doing your research project on?" I ask to change the subject.

"The Great Lakes."

"Excellent choice."

"Did you know that Lake Superior contains enough water to submerge North and South America in a foot of water?"

"I did not. Wow."

"I learned that on Buzzfeed."

I compliment Matthew on his hard-hitting investigative research, and we laugh, and I don't feel so bad for a moment. We say nothing for a few minutes, while Matthew looks through an old copy of *The Hobbit*, his finger tracing a map of the Shire. Then Paige sticks her head around the shelves.

"There you are!" She looks at me, smiling, and then starts when she sees Matthew. "Oh—hello."

He nods a greeting, then looks back at me.

"Come sit with us!" Paige says, grabbing my wrist, pulling me away. "Breanne found the most hilarious thing; you have to see."

I'd be lying if I didn't admit how happy this makes me, my face blushing. Matthew raises a hand as I go, shrugging as though I have no choice in the matter, accepting that bullshit with a resigned smile.

5

Episode 67 1:10
High school sports events: football, basketball, hockey.
Bringing all the rink rats and cheerleaders and fangirls
to the yard. The big game is a breeding ground for con-
flict, romance, and puking: the cornerstone of a classic
film.

There are more nights, meaningless and meaningful group hangs at different houses in rotation. Paige's, Aidan's, the backyard of a guy named Josh, even Lottie's place once—when her parents are out.

I notice that her room has changed a bit. I haven't been for a while, and I see that she's taken down a couple of her parents' old posters and replaced them with new ones of bands she likes. There's a picture of her and Paige stuck into her mirror frame. Everyone fingers Lottie's things and *ooh*s and *ah*s over her room and her hoarded books and music, lying on her bed and tossing her old stuffed animals around. Instead of feeling comfortable, as I should be, I'm paranoid, nervous, watching Lottie, who doesn't seem to care at all.

"Oh my God, it's you and Stevie!" screeches Paige, picking up a photo from her dresser. "So cute!" Me and Lottie, wearing jammies and giving each other full-body hugs, huge grins on our faces. I remember that night. It was our first sleepover. We ate so much junk food that Lottie threw up before we went to sleep, and her mom gave us both flat ginger ale and electric blankets, and Lottie's nausea just became another fun part of the night.

"Nice nightie," Aidan says, leaning over Paige's shoulder and popping some chips in his mouth. "You still got that one, Stevie?" he guffaws, and Paige glares at him. He bugs his eyes out with a *what?* expression, then rolls his eyes and throws himself into a beanbag chair.

"Of course I do," I deadpan, "and I'm saving it for a special someone."

They laugh and move on, to someone, something else. Lottie is speaking animatedly to a girl I don't know.

I glance back at the photo, two sweet girls in their pj's. That room, that corner of my world that seemed so untouched by everything else, feels like some kind of fakery now, different and sullied somehow. But Lottie is completely unbothered. *What is wrong with you, Stevie?* I wonder, looking at myself in the mirror, at my half-grown-out hair. It seems like a metaphor for my whole life. Half finished, unappealing, awkward. I notice Dee in the reflection behind me, smirking at something Josh said to her.

I turn around and see there is nowhere to sit. I look out the open door and walk into the hallway. Her parents are out, so I wander down the hall, looking into the rooms. I notice that the guest room bed is made, that there are a bunch of things on the night table: a book, water glass, notepad. We don't have a spare room at my house, but I recognize the signs of a parent sleeping in another room, and my heart sinks a little.

"What are you doing, Stevie? Casing the joint?"

It's Aidan, an unlit cigarette hanging out of his mouth, lighter in hand. He leans his tall frame over and puts his chin on the top of my head, following my gaze into the spare room.

"Fascinating."

I shove him off, scoffing, and head back toward Lottie's room, a girlish shriek wafting over the music.

*   *   *

There's some kind of big hockey game tonight. I'm not into hockey, and our town is on a decade-long losing streak, but games are shorthand for partying for high-schoolers from everything I've learned from movies, and I guess we're no different. Aidan sends a group text telling everyone that we're going to "pre" at his house before we go to the arena.

In homeroom, I look over at Paige, who's on her phone under her desk. I think about the game, and text her:

You going to Aidans? I mean obvs but just making sure

She sends a thumbs-up emoji.
I ask: *Go together?*

Sure lottie and i will grab u on the way

My stomach clenches in a jealous little knot, but I untangle it and send a thumbs-up back her way.

43

My mind is all over the place. I keep trying to find my way into these friendships—new, old, anything—but I meet road-blocks everywhere. Rhonda calls me a space cadet, but there is something of a look of concern on her face. I laugh and apologize, tuning back in. I look at Paige, her head bent in concentration, texting, but not to me.

* * *

I walk home with Lottie, and it feels weird again. She's quiet.

"You okay?" I venture, looking sideways at her as we walk.

"Hmm?" She smiles. "Oh yeah, sure."

She is silent the rest of the way home. Before long we're at her house, and I walk up the driveway with her by instinct, and we flop into the chairs on the porch.

"So," I try, "What's up here? Like, with your mom."

Lottie laughs, darkly, then heaves a sigh. "Well . . ." She looks at me, like she's deciding if she should go on, and then does. "Don't freak out, Stevie. I mean, I know how you can get."

"Okay," I say, agreeing to anything, not knowing what she means.

"Well . . . the latest is my mom claiming that she wants to 'transition.'"

"Transition? Like, become a man?" My mind races. What does that mean? How will that change things? I think of the bed in the spare room; maybe I don't know Rhonda as well as I thought I did.

"Yes. Yes, a man. Like she didn't just drop a huge bomb on us, she needed to do this, too."

"Oh my God, seriously?" Will she still be the same at all?

"Yes. Seriously."

"Why? I mean, like, what'd she say? When did she tell you?"

"I think a few days ago? I don't even know. It's just been crazy around here."

"Why didn't you tell me?" But also, why didn't Rhonda tell me? My chest feels tight.

Lottie looks exasperated. "I'm sorry. I don't know, I'm just trying to figure it out, Stevie. Don't make me feel guilty."

"Sorry, sorry. For sure. So . . . what happens now? What does this mean?"

"I have no idea. She says that this is how she's felt her whole life, and that it was killing her. Like, literally, she said. Killing her." She blinks, and I see that she's holding back tears. "So, there's that. Hooray. Get out your rainbow flags, everyone. I'm going to have two dads."

I reach over and give her a hug, as much for me as for her. I don't know if this is bad news or good news or what. I don't know anything, not anymore. I am certain we need each other. She accepts it but pulls away and wipes her face.

"Does anyone else know?" I ask.

"Paige does," she says, then adds, "She just happened to be here and I told her. Please don't be jealous, Stevie." She looks tired and irritated.

"What? I'm not jealous," I scoff. Totally jealous. And feeling stupid.

She stretches her legs out straight and then sags in the chair. "Okay. Anyway, she said that I should turn my life into a documentary. Like, my life is literally like a movie."

"Yeah . . ." That knot in my gut turns over into itself and becomes the mother of super knots, like the kind you get in

45

necklaces that seem impossible to untangle. She told Paige before me. I look out at the lawn, at the purple sand cherry tree we used to climb as kids and named Martha. I think about Rhonda and how much I love her.

"Maybe . . . It is kind of cool," I murmur.

"Cool?" Lottie looks at me in disbelief.

"Yeah, I mean . . ."

"It's 'cool' that my mom is going to go from Rhonda to Pete?"

"Pete?"

"Yes. Pete. Fucking Pete. Stupid fucking magic dragon name."

"I think the kid was Pete, actually. Or do you mean Puff?" She glares at me, and I shut up for a second. I let it sink in. "Pete . . ." I say again. It's growing on me already, Rhonda as Pete. I look back at Lottie, who is staring hard at me, and I remember myself. "I'm sorry, Lottie; I'm sure this is really hard on you guys." I give her hand a squeeze.

She relaxes a little. "Well, yeah, my dad is about ready to have a nervous breakdown. So much for him being so cool about this. And, she—'Pete,' that is—is going to tell the staff at school soon. And then the students. So I guess the whole school will know. And she's decided to go to another school for next fall to start fresh, but just felt like she couldn't wait any longer to make the transition public because soon we'll start to notice anyway, whatever that means. Can't wait. Fuck my life." She says nothing for a few minutes, and then: "I'm going to drink my face off tonight."

"Right, I hear that," I say, but I am staring straight ahead. Gutted. Rhonda has always been the one person who was unmovable and stable, no matter what else was happening. I feel horrible for being hurt by this, for thinking of how much it will change my life when I should be glad for her, for him, but all I can feel is panic. I look down at my hands and see that they are gripping the arms of the chair, my knuckles white.

* * *

I toss my backpack on the bench by the door and call out for Mom, thinking that I can talk to her about this. She and Rhonda have always been friendly, although I get the feeling that Mom's a little jealous of her, of how much time I spend there.

But just then Mom appears around the corner with a big smile on her face. Too big.

"Hiiii, honey," she singsongs.

"Um. Hi?"

"I'm so glad you're home. There is someone I want you to meet today." She gestures from the kitchen like she's calling a guest onto a stage. "This," she says, pulling on his arm, "is Reg."

Oh God. The guy who walks in is wearing wooden necklaces, a scarf, and a scruffy face. He is clearly trying out that "rugged manly man" thing. He's good-looking, but he might as well be wearing a sandwich board that says I KNOW I'M GOOD-LOOKING; ISN'T IT AMAZING?.

"Hi, Stevie," says Reg, putting out his hand, "I am so pumped to meet you."

Pumped?

"Um, hi," I say, shaking his hand. "Nice to meet you, too."

"I have heard so much about you. Your mom is really proud of you." He grins and puts his arm around Mom, who is smiling like an idiot.

Then she gushes, "Come on, come on! Reg made us dinner!" and pushes me into the kitchen. The table is set and everything.

47

The dinner itself is good. Not the crappy food we usually have. It's lasagna and Caesar salad but made from scratch.

Reg asks me about school, then says, "So! Tell me about these videos you make. Your mom says you've got your own YouTube channel? That is awesome!"

"Yeah," I mumble, glaring at Mom, who has to tell everyone about every bowel movement I have. She's smiling into his face, and they're holding hands; he's rubbing his thumb over her knuckle, so they're both eating with just one hand on their cutlery. I roll my eyes. "So, what's your job?" I ask him.

"Oh, I'm a millwright." He chuckles at my blank look, wipes his face with a napkin (when did we get napkins?), and says, "I fix machinery. When a farm or winery has a piece of equipment that breaks down, they call me." At this, Mom literally squeezes his arm muscles.

I nod, chewing. He clears his throat and starts again on the school thing. "Your mom says you're really good in school. That's great. Haha, I wish I'd done better in school." Then he points at himself. "Self-taught."

Let me guess: he was a cool guy in school who spent too much time with a hacky sack and a bong. I'm itching all over to just leave.

"Can I be excused? I'm going out tonight and have some stuff for school to do first."

Mom's face hovers between anger and disappointment, and she chooses the easy route of surrender. "Oh, fine. Clear your plate and put it in the dishwasher." I jump up and away, and she calls into the kitchen, "Rinse it first!"

I go to my room, actually planning on doing some homework, but my mind is buzzing. I guess I'm happy for my mom, but she's acting like she's in a romantic comedy, and I'm not used to having anyone in our house. Normally the guys she's dating reveal themselves to be losers before she gets a chance to bring them home. She really does think this one is different, even if I don't. I'm sure he'll screw things up in no time at all— he'll be married or jobless or cheat on her or something else. Take your pick from a game of Loser Bingo. Meanwhile, I can hear them now, murmuring to each other, Mom sighing happily. I don't want to go back out there with them, playing house and family and using napkins and rinsing fucking plates. She obviously wants to be alone with Mr. Reg the Millwright and his machine-fixing hands. My room feels so small, like it's shrinking into a tiny space shuttle cabin on a rocket that won't launch. I sit at my desk, pull out my geography textbook, and stare at it. I check my phone, but it's tight-lipped, looking the other way, pretending I'm not even there. Nothing.

Everything Lottie told me about Rhonda comes back in a sharp stealth whisper in my brain, a song I can't get out of my head. Everything is changing. Will Rhonda still be the same? I feel guilty right away for thinking that. Of course. Of course not. Both. I miss Rhonda already. *Pete.* I wrap my mind around the name. It's so important that I am there for Lottie, I know that, but she doesn't even seem to want me to be or care if I'm affected. Why hasn't Rhonda said anything to me about this? Does she know that Lottie told me?

And then there's this: Rhonda, now Pete, with his new (real) identity, will be changing schools next year. Something sinks inside me, and I put my hand on my stomach as if I can feel it dropping into my guts. I feel like I'm on a fast-moving ice floe and my life is reducing to a speck in the distance. High school already feels weird; home is following suit. What will I do if one of the only adults I can actually count on leaves? I take a deep breath, trying not to listen to the happy sounds of togetherness coming from Mom and Reg in the kitchen as they tidy up. I look around my room at all my stuff: my movies, my TV and VCR for the old flicks. Characters from all the classics stare out at me from posters plastered all over the walls and ceiling. They give me comfort, keep me company, promise never to change. Molly Ringwald sneers, Winona Ryder as Veronica in *Heathers* looks cool and apathetic. *You're not alone, Stevie*, they say. *We got you.* I login to my channel and read some comments from my few loyal subscribers. It's a nice boost. They are with me, these strangers who love the same things I do. YES! one says. I LOOOOOVE HEATHERS! There are people out there, somewhere, for me. A small consolation.

I press my lips together and nod as the doorbell rings and the next part of the night begins. It's game time.

* * *

The pregame party at Aidan's house is already well under way by the time Paige, Lottie, and I get there. His parents are obviously not home, and he greets us at the door like a game show host, arms wide out, sloppy grin, music loud behind him like a gust of wind. I notice that he and Paige seem slightly more formal than usual—a kind of awkward kiss that Aidan covers up by loudly ushering us in. Something is different between them. I'm out of the loop on the constantly shifting social ground. I catch Lottie's eye with a questioning look, but she gives nothing away, smiles, and leads the way into the house like she's been there a million times.

The house is kind-feeling and comfortable, full of flowery cushions and curtains, warm honey-colored oak cupboards and pictures of Aidan and his brothers tacked to the fridge and in frames on tables. On the kitchen table are bottles of liquor and big jugs of soda alongside red cups half filled with swampy concoctions, but underneath is a pretty tablecloth.

By the looks of things, some people will not make it to the game at all. It seems like this has been going for hours. As I walk through the house, I see a couple making out while inside the same enormous jersey, two guys wearing old boxing gloves and drunkenly fighting in the hallway, and some feet sticking out from under a snoring blanket on the couch in the living room. Aidan tells us cheerfully that someone has already puked. He points to a pale-faced guy staring disconsolately from a corner on the kitchen floor, holding a can of soda to his forehead.

A guy I don't recognize comes through the kitchen with a joint hanging out of his mouth, followed by three girls, a skunky cloud behind them.

"Hey!" Aidan yells, "Smoke *outside*, bro! My mom can smell it a mile away! I can't believe people still smoke joints," Aidan complains to us, pouring some rum into a cup. He shakes his head. "Edibles or nothing for me, man."

"Right?" I say, and Lottie raises an eyebrow at me, her bullshit detector calling me out for attempts at coolness, but I grab a beer and walk away from her. Paige has already drifted off. She's looking at some pictures on the mantle. I stroll over and nudge her with my elbow.

"Hey," she says.

"Hey." I bob my head awkwardly. "So . . . what's up with you and Aidan? Everything okay?"

"Why, did he say something to you?" she says, an edge to her voice.

"What? No—" I start, carefully.

"Oh, whatever, you two have your little friendship thing going there," she says, waving her hand dismissively.

"Um, no, not really."

Paige rolls her eyes and looks around the room. "Yeah, well. I dunno what's going on with us. Maybe we're done. I don't even know."

"Oh. Well, I'm sorry." I touch her shoulder, which feels bony and frail, like she's a little teen dinosaur, which she kind of is. Maybe she's not as high up on the food chain as Breanne, but she's got some kind of stomping power. There's a watchful hunger about her. She looks at me now like she's assessing me, deciding something.

"Thanks, Stevie," she says, unsmiling. She looks across the room and says, vaguely, "You're sweet."

*　*　*

We end up at the arena halfway through the hockey game, and our team—the team that I suddenly pretend to care about—is losing, but that does little to dampen the fervor in the place. In fact, everyone just seems more excitable. The stands are full of fans from our town and the opposition. People are shouting and sloshing around drunkenly. It's a messy, chilly uproar, and after an hour or so of watching our team lose and getting a numb ass, I find myself weaving between seats, down the stairs, my head spinning with beer, heading toward the bathrooms. There is a lineup of girls waiting, leaning up against the yellow-painted cinder block walls, scrolling through their phones. Guys totter in and out of their bathroom across the way, checking the girls out, talking to some of them. I can see just inside their bathroom to where the sinks and mirrors are and notice Aidan, inspecting his reflection. He is tall and thin, all angles and limbs. He tosses his floppy hair back, burps, and trots into the hallway.

"Stevie!" he shouts at me, and stumbles my way, his arms open. I don't really want to hug him but don't know how to avoid it, and this is exactly what most guys count on, from what I can tell. Before I know it, he's enveloped me in a bear hug. My face is in his chest, and I breathe in his musky, soapy, boozy smell, blushing. He rocks me around, bumps us into the girl behind us, and apologizes, finally releasing me.

"Easy there, Stevie, stop mauling me."

"Yeah okay, buddy," I laugh, and he smiles and looks at me like he's seeing me for the first time.

"Did you dress up for me, Stevie?" he says, gesturing to my sweater-and-jeans combo.

I look down at what I'm wearing. There is mustard on my shirt.

He laughs. "Ah, Stevie, Stevie . . ." He licks his thumb and leans into me, rubbing the mustard on my shirt, just inches above my left boob. I back away just as the line moves forward a little. The girl ahead of me goes through the doorway into the bathroom itself.

"Uh, unless you're coming in here with me, I think we should part ways now," I say, looking away.

"What? Oh! Right, right. See you later," and he turns and rambles up the stairs like a big puppy, his long arms and legs seeming separate from the rest of his body. I watch him go, shaking my head.

"Stop looking at my ass, Stevie!" he yells behind him, laughing at himself.

After, I wander back toward the stands, but when I glance up at everyone I came with, I don't really feel like going back and sitting with them. I make my way to the concession stand and get in line. I recognize the tall figure in front of me and tap him on the shoulder.

"Hey, Matthew," I say, and he turns around.

"Oh hey, Stevie, how are you?"

"Good, good, you know, getting my hockey on."

Matthew laughs. "That's good. I hardly know what I'm doing here."

"Are you here with friends? I mean, obviously," I say, reddening, "but I mean, who are you here with?"

"Uh, Ava and Antar? Do you know them? Also, of course, Jamie and Mitch," he says, referring to a couple of guys he's hung out with since we were kids. There was a year or so there where I used to do stuff with the three of them all the time: watch baseball games, movies, play board games and goof around. And then we just grew apart, I guess.

"Nice. Yeah, I know those other two. Ava and Antar; they're in our homeroom, right?"

"Yep. What about you?"

"Oh"—I wave my hand—"Paige and them."

Matthew nods a few times, and the corner of his mouth turns up. "Well, look at you—hanging out with the 'cool kids.'" He's busting my balls.

"What? No!" I say, while he laughs. "Seriously. They're nice, if you get to know them."

"Ah, I see." He smiles as I make a face. "No, really, I believe you." The woman at the stand clears her throat, and he turns to make his order.

When the game ends, I wander around the arena. There are cardboard containers on the floor with ketchup smeared on the inside of them, fries hanging out like tongues, puddles of beer that creep all the way under the first rows of seats, where it will be hard to mop. People are milling about, coming down the stairs in clumps of coats and purses, shouting to friends across the way, to other fans, to themselves. I look across the ice and see Lottie and Paige sitting alone on the rival side, midway up the stands. Their arms are linked and Paige is resting her head on Lottie's shoulder. They are moving back and forth to the echoing music that pumps loudly and incoherently in the arena as the players head into the locker rooms and fans vacate the stands. Someone bumps into me, and I stumble, putting my hands out against the Plexiglas. I stay there, momentarily frozen, looking through the scratched window at the scuffed, smudged vision of my friends.

I leave the arena alone. People are stumbling around outside, drunk and laughing. I hear someone barfing in the darkness around the side of the building. It is a desperate, lonely sound.

*   *   *

When I get home, Reg's car is still in our driveway. It's quiet in the house, and dark, but the darkness doesn't stop. I feel like I'm filled with the black ink of all the world's pathetic diary entries. The noise from the arena is still echoing in my ears, rumbling in my fingertips. I left without Lottie or Paige, walking home by myself—not because I wanted to be alone but because I didn't, and thought that if I was with them I'd feel worse.

I take out my phone, but no one has texted me. I reach across a different divide.

Hey dad

He pings back pretty quickly. *Hi kiddo whats up*

Nothing just saying hi

Hi!

We exchange some emojis and then he signs off, says it's too late for an old man to be up. I sit at my desk and look at my geography textbook and its diagram of soil formations. I draw another layer at the bottom in pencil with a small arrow and label: *me.*

6

Episode 68 00:00
The high school cafeteria. The great leveler of high school
movies. It's where the entire mass of beauties and weir-
dos come together to eat and do so much more: try and
fit in, wish lunch would end, laugh with friends or stare
at people they have crushes on. It is universally different
and the same: terrible food, echoing laughter, the screech
of chairs. It's got it all with a side of fries.

The next day, I take my tray across the lunchroom and slide onto the bench beside Paige. Lottie is on her other side. She is giggling at something Luke just said.

Breanne is standing up, her long red hair like a cape. She isn't laughing. She's sipping her drink from a straw and looking at Paige's tray, her eyes narrowing. "Is that all you're having?"

Paige looks at the yogurt container in front of her. "Yeah, I'm full," she says, looking away, her smile fading. Breanne raises an eyebrow.

I look at Paige and smile. "That's how you get to look so great, right? The discipline. Like, remember when you were, like, counting the peanuts the other day? It's impressive."

I look up, and everyone is looking at me.

Breanne laughs. "Wow, Stevie, bold. You think an eating disorder is 'impressive'? Want her to have another week in the hospital so she can *look great*?" She widens her eyes and shakes her head. "Kind of cruel, don't you think?" She smirks, looking at the others. They all look at her and then follow suit: eyes on me, disgust and disbelief.

Paige looks down at her lap, her mouth disappearing.

Oh God. I wish I could slip backward in time and redo the last fifteen seconds.

Breanne takes a sip, watching to see what I'll do.

So. Stupid. I should have known.

"Oh, shit. Paige—"

The bell rings and Paige ignores me, standing up. She walks out of the cafeteria with Lottie, who is shaking her head.

"Uh-oh, Stevie, she's mad," Aidan says unaffectedly. "And trust me, you do not want her mad at you. She's a raging bitch half the time anyway. At least to me," he grumbles.

I spend the rest of the afternoon texting Paige, asking her if she's okay, apologizing.

I didn't know. I'm sorry!! Please!!!

After the bell rings, I shoulder my way through the crowds and get to Paige's locker, but when she doesn't turn up, I head to the doors of the school, where I can see down the little hill, see everyone leaving. Lottie and I always meet at the huge rock at the end of the driveway of the school. Maybe I can talk to her, I think, as I crane my neck to see if she's waiting for me or on her way. Nearby, Matthew is huddled over a book with Mitch and Jamie. He pushes his glasses up on his nose and laughs at something Mitch says. I see Dee, smoking under a tree while a guy from our homeroom talks animatedly to her. She sees me and lifts a hand in greeting. I ignore her, and notice Lottie, her white-blonde hair shining in the sun. Paige is with her, and they are already walking away from the school. I stand on the steps while people jostle and bump into me until someone speaks in my ear.

"Hey, kid, you gonna stand here all day?"

It's Rhonda. *No—Pete*, I correct myself, feeling a sad snag but ignoring it. His satchel over his shoulder, ready to go home as well.

"What? No, I just—"

"Where's your partner in crime?" he says, looking out over the crowd with me.

"Oh, I'm not sure. I think she might have left . . ."

"Huh," he says, looking a little surprised. "Is she being a jerk or something? Do I need to step in?"

"No, no. No."

"So, no?"

"Haha. Everything's fine."

Pete looks at me closely. "If you're sure. You know where to find me if it's not."

I get a lump in my throat and look away. "Yeah, I know. Thanks. Well, I'd better get going," I say. "See you tomorrow!"

I walk home, my hand around my phone, waiting for a vibration that never comes.

* * *

Later I get on my bike and ride over to Lottie's, feeling sick and anxious.

"Hey," she says, leaning against the door.

"Can I come in?"

Lottie looks over her shoulder and heaves a sigh, then stands aside to let me in. I follow her through the house with a pit in my gut. Her parents are in the kitchen, and I wave at them. Jacob lifts his hand and forces a smile. Pete looks super serious also, but when he sees me, he breaks into a grin.

"Hey, Stevie! You tracked her down, eh?"

"We're going outside," Lottie says, ignoring him, heading toward the screen door at the end of the kitchen.

* * *

Outside, Lottie collapses in a patio chair. I pull one out, and it screeches against the deck. I sit down and start right in.

"You know I didn't mean anything," I say.

She blows out her cheeks. "*I* know that. But Stevie, she is *pissed*. And embarrassed. And I don't blame her. You totally betrayed a confidence."

"But I didn't even know!"

Lottie looks at me with her eyebrows raised, like how could I be such a moron. I start to wonder if maybe I did know. Or if maybe I am a moron. I wring my hands.

"Also? Maybe give her a little space. Texting her all the time? It's a little . . . well, I'm sorry, but it's a little desperate."

My face is burning, and I don't say anything.

"I'm sorry, Stevie," she says, quietly. "Don't shoot the messenger." She looks sorry, and that makes me even more mad and embarrassed. "Just, you know. Let it go."

"Right. Okay." A moment passes. Then another one drags

its feet across the yard, yawning. Finally, I clear my throat and make an excuse to leave. Lottie watches me gather my stuff and go out through the yard fence so that no one, especially Pete, who I feel suddenly estranged from, has to see my eyes filling up.

I go home and straight to my room, ignoring Mom's cheerful greeting. I need distractions. I root through all my old movies and notice *Dog Day Afternoon*. I pop it in the ancient VCR and lay on my bed with my head propped up by a teddy bear. It's hardly started when Mom knocks on the door and opens it.

"Oh, I love that one!" she says, looking at the TV. "'Attica! Attica!'"

"You wanna watch with me?" I ask, not looking at her. Knowing the answer.

"Oh, hon. I would love to, but can I take a rain check? Reg is coming over."

Oh goody.

"Oh, yeah. For sure. No problem." I say this like a robot, but she doesn't even pick up on it, so relieved that I'm not giving her a hard time.

Soon I'm immersed in the world of the movie. Love this flick. Classic, and one of the first mainstream movies that featured a trans character, before trans was a household term. I start to think about what Pete has done. How it's really brave, becoming his true self, even if it is hard for Lottie, and for me, to adjust. Maybe I can do something, even something kind of private, to show my support, to help me to get on board. To show Lottie that I love her family. Maybe a vid for my channel. On the best trailblazing trans films, or something. I start working it out, choosing movies in my head, jotting down ideas for a script.

7

Episode 69 00:00
I went out of my usual wheelhouse for this list. I did
what we all need to do: I educated myself. While I may
have thought I knew about the representation of trans
people on the silver screen, I was woefully—and I mean
woefully—ignorant. But something changed in my life;
to be precise, someone is changing in my life, and so I
knew I needed to branch out and watch more than the
usual fare of Boys Don't Cry *and* Dog Day Afternoon.
This person in my life is showing the bravery it takes to
transition. This Top 10 List is for him.

The next day, Paige doesn't speak to me. I try, in homeroom, while Pete is talking, to catch her eye, but she stares straight ahead, ignoring me. I finally buckle, despite Lottie's warning, like I can't help myself. I am desperate, it's true, but I feel like if this isn't resolved, I won't have any peace, and that I'll lose something important—my place in this precarious order, but also, I worry, more than that. I shoot out a couple of texts from under my desk.

Hey. You ok? and *I'm so sorry paige!!!!* And sad emojis, tears, broken hearts.

And then, finally, in the late afternoon, she agrees to come to my house after school, something she's never done before but that I offered up as a last resort. She looks at me, her face hard, and says, "Yeah. Okay, it'd be good to see where you live." Something prickles in my mind, but I push it away.

On the way home, I try to talk to her.

"Look, I'm really sorry."

"I don't want to talk about it."

"That's fine. Just, I—"

"It's *fine*. Seriously. Stop."

"Okay."

She turns and looks at me, and says, "So, like, why *didn't* you want to invite Lottie to the movies with us that time?"

"What?"

"Just that I thought you were such good friends. She told me she wasn't doing anything that night."

"I dunno. I can't remember. I thought she couldn't make it," I mumble, my face reddening.

Paige nods, looking ahead. "Yeah," she says, "okay. Sure. Seems like maybe you lied about that, but I guess I'm wrong."

This isn't how I thought it would go. She is different. Pissed off. There is a chill between us, and we say little the rest of the way to my house.

In my room, I sit nervously on my bed. Mom is out with Reg again, but that's a small comfort. This is awkward.

"What do you want to do?"

"Hmm?" Paige is looking around my room like she's at a zoo exhibit. "What *is* all this shit?" She's staring at all my old tech: TV, VCR, DVD player, and piles of old movies.

"Oh, it's just a bunch of junk I keep around."

She looks at me, unconvinced.

"Remember how I like old movies? So . . . this is how I watch them. I like the, uh, authentic experience." *Oh God*. I roll my eyes at myself.

She crouches down, looking at the stack of movies that starts at the floor. "I've never even heard of any of these."

She looks over her shoulder at me, and I say, "Well, they used to be my mom's."

She says, "No wonder you like that media class so much. I thought it was just because Lottie's mom—well, 'dad'—teaches it."

I don't like how she says that: "dad." It makes my skin itch, makes me want to push or bite.

"Yeah, no," I mumble, "I have a thing for old films."

"'Films'? Wow, you are hard-core." She notices a light set up behind my laptop, and touching it, she says, "Do you make your own 'films'?"

"No, no," I say, and the actors in all my movie posters look the other way. "I just sometimes do videos and stuff. Like, just on YouTube." I aim this shot thinking it will hit a mark, something she knows and likes, but it finds the wrong target.

She raises an eyebrow at me. "Oh yeah? You have your own channel?"

"Kind of," I mumble.

She is looking at some papers beside my laptop, where I write scripts for my channel, and I hop off my bed and say, "Let's go. Get something to eat or something."

Paige nods distractedly and follows me. Some kind of animal instinct in me feels her behind me. My hackles are up, my senses honed. There is blood in her nose, and I'm in her sights; I can feel it.

We go to Tim Hortons, and I grab a doughnut and she gets a coffee. We sit awkwardly for a while, Paige looking at her phone, and finally she says, "Look, I've gotta go."

"Sure, no problem. Um, I'll talk to you later?"

"Yep," she says, throwing her cup in the garbage as she leaves me sitting there. "See you."

I watch her walk away down the street, her head in her phone, and tell myself it's all fine. It's fine.

* * *

The next morning, I'm chewing on the bum end of a bluish loaf of bread in the kitchen. Mom is sucking the death out of a cigarette while reading the local paper. It will tell her when the garden club sales are and about the watercolor classes at the library, but it won't tell her about the real world. My world. I watch her and am amazed by how little she knows about me or my life. About her incredibly shrinking daughter with her secretive, fickle friends. I want to shock her, to get her to snap out of her little dream life she's been in lately.

I clear my throat. "So . . . Lottie's mom is transitioning. Into a man."

Her dull eyes register me out of the fog. "What? Who is? Rhonda?"

"Lottie doesn't have another mom. Yes, Rhonda."

"What do you mean—she's having a sex change operation?"

"I don't think they call it that anymore, Mom."

"What the hell do you mean, 'she's transitioning'?"

"Well, she is a man. He is. That's what he told Lottie."

"Who did? Rhonda?"

"Yes, but that's not going to be his name now."

She thought about this. "Holy. I had no idea. I mean, I haven't seen her in a while, but . . . What's she changing her name to? I guess Ron? At least that part will be easy."

"Actually, his name is Pete."

"Oh, Jesus."

She takes a deep breath, her eyes blinking slowly. "What about school?"

"I guess he's telling the students soon. And then—" A lump in my throat. I can't bear the idea of school without Rhonda. Without Pete. *Come on, Stevie, hold it together.* "Then he's changing schools next fall. Going to teach somewhere else. To start fresh."

She nods, up and down, up and down, while this information sinks in.

"Huh," she says. "That makes sense, I guess." She picks at her nail polish. "I mean. Well. She was always a bit mannish." She exhales. "I don't blame her for wanting to ditch this club. It's a huge racket." She nods some more. "Pete, eh? I bet she can't wait to stop shaving her pits. That's what I'd look forward to if I were her."

"Him."

"Who?"

"Pete. You have to call him 'him.' That's how he's chosen to identify."

"Oh jeez, Stevie, will you cut me some slack? I'm forty-six; sometimes I forget who *I* am. *Him.* God, you're insufferable."

She walks out of the kitchen and leaves me there, and when

I look out the window I see that even the clouds are rushing away from me, sliding across the sky with their eyes averted, pretending they have something else to do. That sky. Always thinking it's so big.

I go to my room. I have a few more edits to do before I publish my latest vid.

*　*　*

School is strange. I still eat at lunch with Paige, Breanne, Lottie, and the rest, but something has changed. There is an invisible wall that I'm suddenly behind. I try to ignore it but feel myself start to disappear, like Marty McFly in *Back to the Future.*

At the end of the day, I wait for Lottie and am relieved when she turns up without Paige.

"Hey," she says, and my heart lifts a little.

The sky is heavy, and it's going to start coming down soon, but we don't rush, just kind of scrape our feet along. And then, without whispering a warning, the rain starts. It's an angry rain, a furious weather system: the sky throwing car keys and coffee cups and its mother's favorite pearl buttons. Raindrops clatter around us like bullets. At first, we just keep walking, going slow, *do your worst*, and then deciding at the same moment, we run: slopping into puddles as they're forming, blinking rain off our eyelashes. We are yelling and laughing. We are crazy wet and cold. Like little kids again. Right then, it doesn't matter why everything feels a little different. Something about rain like this just makes you forget being mad or cool or anything else but being wet. I can ignore it all; I can pretend it's all fine.

We go to Lottie's house because it's the closest, run inside, panting and laughing and shaking like wet dogs. I close the door, and we peel off our jackets and shrug out of our shoes. There is music playing from the radio in the kitchen. Water drips down my neck, and I shiver.

Pete is already at the counter cutting an onion.

"Hey girls," he says. Lottie nods. "I saw you walking home. I would have offered you a ride, but"—twinkling eyes—"rain builds character."

"Hey Pete," I say.

He looks up, surprised, and looks at Lottie. She grabs a cookie out of a tin and glares at me.

"Pete, hmm?" he says. "Looks like you've been talking to my girl here." He gestures to Lottie, who is still staring mutinously at me.

"Yeah, um, she told me. I hope that's okay?"

"I assumed she would. That's what best friends are for. In fact, I'm kind of surprised it's taken you this long to mention it." He looks happy, relaxed, and I feel something lift inside me. "How are you taking it? I know it takes some time to process."

Lottie interrupts. "Can we just—like *not* talk about this all the time?"

"Case in point," Pete says kindly, gesturing with his knife to Lottie.

Lottie rolls her eyes, and I look back and forth between them.

"Yeah, I guess it takes some getting used to."

"And it will continue to as I start to look different. Mind you, at first that'll just be like watching me go through puberty—zits and everyth—"

"*God!*" says Lottie, her eyes bugging out.

I smile and gesture at the cutting board. "What are you making?"

"Chili," says Pete, ignoring Lottie. "You wanna stay?"

"Oh, no, that's okay, thank you. I'm sure that my mom has dinner for me." I am sure this is not true unless Reg the Super Stud is there. I rock back and forth on my heels.

"So," I say, forging ahead again, "I've been listening to a lot of Bowie."

He looks up. "Oh yeah?"

"Yeah. Sad that he died."

"Sure, big loss, that one."

"Yeah. He was a real trailblazer."

Pete raises his eyebrows at me.

"You know, like in terms of gender," I say.

"Ah. Yep, right you are, Stevie." He smiles. "You think I should change my name to Aladdin Sane? It's not too late. I haven't done the paperwork yet."

"Haha. Right."

Lottie throws up her arms and leaves the kitchen, and I follow. We go to her bedroom, and I plunk soggily onto her bed. She is changing into dry clothes.

"What is with you?" she says, peeling wet jeans off and pulling on some comfies.

"What? Just trying to connect, here. You might try it yourself."

"Oh yeah? Should I? Right. Look."

Lottie grabs her phone from where she tossed it on her dresser and comes over to the bed. She opens Instagram and shows me Pete's account, which I guess is private, but Lottie's following him. I scroll through, pausing occasionally at a picture. There is a cute one of him with a coffee mug with a moustache painted on it held to his lips from yesterday. Below it, the hashtags #JOURNEY #TRANSITION #FTM #TRANS #LETSDOTHIS.

"Cool," I say. "He's really doing it."

"Right. Very *cool*," Lottie says, making a face that I guess is supposed to be me, sucking up.

I ignore it. "He seems pretty conservative. Like, with how he's dressing and stuff."

Lottie shakes her head, smiling slightly. "Not living up to your expectations, I see. Why? What were you expecting?"

"What? No, I— No."

"I wish she hadn't changed her name. He."

"Rhonda isn't really a man's name. Not that that matters. Gender is fluid."

"Whatever. He said I can still call him Mom if I want. Or, like, something else if I want."

"He's a nice guy. But, you know," I say carefully, "you should probably make an effort to respect what he wants."

"Excuse me?"

"I just mean that it might be easier for you. And for him. I'm serious. It's tough, I get it, I mean I've been adjusting to it, too . . . but it's kind of cool, too, don't you think?"

"Stevie, God. You do *not* understand."

"Uh, no? I *totally* understand. Or, I'm trying to." I look out her window and think about the significance of all of this, in a larger sense. "We are living in such an interesting time," I say. "People can be who they want to be."

"Oh my God," she says. "This is not a movie. It's my life."

"What? No, it's just that—"

"Stevie." She looks at me, her eyes suddenly angry. "Will

you *please* stop. About this. And, frankly, everything. Just—just leave it alone in general."

"What? Why?"

"*What? Why?* Fuck. Never mind."

"No, what is it? Is it something to do with Paige?"

She snorts. "Paige? Are you serious? You are *obsessed*. Jesus. Forget it."

My face burns up to my hair. She picks up a book, sits back on the bed. I get up, grab my bag, and I look at her once more. I say that I'm leaving. She nods but doesn't look up. I gather my things and head out, just in time to see Lottie's other dad, the original, coming home from work. He waves though the car window as I hold my bag above my head and run in the direction of my house. He calls out to me that he'll drive me home, but I yell back, "That's okay! I love the rain!"

That is bullshit, but I don't want anyone feeling sorry for me, even when it comes to acts of God.

At home, alone, the rain pounding on the windows like a drum, I push PUBLISH, send my video out into the world. I want to show my understanding, my acceptance, my support—even if my loyal subscribers are the only ones who see it

* * *

In the morning, I wake up forgetting why I feel kind of sick, and then remember. I check my phone, but it is giving me the stone-cold freeze. I hear from no one. I decide not to check in with anyone. I'm sure things will blow over.

But Lottie is not at our spot to walk to school. I ignore the shiver that runs down my back. I walk up the hill toward the school, and I see them. Lottie and Paige, together, staring me down. I climb the steps. Time stands still. The air isn't moving.

"Hey," I say.

"Oh, 'hey,'" says Lottie, arching an eyebrow. Something's not right.

"What? What is it?"

People are looking at us as they walk through the doors.

Lottie leans in, her face terrible and contorted. I'd laugh if this wasn't awful.

She lowers her voice and growls, "You made a fucking video about my life?"

"What?" I shrink back. "No!"

Paige snorts. Lottie shakes her head.

"'Brave Trans Film Heroes'?" she spits. "You didn't do that? You didn't make a fucking video where you talk to the camera about how you 'even have a trans hero in your own life'?" She opens her eyes wide, mocking innocence.

I blink quickly. "Well, no, I mean, no one would know that it's—"

"You have no loyalty, Stevie. You keep no secrets. Fuck. You." She turns, hair whipping in a curtain of fury.

"And by the way," says Paige, "we were all talking about you last night. And guess what? Aidan said you threw yourself at him at the hockey game. He is my fucking boyfriend, Stevie. I trusted you! I thought you were my friend. Stupid skank. Like I wouldn't find out. I should have known: 'What's up with you and Aidan?'" She puts on a simpering imitation of me.

"What?" I manage.

"'What?'" she mimics again. "Yeah, I heard all about it. Go to hell, you betraying little asshole."

And she's gone, leaving me on the steps with my mouth hanging open for all the thoughts and words to fall right out of me and onto the pavement, where they break into a million pieces.

*   *   *

The day is a sickening torture. I eat lunch alone, in a corner, and watch as they laugh with each other carelessly. I am called out repeatedly in class for daydreaming.

Breanne stops me in the hallway between classes.

"You thought you could blow Aidan at the game and no one would find out?"

"I did *not*—"

"Right. Like it wasn't obvious that's what you were doing from the beginning. Attention whore. Well, actual whore, too. Lots of guys are talking. Don't worry, we'll make sure you get *all* the attention you deserve," she says ominously.

I am frozen, my mouth opening and closing.

"You know," she says, picking a nail, "I saw your channel last night. We all did. Paige showed it to us. She saw all your weird geek equipment at your house, with your 'scripts.'" She throws back her head and lets out a laugh. "It *sucks*. We couldn't stop laughing at your stupid little episodes," she says, with a lisp that I know comes from my early videos when I wore braces. "Oh my God. Seriously, you have zits *all* over your face in half of them. You are disgusting." She laughs again, then turns serious, staring at me hard. "Listen, I'm *very* protective of my friends. So stay the fuck away from them, Stevie. Stay away from all of us. You"—a finger, pointing—"are garbage."

I cry in the bathroom three times. And at the end of it, there is no one to walk home with. I don't know this is just the beginning.

By the time I get home, it has gained momentum. First, there are comments on my channel.

FREAK

WHORE

SLUT

SHE'LL SUCK YOU OFF ANYWHERE YOU WANT

WHO WOULD WANT THAT LMAO

They keep adding up, quicker than I can refresh. A pile-up. Tears hot on my face, I look at video after video that I have made, carefully, lovingly, and read what's under them. A sickening panic is rising in my gut. Paige? Lottie? I picture them together, laughing at me. No, I know Lottie would never. But . . .

I take down the video about Pete, even though the hateful comments on there are directed mostly at me. I leave the other videos up for now. Maybe it will blow over.

My phone is shaking in my hand. I check Instagram. I have been tagged a bunch of times by accounts I've never even seen before. There is a still image from one of my early videos: my eyes half open, my mouth open, braces on full display. It's a meme. It says ERMAHGERD! MOVIESH! Under it. And another: ERMAHGERD! I LOVE COCK! There are so many tags under them, things that make no sense, with my URL, too: #LOSER #WHORE #NERD #BITCH #TROLL #SCHOOL #STEVIE #SJW #LONER #KILL-YOURSELF, more. I try to trace back who the unknown accounts belong to, who follows them. Deeper and deeper. I see that Breanne Davis is following a couple of them, and Aidan, and then Paige by extension, then Lottie, in six degrees of separation. I look back at my channel. There are more and more comments. I can't keep up.

In every app we all use, they find a way in.

What did I do? What do I do?

"Stevie?" I hear my mom call. "Stevie, hon, we're going out, okay?"

"Bye, Stevie!" Reg yells from the hall.

The door closes with a click.

My phone pings. It's a group text I've just been added to. I don't recognize the number or any of the fifteen people on it. I scroll up and read through the thread.

you know Stevie

who

this loser

There is that old pic of me again.

LMAO yea I know her

i am in one of her classes. She reeks

There are a bunch of shit and barf emojis.

like what

dead tuna

LMAO LMAO

omg

dying

slut

Fish emoji. Skull emoji.

shit is she on this thread

oops

i thought i smelled something

lmao whore

I am removed from the thread. I stare at my phone and feel like I might be sick. My cheeks are burning hot. I don't want to cry, but once it starts, I don't know how to stop. I am gulping and gasping. I hate myself. My head is pounding. I rush to the bathroom and try to stand over the toilet, the last of my sobs coming out with a string of spit. I gag and cough, but nothing comes.

I am invited and removed from more threads all evening long. I turn my phone off, and finally, after crying so hard there is nothing left, I fall asleep.

* * *

I wake and remember. This is my new normal.

Lottie and I have had fights before. We've been best friends our whole lives, so it's not like we've never had periods where we're not speaking. Our parents usually act as peacemakers, bringing us together for movies or pizza or whatever. We get over the awkwardness and grumble apologies. We pretty quickly forget whatever it was we were arguing about.

But this is different. They see me as something I'm not. They turned me into someone I'm not.

It worsens.

I try to fix things. I wait for Lottie after school, a few days in a row, shyly, trying to disappear but hoping she'll see me. But she just walks by me with a bunch of other people. Once she looks back when Breanne makes a face at me and laughs loudly, but she doesn't hold my eyes for long. She looks worried for a second, but then her face hardens, and she just shrugs and turns away. Like she figures this is the price I have to pay.

I text her.

Why are you doing this

Why are u being such a bitch? you know me

I wait a few days and try again.

Wtf I was trying to say your dad/mom is awesome. I love your family you know that. I never did anything with aidan or anyone else. You know that.

She unfollows me on Instagram. I unfollow her, then regret it, but can't go back. School is now something I endure. I come home exhausted every day. Dread and being on the defensive takes all of my energy. I spend the day ready for someone to strike, waiting and watching, weighing the jabs and letting most roll off me. I don't know how or why it changed so quickly. Why they hate me. It's incredible to me that they can hate like that. I try everything, and nothing works. I try to be myself, but no one wants that.

* * *

Another morning. I don't want to go to school. I can't. I would rather die. They'd rather I die. I scratch at my arm with my fingernails under the covers, hard. *Did I do something? Did I give Aidan the wrong idea? Was I flirting? Oh God. Forget. Remember.*

I hear Mom in the kitchen, humming happily. She calls to me, "Rise and shine, sleepyhead!"

The sun is pushing hard on the edges of my blinds. My eyes are swollen. I drag myself out of bed, carefully choosing clothes that have passed my inspection for stains or smells or strangeness that might draw attention. I sniff the pits of my shirt, convinced that they're right, I am repulsive. I shower and scrub myself raw, hard, red. In the mirror, my arms and legs burn, alive, my eyes puffy.

I stare at my blotchy reflection and try to wish my life away.

Pete knows something is up. He pulls me aside when the bell rings.

"Hey, kid," he says.

"Hey," I say, my head down.

"Listen. I know that some kids are giving you a hard time about, well, your videos. I hear there was a trans-positive one? And you know, I gotta applaud you for that, but I don't want you getting any heat. I know that this is affecting you as well, and I'm sure you meant well. I didn't see it, or any of them, honestly—but Lottie mentioned it."

"I took it down."

"Yeah, she was pretty upset that you put it up there. She said that's why you're not coming around. But don't let that bother you. She's going through some stuff. Give her time, okay? I mean, kids are talking, and Lottie figured they knew the video was about me. A couple of kids have said some stupid stuff to her, but they're just scared of what they don't know. I'll talk to all the students soon."

I grunt and look away so I won't cry. A few quiet moments pass. He pats my shoulder.

"So . . . anyway, come with me."

Pete leads me out of the classroom, down a corridor toward where the auto shop is. He swipes a card to unlock a door to a room I've never been in and opens it for me. I know this place: the Makers' Space. I look around: computers, printers, scanners, some big lights, a green screen, what looks like a darkroom, and more. A bunch of students are working away busily, in their own worlds, and take no notice of us at all. There's a whole section for woodworking equipment and long tables, tools, saws, the works, and I see one girl sliding a long piece of wood into a saw to slice it in half. Another girl is on a laptop, editing something. She turns around, and I see that it's Dee. She gives me a nodded greeting and returns to her work.

"Whoa," I say.

"Yeah. Usually– but not always—reserved for upper-year students, but since you're into the media stuff, I wanted to give you a chance to get your hands dirty here. Maybe you can make some of your videos even better."

My face burns, and I mumble a thank-you.

"No problem. Here." Pete reaches into his pocket and hands me a card.

"What's this?"

"It's a key. It'll get you in the back door from outside or from inside the school. You can come whenever you want. Who knows when the creative muse will strike, right?" He pauses while I stare at the card. "I trust you with it. You're smart, Stevie."

"For me? Really?" I ask, not trying to tempt Fate, because

lately Fate has been a spiteful, vengeful bitch who I like to keep at arm's length.

"Really." Pete puts his hand on my shoulder and says, "*Nolite te bastardes carborundorum.*"

"Huh?"

He holds the door open for me, letting it swing shut behind us. "I told them they shouldn't have canceled the Latin program."

MAY

8

Two months and a world later.

It's spring and everything is still fucked.

I walk to school trying to call back that feeling that maybe things will change, maybe today will be different. I have been riding the tide of collective hatred for two months now. Something has to give.

They find me whenever I'm alone. I am a pariah. The catcalls, the comments, even, humiliatingly, the occasional object thrown at my head while walking to school. Whatever was set in motion, whatever match was lit, has become a full-blown forest fire. I am under constant, unrelenting attack.

I never go out anywhere anymore, except to my new part-time job at the Dairy Queen. Mom thought I was hanging around the house a little too much, so I got it a month ago. Occasionally I get bullied there, too, when people from school come—they'll rip open the little packets of sugar and pour them all over the counters or drop ice cream on the floor—but generally it's a refuge; I feel safe there. When there are no customers, it's manageable. I just watch stuff on my phone or do homework. I can have as much soft-serve ice cream as I want, which is always a plus. I like the guys who work in the kitchen at the back. It's fairly mindless work.

Left alone and lonely is preferred to the alternative now. The alternative is a wave of cruelty. Last week, a crowd literally stood in a circle around me. They made it tighter and tighter, some of them touching me, grabbing me, closer and closer, my eyes clenched shut, until I cried out, and they all laughed and turned away. I saw Breanne's curtain of hair in the group as they moved away. They have so much power. They walk around with it like it's nothing.

No one even knows why I'm a loser anymore. I'm slutty, I'm disgusting, I'm stupid, you'll catch something by association. It doesn't matter; it's been verified by collective insistence, persistence, invention. And because, if nothing else, they know they don't want to unpopular by association, everyone avoids me unless they have reason not to.

I don't know who I can talk to. It's too embarrassing. The thought of telling my mom makes me sick. The things I've been accused of, sex stuff . . . I just can't imagine telling her or showing her what people are saying. It's sickening. She'd freak out and probably make it so much worse. I could never tell Pete. He'd go right to Lottie. And she already thinks I'm meddling in her life.

One day after school, I decide to go see my dad. To actually visit him, see if he can help. He's always said that he's there for me if I need him. I just never really have, until now.

I walk to the bus station. Everyone here seems like they're trying to get the hell out of town, and there is an air of desperation, hunger, and a nasty touch of something about to blow. People are snapping at each other. They're irritable. There is a woman arguing with a bus driver about her ticket. There is a couple sniping at one another. There is a mother pushing a stroller back and forth with a vacant look in her eyes, trying to get her toddler to stop crying and go to sleep.

I buy a ticket to downtown Hamilton. I didn't tell him I'm coming; I'm afraid he'd somehow postpone the visit or something. Waiting on the bank of green vinyl chairs for the announcement about my bus, I watch pigeons fly up in a frenzy, then settle down again.

* * *

The sky darkens as we approach the destination. I get my bearings and try to remember where my dad lives, where the coffee shop he owns—Bean There, a name I can't help but like—is in relation to the station. And the apartment, which is walking distance from there. It's all so conveniently close that you'd think I would visit more often. Last time I was here, my dad and Eleanor had me over for dinner. They cooked together and were laughing and flirting while they were standing at the stove. I didn't know what to do, so I fiddled with the little rooster-and-hen salt-and-pepper shakers and spilled a bunch of salt all over the table. Eleanor laughed it off, saying it was no big deal, but that we had to throw some over our left shoulders to ward off bad luck. It was a really nice night, in the end. But it's been a long time since I was here. After the divorce a couple of years ago, he had a kind of agreement with Mom. It wasn't legal or official or anything, but I saw him about one weekend a month. And then less and less.

The bus brakes make a squealing sound as it slows into the station, and I get up with everyone else. People half-stand under the baggage storage above, their heads bent, angling to get out first. The girl in front of me pulls her underwear out of her bum. The driver tells someone in a huge hurry how to make their connecting bus, then helps an old woman down the steps.

Soon I'm standing on the road, a little unsure of where to go next. *Come on, Stevie, you got this.* I start walking, and sure enough, it's coming back to me. I remember where Bean There is, and where the apartment is.

There are two guys fighting in the street, so I cross to the other side but keep watching them out of the corner of my eye. They are puffing out their chests, and I can tell they both want to hit each other but are afraid of getting hit back. It's coming off of them like sweat or sound waves. People are heading out of restaurants and into bars, and apart from those two guys, the area looks a little bit nicer than it did last time I was here, and I figure that my dad was right to buy around here when it was still crappy and cheap. There is a burger place that is dressed up for hipsters, and a little clothing shop that looks like everything is made for fairies and twee musicians. I admire a necklace in the window that has arrows pointing in different directions. As I turn the corner, it sounds like the two men have decided to each get the last loud, furious word before parting ways. Neither of them is ready to say good-bye.

I see the coffee shop, with its sign made of reclaimed lumber. I stand at the window and notice that Eleanor is behind the counter, cleaning the espresso machine. I came all this way, but now I'm so nervous I have trouble going in. Eleanor has an apron tied around her tiny waist, and her black hair is in one of those fancy braids that looks like a fish bone. She looks pretty and untroubled, and I wonder if I should leave her alone and not push open the door and bring with me all my me-ness.

The door chimes as I open it, and she turns and smiles wide at me.

"Hi," I say, shyly, looking down.

"Hey there," she says. Then, "What can I getcha?"

I blink, then realize. She doesn't remember me.

"Oh," I say, like one of those idiots who is surprised they're being asked what they want when there's a line behind them. Except there isn't a line behind me. There are a lot of people at tables, clicking away on laptops with oversized coffee mugs beside them, and none of them are looking at me, but I still feel stupid. "Oh. I'll have, a, uh, a tea, please." I hate tea.

"Sure. I have a nice English Breakfast; how's that?"

"Great."

She turns to make it, and I blurt out, "To go, please!" and knock over a little stack of granola bars. She nods, no problem, just chipper as can be.

I'm outside again, with a cup of tea, and my face is burning. I guess Dad has no photos of me up anywhere, and I'm obviously not memorable. Big surprise there.

I walk down the street and make a turn down a small side street, throwing out the tea in the first garbage can I see. It makes a terrific *splunk* when it hits the inside of the can. I know where they live, and I keep going in that direction. Maybe I can still save this; maybe all is not lost. Maybe I'm not forgotten.

They live on the second floor of a nice, old brick semi. I know there's a fire escape from when I was here last time. I remember wondering if I could jet out that way after I spilled all the salt. There's a small light on inside, but I don't want to ring the bell, feeling suddenly like maybe I don't want to see my dad after all. I just want to look in.

I head around the back and look up at the fire escape. It's folded up, so I have to jump a few times to catch it, scraping my fingers and falling on my knees before I finally get on. I hang there for a little, then hoist myself up, all the while clanging and making a racket. But I'm up, and I'm climbing, and my heart is beating really hard. I don't think about what I'll say if I get caught but just keep climbing until I am level with their living room. There's a landing on the fire escape here, and I sit, catch my breath, and look in the window.

A cat sees me and comes to look through the glass. It meows, its mouth yawing open soundlessly. This is new. I didn't know my dad got a cat, and this tiny fact nearly cracks me open, right down the middle. It's a silvery gray, and I wish I could pet it, scratch its ears. I wonder what its name is and if it's friendly. And I sit there, on the fire escape, tears rolling down my face. My knee falls against the glass, and the cat butts its head against the window, and I imagine that it's purring.

And then, my dad is there.

"Oh my God!" I hear him shout, clutching his chest. Then he starts laughing, relieved. "Stevie!" he says, opening the window, "you scared the bejesus out of me!" He's laughing and he reaches out for my hand, pulling me in. I wipe my cheeks and laugh, too.

"Sorry," I say.

"Oh my God," he repeats, calmer now, running his hand through his hair. Then he remembers himself and gives me a big hug. "What are you doing here? Is everything okay? Is your mom okay?"

"Oh yeah," I say, suddenly a little embarrassed. "For sure. I was just nearby . . . I had a thing . . ." This kind of vagueness wouldn't fly with my mom, but he is nodding, smiling.

"I'm so glad you came by!" he practically shouts, and I realize that he's nervous. "Are you hungry?" He starts rummaging around the kitchen, looking in cupboards.

"No, I'm fine." I sit down at the kitchen table, and the cat winds around my leg. I trace a circular pattern of wood grain on the table with my finger. Dad finds some cheese and crackers and organic lemonade and busies himself bringing it over to the table.

"How's school?" he asks, handing me a glass.

"Uh, good. Good, good." I am nodding. There's a pause. He's smiling at me. "Um. Well, not great, actually." Oh God. I look up at the ceiling as the tears start.

"Oh. Oh, honey." Dad comes over to me, giving me an awkward hug that puts my face in his armpit, but it doesn't matter, because it's really nice, actually. He crouches down and looks at me, wipes tears from under my eyes with his rough thumbs. "What's going on?"

"I don't know," I say. "I just wish everything was different."

"Yeah, I get that. I remember high school. It's a tough place."

I find it hard to imagine my dad having a tough time as a kid.

"It gets better, you know. You just have to find your people. You've got Lottie, right?"

I take a deep breath and let it out, the last of my tears coming out shakily. "I guess. I thought I did, but I dunno."

"Oh, now," he chuckles, "you two have had your bumps before, right?" He gives my shoulders a little shake. "It's just a phase."

"Uh-huh."

A few seconds go by, and he's rubbing my back. I see him glance at the clock, and I jump up.

"Yeah. Thanks, Dad. It's okay. I'm just being dumb. I . . . I should probably go."

"Really?" He stands, runs a hand over his face. "Okay, honey. Want me to drive you anywhere?" He is being so nice that I almost start crying again.

He drives me to the bus station, chattering away about this and that, giving me money and a huge hug when I get out.

"I love you, Stevie. It's gonna be all right." He grabs my shoulders and looks me in the eye. "I promise. Okay?"

I nod. "Okay."

I stand in line for the bus with my ticket, and he waves as he drives away, the music from his radio fading. Soon enough it feels like it didn't happen, like I have never not been standing here alone.

* * *

The next day, I'm on my way to school, keeping to myself, aware of the potential threats everywhere, a cacophony of anxiety in my head.

But in the middle of all the noise, there's one person I can't figure out.

I am on alert, listening for her.

I walk through my neighborhood, waiting to hear.

Dee.

Dee, that girl who hung around, staying out of the fray, for months, seems to have a thing for me. She's everywhere. It's almost like she's following me. I see her in the Makers' Space—always there, working on editing videos. I never look too closely, but it looks like movies that she's cutting. But whenever I look over, she catches me and turns around.

And then there it is: I hear footsteps behind me, matching mine.

Ever since Lottie and Paige dumped me and the world caught fire. Since I was left alone on the school steps gasping for air.

Watching me, following me, trying to get my attention, but not in the same balls-out-cruel way as everyone else. I don't know what she wants, but I'm afraid to trust anyone. I walk faster now, my heart rate going up, my face sweating. I see the school and heft my backpack further up my shoulder. She starts whistling a weird little tune. I resist the urge to look back and go into the school as the bell rings.

My phone buzzes. It's a text from an unknown number.

I like old movies too

*   *   *

I have Media Studies for homeroom. Pete's class. That's how they know him now, too. Not long after he showed me the Makers' Space, he had his big talk with our class.

The classroom was busy and loud, and there was such a layer of hair spray and body spray in the place that I swear you could almost see it. I found my seat by the window and noticed Pete smiling at two guys who were competing for his attention, talking over each other before class started. I felt jumpy. I kept my head down, just willing the class to start so there wasn't any gap where I could attract attention.

Then: Dee. I heard her throw her bag down and sit behind me and to my right. I could sort of see her. Her legs were crossed, and she was bouncing her foot up and down, up and down. She wore oversized, loose clothes, headphones on her neck, her hair wild.

She whispered, like a hiss, "Hey. Hey, Stevie."

No one noticed. Everyone was talking and laughing and getting settled in, on their phones and getting out their laptops and binders.

I ignored her.

"That's okay," I heard her say in a low voice, "I can wait."

Pete walked to the front of the room, and everyone quieted down. He was smiling. *Something is happening,* I thought. *Is this the day?* I was so nervous that my legs jiggled all over the place. I wished Lottie and I were talking again, that I'd known this was going to go down today. But she had Paige, and they'd probably dissect the whole thing in her room, listening to records together.

He turned to face the chalkboard and wrote, in big letters, Pete Sherman, then turned back to us.

"That's my name," he said, gesturing at the board. "I'm Pete. I've been Pete for a very long time, but I was called something else. And I told you to call me something else. And now, if you can, I'd love it if you called me this. It's new to you, but not to me. If you'd like, you can call me Mr. Sherman. But that's really how I see my father, so if Pete is cool with you, it'd be great."

The room was totally quiet. I knew some people were looking at me, that they'd seen my video or heard about it and now were putting two and two together about who it was about. Then someone started clapping. I heard the chair, just behind me to my right, screech as the person clapping—Dee—stood up. I looked over at her, locked eyes, and looked down, my whole body thrumming. But then, within seconds, Matthew and other quiet kids I'd never really noticed stood up. And then more people. Finally almost everyone else joined in, and I looked at Dee again and exchanged a small smile. I stood, shakily, clapping. A few kids stayed seated, raising eyebrows and rolling their eyes and exchanging looks, arms against their chests, looking around like *WTF*, but most of the class was applauding.

Someone whistled and boomed, "Yeah, Pete!"

"All right, all right. Sit down." Pete beamed at us, waving us back to our seats. "Thank you. You folks are great. I know that you'll have lots of questions. Yes, I'll be using the gender-neutral single-person staff bathroom, and no, I won't be saying any more on that topic." He laughed, and others did too. "I'm sure some of your parents will have lots of questions. I'm happy to hear them. Later. But for now, we are here in Media Studies! So, without further ado, let's get back into the Hero's Quest stuff."

That day, and since, I have felt Dee there, buzzing like a fly, in my periphery. I see her smoking outside, listening to something on her earphones, ignoring everyone else, and she always knows when I'm looking. Her eyes will lazily find mine and she'll wink. That girl. She is nothing like me. She doesn't care what anyone thinks. A lone wolf, for the most part, although sometimes I see her talking to other people who are on the edge, other outcasts. I never see her with my former-friends-turned-current-tormentors. Did they excommunicate her as well?

And does she want to be my friend? I can't trust it. I look at the mystery text. I don't respond.

I can see her taking everything in. It seems like she's in most of my classes, but I haven't been paying a lot of attention until now. She's in homeroom, where Pete is now starting to show signs of his public transition: his hair is cut into a sharp fade, and he's been wearing some really cool blazers with a tie. He looks good and seems so happy, but the truth is that I do miss Rhonda, even in small ways, like seeing her name on the classroom door. She's someone else now, someone better, but not really someone I know well.

Dee is there in Science, leaning back in her chair and twiddling a pen in her fingers like a magician when Matthew answers questions like a science boss. She whispers to me in class. She only volunteers to participate when I get called on and don't know the answer. I see her scoff when Luke, with his posse of hockey goons, imitates Matthew, sticking out his teeth and raising his hand. I look at her when the gym teacher, Mr. Cavalier, tells the guys they're throwing like girls and calls them ladies and Nancys. She stares him down, furious. Or when kids like Carol or Mahir get racist darts thrown their way, some of them really hitting the mark, others deflected and thrown back. She never laughs at cruelty. I know she's watching what's been happening to me, too. It's like she's keeping score.

9

At dinner tonight, Mom wanted to discuss Reg.

"Stevie, honey, I'd like to talk to you about something," Mom said, while she opened the bucket of KFC she'd picked up for us. I was so happy that it was just us at home for dinner, that he wasn't there, talking about his favorite concerts or trying to simultaneously be my best friend and my mother's lover. Ugh.

"Uh-huh," I said, picking up a piece of chicken in my fingers gingerly and taking a bite.

"Things with Reg are getting pretty serious," she ventured, avoiding my eyes.

Uh. I froze. What was happening? I stared at her, the chicken hanging from my hand.

"And, well, it doesn't make much sense for him to be paying rent at his own place since he's here so often."

I briefly imagined Reg's house. He'd probably tried to decorate it like it was the green room at CBGBs where he was high-fiving celebrities and acting like God's gift to everything, but really it was just a boring craphole.

"And God knows I deserve to be happy, and he makes me happy. You want that for me, don't you?" My mom has this idea that she has been dealt a bum hand in life and is always going on about how hard it is being a single mom. "You know, he actually knows a lot about music and movies and stuff. You and Lottie should talk to him sometime."

The rest of the conversation was a foggy blur of reasoning that began and ended with me having zero say in the matter. He was moving in. I provided her with what she needed to hear:

"Right. Okay. Whatever you want, Mom."

My ears buzzed, and I decided I wasn't hungry at all. My mom chose to believe this. I went to my room, where I listened to her calling Reg to tell him how our conversation had gone. *Pretty well. I think it will be good for her.*

I picked up my phone and texted Dad. There was always a way out.

Hey dad.

He answered right away. *Hey kiddo! How are you feeling?*

Fine. Question:

Shoot!

If I wanted to could I come live with you

Ellipses, on, off, on, then: *Wow. I would love that. But I don't think makes sense. mom would be pissed. would be*

*hard. school and friends are there. Are things really that bad?
Give it time?*

I didn't respond. He texted a few more times; then he called
me, but I didn't answer.

Its fine dad. just wondering. Not a big deal.

Nothing's a big deal until everything is. I watched my
phone humming as he tried to call again, and then stopped.
Gave up just like that.

Ok kiddo call me later if u want xo

And then: *You know me and eleanor would love you to
visit again*

Right. Eleanor who doesn't even remember who I am. And
so I have spent the evening editing, commenting, dissecting
the rare, the camp, the cult films I love.

I'm alone. I know that the storm rages on against me online.
I try not to check, but then I do. Each time, there are more—
people I've never heard of trolling me, which isn't all that
unusual—but I thought it would have died down by now. But it
keeps up, steady, unstoppable. It never sleeps. Ever since Lottie
and Paige screamed at me, then ghosted me, dropped me like
they never knew me and made me feel invisible, they passed
the torch: I have become visible to the rest of the school, fun to
play with, just a joke. At the least, no one wants to be my friend;
at the worst, everyone wants to be my enemy.

I decided to continue making my videos about old movies.
I can't help it. It's always made me feel better, but I guess it's

different now. Maybe it's kind of like I'm making a target for myself, but some part of me can't shut it off. These old flicks are what I've always used to distract me from anything bad. I considered starting a new channel, or disabling the comments, but I haven't because there are, even among the harshest and cruelest comments, sweet ones from strangers.

I DON'T KNOW WHATS GOING ON WITH THESE COMMENTS BUT YOU DO YOU GIRL KEEP IT UP

I LOVE YOUR CHANNEL DON'T LISTEN TO THESE TROLLS

KEEP MAKING GREAT VIDS YOU MAKE ME HAPPY YOUR FUNNY AND CUTE

Because of them, I keep going and keep looking at the comments. It's a reflex, it's a drug. I never reply to the comments, but I hope for them, I wait for them to reach me across the void.

I look out the window and see Reg's car, shining in the pouring rain. I take off my headphones and then I hear him, chitchatting with Mom, making himself at home, keeping her away from me. I think of Lottie, at home, probably about to play a board game and hold hands around the table with her two dads and Paige. Assholes.

I lie on my bed, and with a sick feeling, I do what I can't stop doing: I scroll through my phone. Insta, Snapchat, pictures, comments, likes, memes, videos, more, more, more, more. Our entire school is like a social media creature that never rests. They won't forget me; their memories are long. I drop the phone beside me, where it pants and throbs like a living thing. I swallow a sob.

I am still, listening. The rain thuds, pounding and rattling, the best noise. Cars cutting through it with their *wiiishhh wiiiishhhhh*. I close my eyes. I remember being sick as a kid, lying here in the summer while everyone else was outside, and my room felt close and small and comforting while the noise outside was just background cushioning. Skateboards and scooters and feet on the sidewalk, all the kids yelling, summertime. Comfy and happy. I try to bring it back, that feeling, but it slipped out and went to another, younger kid's house when I wasn't looking. You can't get that back, that kid stuff. I remember trying to play with my toys in the bath one day and realizing I didn't really know how to do it anymore, and so I just lined them up on the edge and knocked them off, one by one.

I hear footsteps, and my mom taps on my door, pushing it open as she does.

"Hey Stevie, honey."

"Hi."

"Listen," she says, pushing her bangs out of her face, "Reg and I are going out to see a movie. You okay here?"

I think for a minute of what it would be like to try to tell her how I feel, about what's happened. I worry that she'd bring Reg in, that she'd share it on Facebook in some attempt to protect other kids, that somehow she would make matters worse. She's just like all the parents who think they're keeping an eye on what we're doing by being on Facebook or reading articles, but we're slippery and fast. We're so far ahead that they couldn't catch up if they tried.

"Yeah, sure." I smile, because she needs me to, because I am careful.

"That's my girl." She looks so relieved. "Okay, gotta get ready!" And she's gone, and I hear her in her room, humming and getting changed.

Later, I watch them get into the Reg-mobile and drive away on a date, and the ground opens up like a gaping mouth and swallows all the birds and worms and raindrops until the street is empty and quiet except for the rain. I let the curtain fall back.

I play around on my laptop, editing for a while; then I look at the comments on my last vid. There's a new one:

SHOW US YOUR TITS.

And another:

GOD NO PLEASE DON'T

LOL

LMAO

My phone buzzes. There is another message from that same unknown number.

Let's meet up. I won't bite.

My curiosity is piqued. But no. Too risky. I need to think. Because I know that everybody bites.

10

The next night, I go to the bathroom and turn the tap on for a bath. I sit on the counter and chew my nails until the tub is full, then step in. It is boiling hot, but I keep lowering myself into it, loving and hating the heat. I always make my baths scalding hot, so hot it feels cold. I freeze in position with my ass half in, holding on to the sides, making some *oh oh oh oh* sounds, but then get all the way in. When I get out, there will be a red imprint like a sunburn over most of my body. I love how everything seems to shrink back, like my nails separating from my fingers, when I get in. It's the best, that terrible heat.

Let's meet up. I won't bite.

The radio on the counter is playing some weird station I found. It's old sixties-sounding French music.

I sit quietly for a while, thinking about the text, then wet my hands and run them over my face. I lift my feet out and put them on the edge of the tub, relishing the cold air. Close my eyes. I am just starting to relax, so naturally, there is a sudden pounding on the door.

"Stevie." It's Mom.

"Hmmm?" Eyes still closed.

"Stevie, I need to get in there."

"Well, it seems that the door is locked."

She turns the knob several times to prove my point.

"Stevie, come on, please. Open the door."

Jesus. This house, I tell you. I don't even know why we have a bathtub.

I lean my head back and put my ears under the water. I can't hear her or the French music, but I can feel the thudding of her knocking, and my ears are burning. I come up for air.

"Okay, okay, keep your hair on."

I splash out, unlocking the door, and then almost break my neck getting back into the tub and pulling the curtain across before she comes rattling in like a tornado made of cigarette smoke and instant coffee grounds. Part of the shower curtain falls down, and the shower rings clatter all over the floor. She turns off the radio with a click and starts rooting around her enormous makeup bag, pulling out mascara and lipstick.

"You know, it's really hard to relax around here," I grumble.

"Oh, I feel so sorry for you. It must be really stressful being a fifteen-year-old with no responsibilities."

I give her a stink-eye because she has obviously forgotten what it's like to be fifteen, but it hits the remaining curtain, so she doesn't see it.

"I have a client coming in this evening. I'll be downstairs. You can have someone over if you want."

"No thanks," I say.

"What about Lottie? I haven't seen her in a while. You two okay?" she asks.

She has no idea what is going on or that I no longer have a best friend. "I guess."

"Teenage friendships. God, I remember those." She pauses, and I hear her snap the cap on her lipstick. "You know, I ran into her dad today."

"Which one?"

"What?" She clues in. "Oh God, Stevie, her *dad*, Jacob. God. Anyway, he told me that Rhonda is moving out, like soon."

I sit up. "What? Already? Pete's moving?"

"Right. *Pete*, my apologies. Didn't Lottie tell you? Yeah, apparently, things are bonkers over there. Her dad said that 'Pete' is trying to find out who 'he' is." I could hear her making air quotes around words out there. "There might be a woman on the scene, too, just to make matters even more complicated."

"A woman for Pete?"

"I *guess*. I think that's what he said. I don't know, maybe Jacob just thinks there is. I can't even figure this stuff out, and I haven't seen any of them for ages. He looks like a wreck, that's all I know." I hear the doorbell from the basement door. "Oops," Mom says, "I gotta go. Bye, hon. I'll be downstairs if you need me!"

I sigh for years and lower my mouth to the water and make bubbles with my lips. It is deliciously silent. A deep quiet, where you can hear the hum of all the whirring things in the house, everything waiting to be used. And I feel in that moment that I could sink down, down, below the surface, into the hot center of the earth. Raising my arms in surrender, my body buzzing like an engine, like another thing to be turned on and up and into something else. I could just melt into the silence and loneliness.

I lie like this for a long time. A song runs through my head and I nod to the rhythm, and eventually the water feels cold and a chill runs across my arms, making the skin rise in tiny goose bumps. I pull the plug and stand, shivering, grabbing a towel that smells faintly of mildew.

In my mom's room, there is a long full-length mirror that swings on a frame. I stand in front of it in the buff. I'm not hairless like most of the girls I know. *You're going full bush*, Lottie said once. She shaves herself, but I'm afraid of putting the razor down there and have no intention of waxing. I'm just getting the hang of shaving my pits without cutting myself; I'm not risking any injuries to my nether regions. It's not like anyone is seeing them anyway, despite what anyone says.

I think about how earlier today, Luke was all over Matthew for answering a question about black holes in Science.

"Yeah, you know that, but could you find a real hole?" he muttered, loud enough for a few of us to hear. Would I have laughed at that a few months ago?

"What?" asked Matthew. Luke and his buddies scoffed.

Then I heard Dee, who sits beside me, say under her breath, "Why doesn't anyone ever stop these guys?"

Without thinking, I grabbed an eraser and threw it at Luke. It hit him squarely in the head and he whipped around, his eyes angry as hell.

"What the *fuck*?" he snarled.

"Stevie!" our teacher called, surprised. "Settle down, please."

Luke rubbed his head and leaned toward Matthew, whispering, "You could find Skeevie's hole, because it's all stretched out and overused. But it probably has teeth. It'd probably bite your hand off."

"Shut up," said Matthew quietly, looking back at me apologetically.

Dee leaned over and picked my eraser up off the floor. She tossed it onto my desk and said, "Nice."

* * *

The next morning, on the way to school, I am thinking about what Dee said. *Why doesn't anyone ever stop these guys?*

How different would the school be if they were as afraid as I am, if there were actual consequences for their actions, if they were somehow kept in line?

I text the mystery number back. I know it's her.

Ok. Let's meet.

And it begins.

11

Episode 70 2:01
Some of my favorite movie heroes are just searching for
someone who understands them or who can help them
reach their potential. And when they find someone?
That's when things really get interesting. Look at Veron-
ica Sawyer, from Heathers, *for instance; look how JD*
lights a fire under her ass, how she gets caught up in his
energy.

"My specialty is teen revenge films," Dee says.

I nod, but I'm just taking her in. Until now, I've mostly avoided her, but now, sitting here, I can't take my eyes off her. She is tall, confident, wild haired, like she's made of steel wool and leather, Pop Rocks and gasoline. A stranger-cowgirl. She looks right into my eyes when she talks, like there is no one else.

She is nothing like me.

And I realize it's something else: I don't feel alone.

"I like your channel. You know a lot—like, a shit-ton, actually—about films."

I smile. "Uh, thanks. So . . . why did you only join partway through the year?"

"Dad changed jobs. You know," she says, rolling her eyes. "Lucky me."

We met at the spot where I used to meet Lottie before school. Lottie, who is never there anymore. Dee met me here, knew right away where to find me. I steal a look at her, and she catches me and grins. A shiver, a ripple runs through me. We are approaching the school parking lot, where kids are pulling up in all manner of nice and shitty cars; others are outside smoking and gathering in groups. Dee stops, and I look over at her.

"So, hey," she says, tugging my arm, looking up at the parking lot, a little surreptitiously. "Do you wanna have some fun?"

"What do you mean? We have school."

Luke and his friends walk by, and he knocks into me and mutters, "Fucking weirdo."

Dee glares after him, then turns back to me. "Do we?"

"What else are we going to do?"

"The possibilities are endless. I don't know about you, but I do not feel like going today." She gestures at the sky, where the clouds have made themselves scarce, where the sun is shining like a big, gorgeous attention whore. "It's a beautiful day."

I nod *yeah, it is.* But.

"It's up to you. But I'm not going to school."

I look at the school. That ugly beast, with its writhing insides, its sour, nauseous belly full of unhappy adolescence. I look back at the sky, with its infinite possibilities. It looks like it could just turn itself inside out like a giant piñata and rain candy all over us until we are buried—chocolate-smudged faces and happy toothaches. I look at Dee, who grins, and makes my heart heat up with some real, actual happiness. I reconsider.

* * *

Dee says she'll wait on the big boulder outside the school. Me and Lottie's rock.

"You'd better get going if we're doing this."

I hurry through the front doors as the bell rings. I have, scrunched up in my hand, a note that Dee just scribbled for me, using my back as a surface to write against. She folded it up and handed it to me, telling me to give it to my teacher.

"What's it say?" I asked her.

"Says that you're fed up and you're taking a personal day."

I opened it.

Please excuse Stevie from school today. She is spending the day with her father.

She'd signed it with a pretty good estimation of my mom's loopy *Tiffany.* It's brilliant. For starters, the excuse of visiting with my dad is an ace in the hole. I mean, what teacher, let alone Pete, is going to deny a kid from a clearly broken home the chance to visit with her dad?

The corridors are loud; it rings in my ears. I stride past my locker, not looking for Lottie, not caring, right into homeroom and zero in on Pete, who is at his desk rummaging through a bag. He sees me coming, and his face lights up.

"Hi there, Stevie! How's the morning going so far?"

He seems so far away to me now. I never go to their house anymore; it feels like a different life, back when he was someone I would confide in, someone I could talk to and trust. Now he's just my teacher.

"Um, good." I hand over the note. "I'm spending the day with my dad." I look away. "Hope that's all right with you," I mumble. And I am hoping that he doesn't run into my mom anywhere in town and mention this.

He reads it and nods, a somber look on his face.

"Of course, Stevie. I know how much you must be looking forward to that. Say hi for me." He doesn't even know when he's being blatantly lied to. I can't believe I used to think he got me, that he got anything.

"Yeah, okay, I will," I bullshit. "He doesn't come around much, so we kind of have to jump on it when he does."

"That's great. Make sure you catch up on what you miss from someone in the class." Then he tells me to have a good day, and I don't even feel a twinge of guilt when I walk right back out of there again. It just goes to show that even people who really know you well may not have any kind of bullshit radar. You could just spend your days lying your ass off to everyone.

Dee is right. I *am* fed up.

And so, when a group of senior-year Barbie clones gives me the once-over on my way out, I flip them not one, but two birds—*ka-pow!*—one in each hand. Boom. And then I slam open the front door, or at least I try to, but it's one of those really heavy metal ones that takes forever to actually open, and so the moment is not actually that momentous.

Dee stands up and I can't help but smile.

* * *

We are winding our way through the suburban streets of my childhood. It is a warmish day, and the sun is in our faces, and I feel, even with everything—everything bad—pretty good. Not alone, anyway, and that's something.

I kick some pebbles. "Where are we going, anyway?"

"Exploring," she says, just like that. Decisive.

I don't say anything, but the silence isn't awkward. We walk through the quiet streets, Dee with her hands jammed in her pockets, occasionally looking at me mischievously. I don't tell her that I have never skipped school before, that I have never, in fact, "explored" and don't even know what she means. I am buzzing with the newness and badness of this. These are streets I grew up on, but they suddenly seem fresh and different; I never see them during the weekday school hours.

"What's your mom like?" Dee says, out of nowhere.

"How do you know my mom?" I ask, alarmed.

"I've seen her around . . ." She pauses; then, "She's pretty."

"I'm sure she'd love to hear that."

"You look like her, you know. Except"—she looks at my clothes—"you don't dress at all the same."

I laugh. "Oh, you mean because I'm not vacuum-packed into my clothes?"

"Yeah, I guess." She says. "I've never seen your dad, though. Is he not around?"

I glare at her. "What is this, therapy?"

She shrugs. "God, defensive. Why, do you need therapy?"

"No, I just mean . . . No. Whatever." I jump up to pull a leaf off a tree we're passing under. "My dad left, okay? Why the hell do you want to know so much about my family?"

"I like to watch people. See what makes them tick." She

looks over at me. "My mom took off, too. And my dad has a new girlfriend who could give two shits about me."

I pull the skin of the leaf away from the bones of it. It looks like a skeleton. "Sounds familiar." I don't know how to say that I miss my mom, but Dee nods like she knows, she knows exactly, and her hair bounces slowly around her face like a lazy forest in a breeze. She has the hair I've been trying to grow out and into, a style I've been trying to own. It is black and curly, and she does nothing with it from what I can tell, but it works. Same with her body and the way she holds herself: strong, relaxed. She's got swagger, a kind of stomp that just seems to come so easily.

"You hungry?" she asks.

"Sure, but—"

Dee looks behind us and quickly grabs me by the hand. Her touch feels like a current running up my arm as she pulls me between two houses. We lean against the brick wall of one of them, and then Dee walks toward the backyard. She peeks over the fence. Looks at me, eyebrows raised.

"What?" I whisper frantically. "What are you doing?"

She grins, oblivious to my concerns. "Come on. Let's see if anyone here has something we can snack on."

The sun darts behind the only cloud up there like it's trying to hide, too. My mind races, but while I'm trying to decide what to do, Dee has opened the gate and is looking under a mat by the back door. She holds up a key like a talisman, her face split by a wonderful, terrible smile.

"Aha! People are so predictable."

And in that moment, those exact words, things begin to slide forward for me. Forward and fast and off course from where I was going in the first place. I can almost see my other self, what I would be doing, sitting in Pete's class, looking out the window at the cloudless sky, looking at a squirrel, remembering Lottie and Paige and how things used to be—like there are two of me in that moment, but one of me chose a new life.

People are so predictable.

I follow Dee inside.

The house is comfortable, cozy, decorated like a candy cottage with flowers and candles and little bowls of potpourri on the tables. I am afraid to touch anything, including the orange cat that has come over to me, winding itself around my legs as I stand frozen in fear. Can the police find fingerprints on a cat? Dee, meantime, is in the fridge, in the cupboards, humming to herself.

"Relax," she says, over her shoulder. "People have way more than they need. No one is ever going to know we were here." She pockets an apple and a couple of small bags of pretzels and cookies and other things from a cupboard that, yes, in truth, appears to be overflowing with snacks.

"Let's look around."

And so we do, and the cat follows me, questioning my judgment, asking with its bitchy little face why I'm doing this, why I've abandoned reason. It jumps up on a bookshelf as we enter the living room, and I want to ask it if it's ever had a best friend who snipped the whole communication thread, which was until then reliably woven into the fabric of its being, just because she suddenly had two amazing dads instead of one, just because there was a new girl with perfectly flippy hair. The cat looks away then and licks itself, which is an answer in itself.

Dee pulls a framed photo off the shelf, and together we notice the same thing. A picture-perfect family with one very familiar face.

"Hey . . . look who it is . . ."

"Breanne," I whisper fearfully, reverently, starting to get very uncomfortable. *Shit.* Now I remember why the house looked familiar. I saw Breanne once on my way home, coming in here. And it suddenly occurs to me that maybe this is a trap. Maybe this whole thing has been some way of luring me away from school, away from any form of protection. My blood runs cold, and I consider bolting. "What's going on, Dee?" I say, edging backward. Who else is here? I wonder. Are they going to swarm me, kill me?

But she's not looking at me. She's looking at the photo. "Breanne." She puts a finger to Breanne's beautiful, evil face. "You know, I've never been a fan of hers." She's wiggles her eyebrows.

I say nothing to this but look back at the door.

"I don't like this," I murmur.

Dee puts the picture down. "We'll go. Don't worry. But not yet. Not quite yet. I wanna look around upstairs."

I freeze, watching her. She moseys, hands in pockets, out of the room. I follow her a couple of steps, cautiously, at a distance, and see her climb the spiraling, entrance-hall staircase, feet making no noise on the cushy cream wall-to-wall carpet. All the time in the world. I look at the cat, which is poised, ears perked, knowing this is one step too far.

I won't go up Breanne's stairs. I keep my eyes on the door. My body tensed.

"What are you doing?" I yell.

Silence.

"Come down!"

This girl is bad news.

"I'm leaving now," I shout, and even though I sound

confident at the start of the sentence, I lose it by the end, barely muttering the *now*. But then I hear her close a door, and she's bumping down the stairs at a hustle.

"Okay," she says gently, and touches my arm when she reaches the bottom. "I'm here."

"What the hell is this about?" I demand, practically running out of Breanne's house. "Are you fucking with me?"

She grins and nudges me with her arm and tells me to relax. We're out of the house. Maybe it's the relief or adrenaline, but I feel a charge of energy. Trouble. But the kind of trouble I gravitate toward, the kind that's bold and fun and makes me momentarily forget everything that weighs me down. It makes my skin tighten and my eyes focus, like someone has blown cool air in my face and the dim fog I've been under is finally lifting. I am awake again and don't really care about the risks, not now when we're outside and the sun is shining down like a kiss. Not now.

We walk down toward the lake, and Dee buys some ice cream from a sad little truck parked at the curb. I wonder what Lottie's doing, and then I don't care. We clamor down over some rocks toward the water's edge and choose a couple of big ones where the sun is shining all over the place. Dee stretches out, way out, her legs and arms going straight as she gets long and yawns and reaches out like a huge lazy cat. She almost drops her ice cream but saves it, sucking it from the bottom. It's sweet and obscene, and I look away, out across the lake.

"So what other movies do you like?" I ask, my back to her.

"I told you, old high school revenge flicks are my jam. *Heathers*, *Pump Up the Volume*, *Carrie*; I even like things like *Revenge of the Nerds* and *Back to the Future*, but for me, there has to be some real payoff at the end. The assholes have to get theirs."

"What do you consider 'getting theirs'?"

"Like, they need to suffer. How else are they supposed to learn?"

I turn back to look at her, and she is taking off her shirt. I look away again, my face going red.

"What?" she asks, laughing at me. "It's hot. I'm hot. I am going to enjoy it."

I watch a boat in the distance and say nothing. She lets out a satisfied sigh. I turn my head again and take a small peek. She is stretched out on her rock, arms over her head, brown nipples looking straight up and daring me to defy them.

Her eyes are closed, but she says, "It's not going to kill you to loosen up a bit, Stevie."

I roll my eyes.

"I'm serious. What's the worst that will happen to you?"

I spend so much time worrying about the worst things. I can't imagine anymore what it feels like not to care, every second, what people think, what kind of danger I'm in. I look at Dee again, she's smiling sleepily, bare to the world. I consider my shirt, sticking to me in the heat. What if someone sees us?

"Just do it, for Christ's sake," Dee laughs.

So I do.

The rock on my bare back is uncomfortable at first, so I put my T-shirt under me. A shiver runs across my body, and I feel like I might be having an embarrassment-induced heart attack, but I try to relax. And then I actually do. Dee keeps her eyes closed against the sun, which is warm and inviting. "Feel good?" she asks me, and I tell her the jury is still out on it, and she chuckles. I look over at her and try to soak up some of her ability to lay back and chill. We stay like this for a while, listening to the water lapping against the rocks, and to the sounds of voices and dogs around the waterfront paths. Then I hear a kid ask, "Is she bare naked?" and turn to see him pointing at me to his mom, who shushes him and pulls him away, and I giggle, and so does Dee.

"So: what do you think of our town?" I ask her.

"It's got that innocent-until-proven-guilty thing going for it."

"Oh yeah?"

"I mean, it seems quaint, but it's actually crawling with terrible people."

I laugh and cross my hands over my chest self-consciously. I roll over and look at Dee. "Like who?"

She turns her head to me and opens her eyes. "Like who? Like those people at school who are all over your ass, even though you act like it's nothing. Paige, Aidan, Luke and Breanne, and the rest of the fucking assholes who run it like some kind of *Orange Is the New Black* version of high school. And even what's-her-name, Lottie. Wasn't she your best friend? What got up her ass? How could you let her treat you like that?"

I don't know. I blink away tears that came fast to my eyes and say nothing, sitting up to put on my T-shirt again.

Dee scoffs. "And the teachers are no better. There's all this 'zero-tolerance' bullshit, but half the time they haven't got a clue what is going on, and they turn a blind eye the other half. And sometimes *they're* the bullies."

"I should get going," I say, because suddenly the clouds are filling up the sky and I don't want to talk anymore. Dee sits up and pulls her own shirt on.

"And what about your mom?" she asks, scrambling up with me.

I turn to Dee sharply. "What about her?"

"You tell me. Seems like she forgot about you." Her eyes are holding mine, and I can feel myself about to full-on cry.

I start climbing up toward the pathway, and Dee grabs my shoulder. "Hey," she says, gently, then takes her hand off me and smiles. "I just want to say, I—I'm here. I've got your back."

"What the hell does that mean?"

"It means that I am not like them."

We are standing on the gravel pathway that runs along the lakefront. I look at her, this bold new friend. She grabs my hand and squeezes it. Like a best friend.

"It's people like us against the world, Stevie."

I roll my eyes and mutter, "You don't even know me."

"Sure I do. You and me? We're the same."

And looking back, after all of it, it might have been here, here in this moment, that I finally felt like I could rebuild myself.

12

On Saturday, Sunday, Monday, and Tuesday, I stay away if I see Reg's car at our house. I don't want to see him—or Mom with him. They're building a two-person raft to sail away to their new life. There is no room for me. He's almost totally moved in now. Every time I see him, he's carrying a box and telling me, "It's the last one, I swear, Stevie! Hahaha." I go to my job. I hide in my room at night, claiming to have a mountain of homework. I make myself disappear. All those hours I used to spend at Lottie's place—I realize now how much time that was, how much it took me out of this house. Mom used to kind of resent me being there so often, but now she doesn't care that I'm around.

Dee came over for the first time the other day, and Reg almost fell over himself to prove how cool he was by complimenting her on her *Stranger Things* T-shirt: "Great show! You have good taste!" I scoffed, and we went into my room together. It was so completely different from Paige being there. Dee ran her hands over all my old movies with reverence, like they were part of some kind of shrine.

"The. Best," she said, holding up *Heathers*.

"Classic."

She threw herself on my bed like she'd been there a thousand times. She gazed at all my movie posters.

"Ahh. What a great room. A total sanctuary," she said, grinning. She sat up then and looked at me, a glint in her eye. "It's almost like a war room in a movie, you know? Like, you could plot some dangerous shit in here." She paused, then looked serious, and I couldn't even tell if she was kidding when she said, "I mean, if you ever wanted to, like, seize the town by force."

I laughed and looked around my room, seeing it in a new light. There is hardly an inch of wall space not covered in some homage to movies; my desk is covered in scripts and notes for my videos; there are piles of DVDs and VHS tapes everywhere.

"Ha. Yeah. I guess."

We spent a lot of time together that weekend. That's the good thing about being a social outcast: your schedule opens right up. Dee doesn't seem to have a lot of demands on her time, either. And we join up in those wedges of time between school, before bed, on the weekends. I have my part-time job, but Dee doesn't have a job, so she just goes with me and waits in one of the booths writing in her journal.

"What are you always writing in that thing?" I ask her one night when we're walking back to our neighborhood after one of my shifts. The days are getting longer, but it's dark by now, and the streetlights are like bright teeth in an open mouth.

"All kinds of stuff. Notes. Observations. Lists. Goals."

"Like, you look at me making a soft serve and are all, like, 'hashtag goals,'" I say, turning my fingers into a hashtag.

"Oh yeah," she jokes, "and the hairnet is 'hashtag fashion goals.'"

"Of course, the hashtag written in the notebook doesn't have *quite* the same effect."

"Right. It's more of an *homage* or a reference to our digital age, if you will."

"Haha. Okay, there, Pete," I laugh.

"Yes, I think I might be securing myself an A in Media Studies this term."

"Oh God, don't remind me. I haven't even started to think about that final assignment yet."

Dee jumps up on a curb beside me and walks along it, her shadow looming above mine. "Oh please, that assignment was made for people like us. 'A new interpretation of a classic film or TV show'? Honestly, I think Pete might have actually written that for you."

"I don't think that's how teaching works."

Dee deadpans with her fingers crossed. "Hashtag 'teaching goals.'"

I groan.

"Well, I'm going to do something completely over the top," she says, jumping down from the curb. "I'm already planning it. Go out with a bang."

Our friendship is easy and exciting and a little risky, only because Dee could give literally zero fucks. She is fearless. Maybe it sounds weird, but it's like we have known each other for years. It's different than with Lottie, because we weren't thrown together as children just because we lived close by and were in the same class. We've actually chosen to be friends. She gets me. She never tells me to calm down or take it down a notch. It's the opposite: she draws me out, pushes me. She likes the same movies and books and music, and we make each other laugh so hard we cry. We loop arms and entwine legs and are so comfortable in silence, sometimes I forget she's there. It all went from zero to two hundred so quickly, but just having a friend at all in these troubled times is a win for me. All the other shit, the everyday nightmare of high school, is starting to feel like something I can take on, that we can take on together.

* * *

Our school doesn't have a track, so during gym we run through the streets of town: a long line of joggers in matching T-shirts and varying degrees of athleticism ritually winding in and out of neighborhoods and past people picking up their mail or gardening. Our teacher, Ms. Kwan, young and peppy and excitable, leads the pack, her ponytail swinging to her steps, then loops back like a border collie to make sure she doesn't lose the stragglers, the uninspired and asthmatic members of the herd who pull up the eventual rear.

Dee and I are about midway in the line, slightly out of breath but keeping a good pace. There's a big gap between the people ahead and behind us. The sun is busting out the big guns today, bearing down on us, making us squint and sweat.

"I can't wait until we don't have to do this anymore," I say, my feet slapping the pavement.

"No shit," says Dee. "A few more weeks. I bet Kwan can't wait until she has a whole summer of unadulterated running. I can just see her"—she holds her arms out in ecstasy—"'Yes! Yes! Running! My one true love!'"

I grin, then look around as I hear someone coming up behind us. It's Aidan, jogging alone, and looking the worse for wear in spite of what would appear to be a body made for sports. He is covered in sweat and wheezing as he makes his way toward us.

"Oh great," I mutter.

He gets closer, and I notice that Dee is picking up the pace.

"What are you doing?" I ask, alarmed, as I try to keep up.

"Getting in shape," she growls, faster now. We put some distance between us and Aidan, and I hear him coughing but matching our pace. We pass a few other kids, who look at us, surprised; Aidan's feet are still rhythmically hitting the sidewalk behind us, closer now. I laugh nervously but keep going.

"Shit!" I hear him grumble as he begins to close the distance between us.

"Stevie, come *on*," Dee urges me, speeding up.

I look nervously behind us. Aidan spits and shakes his wet hair out of his eyes; he looks like he's going to puke. I turn to Dee, who stares ahead with grim determination. People are moving to the side, slowing down to watch us now. The school is in sight. Faster now. My lungs are aching, but I feel the urgency; I tap into something. I have to beat him. I notice Ms. Kwan now, lifting her head and turning, running backward, watching what has become a race. Dee is falling back, behind me, but I have gained a second wind.

"Come on, Stevie!" Ms. Kwan shouts as I start to lag, as I feel like my heart will burst, as I hear Aidan hissing *you cunt, you bitch* behind me. "Push yourself! Go! Go! Go!"

And we're almost there, and I hear Dee's laugh now, because suddenly, *listen*—Aidan's feet have taken on a fainter sound, and he swears loudly as we cross through the school gates, and at the very least Ms. Kwan is clapping. She slaps my back and I stumble forward, gasping but smiling.

"Nothing like competition to fill your lungs, hey? Sorry McPhearson," she calls to Aidan, "she beat you fair and square."

I lift a water bottle to my mouth and close my eyes against the sun.

"I knew you had that in you," I hear Dee say, and I can tell, even without look at her, that she's grinning. Something that had long gone to sleep flickers its eyes open inside me: pride.

*   *   *

There's a new me, better than the old me, and it is because of Dee, who is bigger, brighter, bolder than Lottie, than all of them. She is rubbing off on me like a marker you write on a birthday card, and realize too late that it won't dry, leaving backward salutations on your fingers. She's imprinted on me. It's not sexual—it's more, better, stronger. It's best friendship. I am returning to myself and becoming *more*. She has less patience for the fools around her. It seems she doesn't want to just watch anymore.

Other people are noticing her, too. I've never been friends with someone like this: someone so unafraid, someone people see. Just when I think she's embarrassing, she passes that point and moves into the bizarre, and I watch, in wonder, as people are surprised and then become caught up in her momentum. She speaks out when she's not supposed to, moves when she should be still, says nothing when she's meant to speak. When people make fun of her, she joins right in the laughter or sends a zinger back, and then it seems like other people defend her also, call out the assholes who try to take her down. Sometimes before class starts, she stands on a chair and does a little dance, and when anyone tries to talk to her, she calls out in a really loud voice that she can't hear them over the music. She does the boogaloo, whatever that is. She parades around the cafeteria like she doesn't know the rules: she walks past tables of popular kids, like Breanne and Paige, Aidan, and sometimes Lottie, tapping them on the head, saying, "Duck, duck, duck," but never "goose," which secretly drives everyone a bit crazy. People are talking about her, laughing when she sings loudly in the halls. She tells rude jokes about nuns having sex, pinches her own butt and howls in outrage, shakes and shimmies while she's opening her locker. People are being pulled into her orbit.

For me, she takes the edge off my worries. She's changed the conversation. When the trolls come for me—on the way to school, after, in class under the radar of teachers—Dee sticks up for me. She shuts them down, tells them to fuck right off, laughs at them, and more. The other day, Luke tried to pin me in front of the water fountain and turn it on. Dee managed to get between us and kick him in the nuts. On the way home from school, some kids I didn't recognize got really close, heckling me. Dee was right there, rooting around in her bag and then suddenly pulling out pepper spray and threatening them. They scoffed but left us alone.

"Where'd you get that?" I asked her as she threw it back in her bag.

"I've had reason to be prepared," she answered, cryptically.

They still find me online, and there isn't much Dee can do about that, but I feel her, like a kind of shield.

Other, different people are noticing me too, and it's not entirely bad. I get the occasional smile of recognition, a wink of association, like they're in on Dee's jokes. It feels good.

Today, for now, it is lunchtime.

In the cafeteria, I'm with Dee and a few other kids who have started sitting with us—or at least near us. I don't know them all that well, but they're all right. I see Lottie come in. She looks right at me, and there is a moment: she raises her eyebrows like a question. I turn, like I didn't see her. I laugh like Dee just said the funniest thing. It's a relief not to be so worried. If I crank up the volume, I can't hear the whispers in my mind.

"What's her problem?" Dee asks me between mouthfuls, gesturing at Lottie.

I shrug. Lottie sits at the end of the table with Breanne and Paige and their popular puppets, but she pulls out a book and starts to read. Breanne is laughing at someone at another table. I follow her eyes to see. There's a girl in our grade with a skin condition, and Breanne has it out for her. It's stupid; the girl is beautiful and nice. Her skin is white and brown in spots and patches, like she's been splashed by a magic potion, from her cheeks going down into her collar and coming out her sleeves onto her wrists and hands. Her name is Michelle, and now she is staring back at the girls with her own group of friends backing her up, but I can tell by her eyes that she's scared. There's a silence. Breanne opens her eyes wide, bats her eyelashes, and lets out a low *mooooo*. Michelle turns away, her cheeks red, and one of her friends puts a hand on her back. She brushes it off.

"I can't stand that girl," says Dee, looking at Breanne.

"Yeah, she's the worst."

Lottie and I make eye contact again briefly. She turns away, and there is a little pang in my gut. Soon I see her get up and leave the cafeteria with her book under her arm. Paige calls something to her, and she turns her head and nods briefly. I wonder if she still likes Paige, if she sees what they're like now. Maybe she's just hanging out with them out of self-defense. I wish we could talk about it.

"Someone should teach her a lesson," Dee says quietly.

"Well, good luck with that," I say. "She's got a monopoly on meanness."

"You don't have to be mean to fix a problem. You have to be just."

"How very gangster of you," I laugh, nervously. But actually, she is like a gangster, like Tommy from *Goodfellas*, that guy who goes from laughing to losing his shit in seconds. She's like characters from all of my favorite movies.

* * *

Dee and I walk home together, which is the norm now. There is no one else to wait for. It feels like a lifetime ago that Lottie and I were friends, like someone else's life, the memory of a dream. As we pass her house, I can see part of the treehouse in the backyard. There are faded blues and reds of paint from when Lottie and I decorated it one summer. That feels like eons ago now.

Pete knows, I can tell. He made a comment today when I was gathering my things at the end of class.

"Haven't seen you around the house in a while, Stevie. I know that you and Lottie are kind of going in different directions these days. I'm not crazy about the kids she's hanging out with, just between you and me." He paused while I rooted around my backpack like it was the most interesting thing in the world. "But honestly, that is par for the course at your age. You two will find your way back to each other. You just have to give it time."

I looked out the window and he continued, "But is everything okay with you? Have things improved, you know, with the kids giving you a tough time?"

"Oh yeah, for sure; everything is fine." I forced a smile, stuffing my binders into my backpack. I was thinking about how he is planning on moving out of Lottie's house, how he is leaving that family, leaving the school—and me by extension— and I could feel the color in my face rising a little. "How are *you*?"

Here's the thing. Pete has been like a mother and a father to me my entire life. He always made me feel like he had time for me, which is, though not a lot of adults realize it, the most important thing you can give a kid. And you can't fake it. Parents try to fake it all the time. They say, "Yep, I'll be right there" when you're little and ask them to play Lego with you, but then they never come, or they'll pretend to be watching when you are practicing handstands underwater, and even though you're holding your breath, you're not holding your breath that they'll still be looking when you burst out of the water to see their reaction. They'll be looking at their phone or at a book or at another grown-up.

But Pete never made me feel that way. He was like a kid, fun and adventurous, but would also sit at the kitchen table and ask me what was wrong even before I knew anything was. He treated me like I was his second daughter.

I remember, just after I turned eleven, I slept over at their house. On that particular day, Lottie was doing her thing, just had her headphones on in her room, and I was sitting at the kitchen table, fiddling with a pad of Post-its.

"How do you feel being eleven, Stevie?" Pete asked me, pulling up a chair.

I thought about it. I felt weird, kind of.

"Nine felt like ten," I said. "And ten felt like eleven. But eleven feels like ten did . . . and I think that twelve . . . twelve will feel like one." I meant that it felt like a galaxy away, a life-time. Because I knew that I was on my way out of being a kid.

But he knew what I meant. He took the Post-its out of my hands and wrote down what I said and put my name and the date. He folded it in half and put it in the case of his phone to carry around with him. He was always doing stuff like that. We cooked dinners together, made birthday cakes, laughed about how solitary Lottie was sometimes while she just sat at the table reading while we gabbled away together. He was my friend, of a completely different kind.

Look, I have my own mom and dad. Lots of people do. But not many people ever get to have a Pete. And at least I did, if only for a time, even if that's over. Now he doesn't know how I feel; he doesn't know what's going on with me or Lottie or any-one else. And I'll just add him to the list.

"I'm fine, kiddo. Thanks for asking." He rapped my desk with his fist and told me I'd better get the lead out so I wouldn't be late for class.

* * *

Dee and I are rounding the corner, and I can see, from the end of the street, that Reg's car is in the driveway. Dee loops her arm into mine and gives me a *buck up, soldier* squeeze.

She comes in with me like a shadow, and I feel stronger.

I can hear them in the kitchen, laughing and flirting.

"Hey! Stevie!" Reg calls out as we try to go past. "Come try my world-famous barbecue chicken!"

"No thanks," I mumble, glancing at Mom and wondering why our little family of two wasn't enough anymore, and why he seems more comfortable in our kitchen than she does. I look at her face—beautiful, overly made up, her mascara making stamps on her eyelids—she's a bowling alley queen, a mall deb-utant, and I love her and miss her. I'm always missing someone.

It makes me tired, and my shoulders sag, but then Dee gives my hand a tug and we go hide out in my room, which expands and is more interesting and full of potential just because she waltzes in. We watch *The Goonies*, and when Reg hears what we're watching and yells, in his trying-too-hard voice, "Heeeey yoooou guys!" I have someone to roll my eyes with.

13

t's been a couple of weeks since Dee arrived on the scene, at least for me. And then something happens that make everyone stop and pay attention.

First, Breanne makes fun of Michelle again at lunch, who runs out of the room, clearly crying. Breanne and Paige put their manicured hands over their open mouths in mock surprise, giggles slipping out like the barks of tiny dogs with sharp little teeth. I notice that Lottie is scowling at them but says nothing.

And then, a loud and laughing crowd bears witness when, after lunch, Breanne discovers that her locker has been defaced. Taped to the door is a set of headgear: one of those medieval teeth straighteners that evoke mortal embarrassment for anyone with a sadistic orthodontist. Her name is on a label taped to the band that goes over your head. Written above it, in red lipstick, are the words BACK OFF, BITCH.

Under this, a scrawled heart:

LOVE, HEATHER

"Who did that?" someone asks. "Who's Heather?"

There's laughing as Breanne yanks the thing from her locker, her face beet red, her eyes brimming with pretty tears. The crowd disperses as the bell rings, and I see Dee at my side.

"You stole that from her house, didn't you?" I whisper, as we walk away with the herd.

"Did I?"

"Why?"

"Be the change you want to see, Stevie."

"Haha, 'how very,'" I mutter, a quote I know she'll recognize.

We bump fists.

Heathers, that queen bee of high school films, of righting the wrongs of the high school popularity machine, by any means necessary.

"I can't believe you did that," I whisper.

"Well," she says, grinning, "the meek shall inherit the earth and all that." She opens the door to our science class. "But sometimes they need a little shove."

* * *

And she shoves.

The next day, while everyone is still talking about the prank on Breanne and who Heather is, it happens again. Dee gets another chance. On Luke's locker is a blown-up picture of him sobbing, his face contorted like a child, puke running down the front of his hockey uniform. The backdrop is the outside of the arena, and it looks like it was taken after the recent game. I recognize a sign in the background for upcoming events. Below, written in the same red lipstick as the day before, it says:

DON'T CRY, BABY. LOVE, HEATHER.

Everyone is talking now.

We are doing this.

We hear a commotion during lunch, and everyone bolts into the hallway to see Luke and Josh scuffling: headlocks and punches and bodies thrown up against lockers.

"What happened?" someone asks.

"Josh told him he should quit the team because he's a pussy," I hear.

Pete rushes out of the staff room and hauls them apart.

"What the hell are you two doing?" he shouts, panting, his own shirt coming untucked. Luke wipes the blood off his face and glowers at Josh, who glares back. I look across the hallway through the gathering of spectators and see Dee, holding my lunch sandwich. She takes a bite and holds it up at me—*Cheers!*—and turns, walking back into the cafeteria. I see Lottie looking on, watching Pete separating Luke and Josh with her head cocked in concern. She catches me watching her, and I spin on my heels, following Dee.

The room is buzzing when I go back in, and I sit at our table feeling an adrenaline rush that comes only from watching someone get theirs, watching someone else give it to them.

Two girls and a boy plop down at our table with a thump. I know them the way we all know each other, which is to say I pretend not to know them at all, even though they're in homeroom with us. They are friends with Matthew, I remember. I've seen one of them, Ava, I think, getting harassed by Breanne for being a kind of social justice warrior. I've always liked her from afar.

"Um, hi," I say, taking a swig from my carton of milk. Dee nods at them in greeting. The rest of the kids at our table—those who have slowly, over the past couple of weeks, joined Dee and me—turn, listening.

"Hi," Ava says. I like her look: she has black lipstick and a deep side cut in her black hair. "I'm Ava. This is Antar and Marta." Antar puts up with a pretty consistent run of bullying from Breanne and Josh that runs right under Pete and the other teachers' noses. Antar is Sikh and wears a turban, which they seem to think is reason enough to harass him daily. Marta is a redheaded girl so painfully shy that, while I've seen her many times, I've never heard her speak.

Ava looks down the table and I see Michelle, the girl Breanne bullied, watching us. Ava jerks her head, calling Michelle over. She scoots down and sits with us, and I smile at her. She lifts a hand in greeting.

Ava juts her chin out. "So. Is it you?"

Dee shrugs.

"I mean, maybe I'm wrong, but it's a hunch, and I'm not usually wrong with my hunches. You seem like the only person here who's that kind of baller."

"Not admitting anything, but . . . maybe," Dee says, holding Ava's gaze.

Finally, Ava says, at almost a whisper, "So . . . why exactly are you doing this?"

"Because I'm not blind to the injustices of this place like everyone else seems to be."

"What's the deal?" Antar asks. "Like, do you have a plan? Who are you after?"

Dee lays her hands on the table and looks at all three in turn, like she's sizing them up. They're watching her every move.

"Look," she goes on, their eyes glued to hers, "what we need are bandits. Cowgirls. Highwaymen. Hunters. Vigilantes."

Vigilantes?

"I mean," I say, carefully, looking at Dee, holding my hands out cautiously, "we don't want to get carried away or anything, but . . ."

"But it feels like it's time to fuck shit up on who's in power around here," finishes Dee.

I watch the others falling under her spell.

Ava nods slowly, and so do Antar and Marta. Marta opens her mouth, then closes it again.

"Is it, like, a revenge squad?" asks Antar, leaning in.

"God, no," I say at the same time that Dee says, "Sort of."

She continues, "I figure it's time for people to fight back. To take down the top dogs. For *them* to be fearful for once."

Antar laughs and fist-bumps her. "Hell. Yes."

"How'd you get Breanne's headgear? That was hers, right?" Marta asks, her eyes glittering with awe.

Dee scans the room and shrugs again indifferently.

The bell rings to signal that lunch is over and classes are starting again. People all over are standing up, chairs screeching across the floor. Those at our table haven't moved. They are watching Dee. She stands up, looking over the table.

"Well? Let's get moving. We have unfinished business."

* * *

On the way home from school, I say very little, my hands shoved in my hoodie pockets. Things feel like they're moving quickly, and I've barely had a chance to catch up with Dee's plans and she's already enlisted other kids.

"What?" Dee asks.

"Nothing," I say, but she's watching me. She gives me a little elbow to urge me on. "I'm just thinking," I say. Then, after a moment, "Is this the right thing to do?"

"The 'right thing to do'? Fuck, yeah! You're telling me that they didn't have it coming?"

"Okay, yes, sure, but . . . you're gonna get busted."

"Nah. And even if we do, it's worth it. 'Bout time someone held them accountable." She stops and looks me in the face. "It's gone on long enough, Stevie. It's time to stand up for yourself."

We start walking again. I think about the day. "Did you see the look on Pete's face, though, when he came out to split up the fight? He was *pissed*."

"That's his job. And to be honest, he's been way too oblivious to some of the stuff going on at school."

"Yeah," I admit, sadly, remembering how much Pete and I used to talk, how easy it used to be.

We turn a corner onto Lottie's street, and I see her heading into her house. My heart aches a little as she reaches into the mailbox to grab whatever's in there, the screen door banging behind her as she goes inside. I know her routine like a forgotten language. I miss her, but I feel a burning anger bubbling under that.

"You okay?" Dee asks, looking at me.

"Hmm? Oh yeah, sure. You going to come by the DQ tonight? I work till ten."

"I've got nowhere else to be."

I know this is true. Dee rarely talks about her dad or her much older brother. I know she lives close by, but we never go there. She says her dad works the night shift and is always sleeping during the day.

"We'll celebrate," she says, calling at me over her shoulder as I walk up my driveway.

"Celebrate what?"

She lets out a laugh like a bark and shakes her head, shouting, "You're part of something, now, Stevie!"

She puts her headphones back over her ears and disappears around a corner as I put my key in the door.

* * *

The DQ. It is exactly the kind of monotonous, soul-sucking job that my mom thinks should be the staple of every teenager's existence. But since Dee came along, if there's nothing to do and no customers, it's not bad. I can hang out with her, which is always a plus. We work on homework, goof off, eat ice cream, and life feels bearable.

Tonight I am working on an assignment that Pete gave us for Media Studies class. I lean over the counter, the assignment sheet in front of me, while I pick at a Blizzard I made myself.

CHOOSE A FILM OR TV SHOW 10 YEARS OR OLDER, AND GIVE IT A NEW, MODERN MEANING AND CONTEXT. YOU CAN PRESENT THIS IN ANY CREATIVE MEANS POSSIBLE. REWRITE THE SCRIPT, AS IT WERE. WEIGHT: 30% OF FINAL GRADE.

We've been watching bits of movies and TV shows all year, dissecting them, deconstructing them. I love this class. Most people do, actually; it's like we've been training all our lives to have a class like this. Still, I'm thinking of how I can make this project mine, how I can bring a little Stevie into the assignment. I am scrolling through IMBD, but really I'm thinking about Dee and her stunts. How satisfying they were to see. How it finally feels like someone is doing something. I think of the Breannes and the Paiges, the Aidans, Joshes and the Lukes, the white, rich, privileged dicks that roam the school, our town—*our online life, too*—like medieval lords. It's like other people all own a part of you. And I get it—it's our fault for sharing so much of ourselves, but we're now in this trap, where we can't look outside ourselves without getting caught, and judged or worse. I feel my eyes starting to water, and then the door jingles, and it's Dee, bustling in with a smile.

"I need a Blizzard, STAT!"

I take a deep breath and laugh. She's here. She's always here when I need her.

14

"Hey Stevie!"

It's Ava, calling me from the doorway of one of the classrooms. The bell between classes just rang, and the hallways are full of students changing classes. I wait for her to catch up. She's wearing a huge oversized sweatshirt that looks like it might swallow her whole. I'm not used to anyone other than Dee calling to me at school because they actually want to hang out with me, but that's been changing lately. The past few weeks, there has been a shift. I don't dread the minutes between classes and actually turn when someone calls my name. I smile at her as she hurries up beside me.

"Hey," I say. "What's up?"

"Not much. Just on my way to Environmental Science Club. It's actually kind of fun. You should come sometime."

"Oh, really? But isn't climate change a hoax?" I say, sarcastically, "I feel like I heard that somewhere."

"Har-har. I go because there's always pizza, and we like to see how much hemp Mr. Wilson can work into his wardrobe."

She notices that she's accidentally passed the Science room

and darts away, waving. I almost run full-on into Matthew, who is passing in the other direction.

"Oops! Sorry!" he says, catching my arm as I stumble. "Gotcha!"

"Thanks," I say.

"How are you?" Matthew says in that way that he has of seeming to see into my soul. We pull to the side to let a bunch of rowdy kids walk by and lean against some lockers.

"I'm really good, actually."

"Yeah. You seem, well . . . I know that for a while there you were, um, well, you know." Matthew, no stranger to bullying, does me the favor of not naming the thing.

"Things were definitely shit for a while."

He nods knowingly. "I'm sorry I never—"

"Don't worry about it," I say, my face growing red.

"Okay. Anyway, glad you've got some solid people with you now. Ava and Antar are awesome."

"True that."

"And if you ever get into Magic: The Gathering, Jamie and Mitch and I would be happy to have you." He turns to leave and I head into my own classroom, a smile on my face.

I have friends now. It's not just Dee, although she is at the core of it. She is my ride-or-die bitch, ever since Lottie jumped. But there's a proper group of us, now. A bunch of misfits and nerds and freaks who have become my people. Antar and Marta and Ava, and sometimes even Matthew, but also some music and arty kids, a couple of second-string athletes, some gifted students and a few other of the dispossessed seeking sanctuary from the high school melting pot.

I remember being a kid, and then being a slightly older kid (*preteen*, my mom would say, rolling her eyes at everything I did), and still wanting to hang out with my mom, or having the occasional playdate with other kids, and that was enough. But then, it felt like overnight, all I wanted was this: friends I could hang out with *all the time*. And now that it's here, I want it constantly. I need it like a high. Every joke is hilarious; every shitty thing that happens to any one of us is a tragedy. I suffer terrible bouts of FOMO when I can't meet up with them. We are all up in each other's social media; we compliment one another's pics with a range of fire and heart emojis because we are the most gorgeous, hilarious, brilliant, and strong creatures any of us has ever encountered. Love, hate, school, clothes, hair, TV, movies, food, parents: it is all fodder for Snapchat and group texts. We are puppies! We are kittens! We have huge eyes and bunny ears and hearts and tiny birds flying around our heads! We're dead. We're dying. We're expressing our constant devotion. It is therapy: balm for the soul, soothing the cockles of my nearly deadened heart. They know, they knew, that I was a target at school, and they buffer me. They shut people down and boost me up. They are saving me. They know it, too, what it's like; all of them. The shared experience of being a loser. And maybe it's that: the being part of something, as Dee said, the belonging that makes me hardly question her tactics, helps me to adopt them as my own.

Over the past couple of weeks, Dee has spearheaded about a stunt per week on someone tapped as a bully, a bitch, a bastard who needs to be taken down a few notches. Taught a lesson. Her excitement is contagious. I'm helping her now, and so are the others. I'll be honest. It is exhilarating. It's a rush. It quenches something we have all been thirsting for. Justice. We've all been there. Bullied, touched, harassed, tormented. Some more than others. It fills a need we have to be vindicated. It is thrilling, and as soon as one is finished, we want to do another. Sometimes they're universal pranks that could be for or from anyone; other times they are more personal. Burning bags of shit in doorways that need to be stomped out. Keying cars with a personal message of vengeance. Some people frown upon doing any actual acts of mischief or pranks, but they are always game to hear about them afterward.

Some people, though, are all in.

Just last week, Dee showed up on my front porch with four dozen eggs in her backpack, which she gleefully showed me after I opened the door.

"What's with the eggs?" I said, joining Dee outside.

"It is more of a traditional prank, I admit, but it is *so* satisfying," she replied, a glint in her eye. I had to admit, I was itching to give it a try.

"That's a lot of eggs; who else is coming?"

"Ava, Antai, the usual. Plus, I think they're bringing a couple of people."

"Okay," I said. "Who's the target?"

This time it was a girl named Justine. Justine is tall, beautiful, and a complete snob. She quite literally thinks she's better than everyone, and it's not hard to see why, I guess, if you're into perfection. She's the captain of the Cheer Squad, which is what they call cheerleaders here. Her squad is full of Justine clones, and she has a reputation for cutting anyone who doesn't fit the physical requirements she has decided on. In fact, there's a rumor that during tryouts, she and one of her henchwomen rate girls according to their height, waist size, legs, and boobs. This year, a large, curvy, confident girl named Beth started her own cheer team called CheerFull, and has accepted anyone who wants to dance, or bang pom-poms around, or whatever cheerleaders do. Justine has been dragging them online. Something about the purity of tradition or some bullshit.

"Good enough for me," I said, taking a box of eggs out of the bag. "Let's go."

*   *   *

"I *love* this!" Antar screeched as he launched an egg at Justine's house half an hour later.

"We don't have enough eggs!" Ava called, using up the last of hers on the front door. She rooted around on the ground and picked up a rock.

A light came on, and a woman opened the door just as Ava launched her rock straight at the doorway. We heard a scream, and the woman's hands flew up around her face. We froze momentarily, then ran.

As we raced through the neighborhood, the evening air and our adrenaline filling us up like lifeblood, I shouted at Ava, "What the fuck, dude? A rock?"

She looked guilty for a second, then shrugged. "I'm sure she's fine. She's Justine's fucking mother; I'm sure she had it coming too," she said, her face suddenly cruel. Another kid, one I hardly know, high-fived her, and I realized there were more people with us than I thought, running through the streets causing shit in the name of justice . . . or something.

We hurtled around corners and ran through the streets like radical children, following Dee as she ducked into a walkway near the school. We leaned against the walls, gasping, out of breath and full of purpose. Everyone was talking at once, and Dee looked around at everyone, her face flushed and glowing like some unreal thing. She pulled a can of red spray paint out of her backpack, and I watched them watching her, thrilled that there was more. She shook the can and drew a large heart on the wooden wall of the walkway and scrawled HEATHER under it. Everyone whistled and clapped, chests heaving in excitement.

Dee lifted her chin up and howled at the moon, and they all chorused after her. I stood quietly, feeling like I'd lost a hold on something.

*   *   *

Tonight we are going up to the Ridge, high above our dreary town, to have a campfire. Antar is going to pick Dee and me up at my house in his perfectly run-down old beater of a car, then push it to its limits in the steep climb up the hill, where whoever else can make it will meet us for a night of cozy bonding as the sun, weighed down by the burden of its job of cheering every bored and hardened adolescent, sinks below the horizon in exhaustion.

Dee and I sit on my porch, and she lights a cigarette, coughing as she inhales. The days are getting so long now that even though it's evening, it feels like there are still hours to go before the streaky sky will darken. Dee moves her hand behind her bent legs to keep the smoke out of my face. She knocks her knee into mine and smiles.

"So," I say, not looking at her, but at two little sparrows who are squabbling on a low branch on a tree near the road.

"So . . . ?" She laughs.

"So, I'm . . . I just wanted to say that I'm glad you're here. I'm glad you came. Like, in general, not tonight. But that too." I feel my face get hot.

"Aw, Stevie." She turns to face me. "You love me! You really, really love me!" She folds me into her arms in a gust of smoke and hair.

"Yeah, yeah. Don't let it go to your head."

"Got it." She ashes her cigarette over the porch stairs. "For the record, I'm glad I'm here, too. I didn't know if I would make any friends here, but here you are. There are actually some pretty cool people here."

I nod, slowly. "They sure like *you*," I say, and I can feel the damp corner of a wet blanket of envy in my voice.

"Oh, now. They just tolerate me. I'm good in small doses."

"Yeah . . . right. Looks like some people are really getting into this stuff. I just wonder—"

But then there is a rumble coming around the corner, and Dee stands, flicking her butt into the garden. Antar's car rounds onto my street, and he rolls down the window as he pulls up to the house.

"Want a ride?" And then, "Hang on . . ." He turns up the music, louder, louder, so loud it seems that the roof of his car will come off, while he dances at the wheel in an increasing frenzy. Dee leaps into the front seat and joins him, and I slide in back and cover my ears, laughing.

It is a warm, deliciously fresh evening. The sun is glinting off the edges of leaves as they shiver and shimmer and preen, shaking their tits because they know they're at their peak and that in a few months they'll be dried up and dead. We roll down all the windows and breathe in deeply, that almost summer—practically summer! just on the edge of summer!— air that smells like barbecue and sunscreen and grass. Somewhere in the back of my mind I remember childhood summers: sliding down a Wet Banana and hurting my back on a rock, running barefoot over a hot blacktop driveway, sipping Slurpees while walking home from the Mac's Milk with Lottie. All at once, just with a couple of inhales from the summer air, those memories hit my brain like an electric shock, and I am happy and sad and nostalgic and excited all at once. Dee is talking away, a mile a minute, her happy chatter filling the car, layered on top of the music like a rhythm, and I close my eyes and take it all in. Antar's car climbs Woolverton Road, the steepest and curviest road in town, and it is struggling, we can hear it, and he laughs and urges it on, "Come on, girl. You can do it."

"Lean forward, everyone!" Dee yells, and we cling to our knees, like we're cajoling an old horse, a boat in a sea storm, and up we go. Up and up and up.

The Ridge. Named after the road it's on, the Ridge is the top of the escarpment and offers views of the town that stretch all the way across to the lake and beyond. There are lookout points and tiny gravel parking spots with unreliable railings. The Bruce Trail cuts through here, and there are always people hiking and walking their dogs, clamoring over the rocks and roots, breathing hard with the healthy work of it, their cheeks rosy. It's also the site of many a teenage campfire, littered with a rotation of bottles and trash and the occasional used condom. The environmental Good Samaritans of the town clean it all up, and the cycle starts again the following weekend. I had a friend when I was little who lived up on the Ridge, and I remember running around her huge backyard that stretched into the protected land of the escarpment, pretending we were in the grounds of a medieval castle overlooking the village.

Antar deftly rounds the curves leading us up higher, and my stomach gives a lurch as we gain precarious altitude above the town. Dee lets out a whoop as her hair flies all over the car, expands and fills the space like her own airbag. I know in that happy moment, seeing our life from above in miniature, how delicate everything is. How fragile and risky and in danger we are of tipping over the edge. I feel so good right now, I know I do. But there is a fuzz, a dark-gray edge to the picture, bleeding into the joy. I shake my head, shake it off, grinning, then laughing at Dee. If nothing else, if no one else, I have this, right now.

"Hold tight!" Antar yells over the music as he takes a corner at top speed, and then we are careening along the top of the Ridge, Dee's hand out the window, riding the warm wind. The sun is straight ahead of us, painfully bright and inviting, daring us to fly right into the fireball. *Close your eyes against the heat of it, Stevie, against the blinding light.*

When we get to the spot we all agreed on, sent through map pins and texts, pinpointing the scraggy dirt clearing where we'll spend the evening, there are already a few people there. Ava is a master when it comes to making fires, I guess, because she is directing the project with serious expertise.

"You have to put the logs up like this," she says, exasperated, to Marta, who laid them flat. Marta sits on a log sulkily and waves at us.

"Okay, Ava, who died and made you queen of fires?" jokes Dee, tossing a backpack on the ground and joining Marta. I sit down beside her.

There are other kids there already, relaxing, listening to music coming from a portable speaker someone brought. A girl named Annie takes a gummy from a bag and passes it around. Others are smoking; it wafts about in a skunky cloud.

"Okay, ready!" says Ava, hands on hips. "Hand me the matches!"

Three hands extend holding lighters, and she smirks. "Or a lighter."

She lights the fire, and it really is perfect. Like a campfire straight from a Girl Guide's iron-on patch: triangular logs, a curvy orange flame, a swirl of smoke. There is scattered applause, and Ava bows, grinning, her face beautiful in the firelight. She leans over to take a toke as her reward, sitting heavily beside Antar, who has his eyes closed, moving his head to the music. A guy named Jesse, who is very small for his age, with glasses and a pile of curly hair that is more statement than style, opens a beer from his bag. I look around and see that my life is a movie: we look like we're in *Friday the 13th*, at camp, and are just too happy and relaxed not to be punished by a murderous psychopath who must be crashing through the path toward us at this moment.

"I love this cut," says Jesse, gesturing at the speaker. "Saw them last summer; it was amazing." There are some nods and murmured agreement. People are laughing and cozying up to each other on the scattered logs.

Dee struggles to stand up, and I give her a shove from behind. She hams it up, staggering to the rickety railing that overlooks the town. The sun is going down, and it's licking all the rooftops like a giant, sleepy cat on its way to bed. Dee opens her arms, taking it all in, and everyone giggles. Antar throws a wood chip at her back. She leans forward over the railing, and we all instinctively put out our arms, as though we'd ever be able to stop her if she fell. She starts humming, moving her head to her own music.

"Teenage suicide," she sings, and I recognize the tune from *Heathers*. "Don't do it! Teenage suiciiiiide"—and she reaches ever forward—"don't do it!"

"Jesus, be careful!" Jesse grumbles.

Dee ignores him, sweeping her arms around, like she's performing on a huge stage.

"What is that?" Marta asks, taking a swig from a beer can. "Did she make that song up?"

"Who knows," someone else says, then yells, "Get back here before you fall over!"

"All right, crazy, come sit down," says Antar, reaching out his hand to Dee.

Dee leaps over some branches and takes her spot by the fire, nudging me with her shoulder. I shake my head at her bravado. Is it too much?

Talk turns to school, to the people we like, we hate, to what's been going on lately, to who deserves it, who has it coming. Ava mentions Paige, and there is a collective groan.

"She's just Breanne's puppet," says Ava.

"Have you seen her run?" Jesse asks, laughing. "She can only go about two feet before stopping."

"Honestly, I think she must have an eating disorder," says Ava.

"Meanwhile her best friend is like a mutant athlete," someone else chimes in.

"Who, Breanne?" I say. "I don't think they're best friends. Breanne is a total bitch."

"That's probably why they're friends, hello!" Jesse laughs.

"I dunno," I mumble, "Paige isn't that bad." I can feel Dee looking at me. *Really?* she's thinking. And yes, I know she's right, but I feel protective of Paige for some reason.

"Some people are mysterious," Marta says quietly, smiling, and I am grateful for her slightly loopy niceties.

"Whatever, and some people just need you to fuck their shit up," says Jesse, and others grumble in agreement.

The night comes, and the town slips on it like a patch of oil, falling into darkness. The fire crackles and throws light up against all our faces. Dee listens, chewing on the cuff of her hoodie, nodding and laughing along with everyone else, but her eyes are alert. She is sitting up straight, taking it all in.

Later, when I am home, my hair on my pillow smelling like campfire, my comforter up around my shoulders, she texts me.

Keep your eyes on the prize

I type back.

Just not sure I want to win

You do, she texts. *Or at least, you don't want to lose. Eventually we'll do something so big, they'll see they have no power over us*

Back and forth, until I'm too tired and I sign off, my eyes shutting with dreams like movies: wide shots and close-ups, music that tells us that something's happening, something we should be wary of, nervous about, even if we don't know quite what it is.

15

On Monday, everybody is talking about the pranks, and if there will be more. Breanne has apparently already had her parents speak to the principal about how she doesn't feel the school is a "safe space," which is, as we all well know, the silver bullet for getting grown-ups to do what you want.

Before lunch today, there was an announcement on the PA system reminding students that vandalism and bullying will not be tolerated at the school, and anyone who is found to be committing acts of either will be dealt with accordingly.

Breanne appears at her lunch table with shimmering eyes, surrounded by supportive friends who glower at everyone outside their group.

Dee walks through the cafeteria, whistling loudly, hands in her pockets, her customary stomp. People are watching her; a couple of hands reach out and high-five her. She sits down at our table with Antar and Ava, Marta and Jesse, who smile at her, amused. She scoots in right next to me, and our arms and legs touch. A jolt runs through me.

"Hey guys," she says. They look at her expectantly. She

giggles, looking at each person in turn, and squeezing my hand under the table. "So, crazy shit around here, hey?" Everyone nods, murmuring and laughing. Dee nods also, her gaze taking in the whole room. "Looks like the tables are finally turning in this shithole."

And then she stands up and looks right over at Breanne and calls out, "The queen is dead!" There is applause, actual applause, and table banging. Someone yells, pointing at Dee, "God save the queen!" and Dee does a little wave like royalty. I watch her, soaking it all in, and see Lottie, a look of disbelief on her face. I feel a small surge of embarrassment, but I ignore it, putting my hands around my mouth and cheering.

*　*　*

In Art class, later in the week, we are making papier-mâché masks. Our teacher, Mr. DiFranco, has paired me with Lottie, oblivious to the ebb and flow of what actually goes on in friendships for those under forty.

Everyone sits with their partners, a pile of newspaper strips and a bowl of paste between them. One person will apply the mask to the other, and then they'll switch. I sit facing Lottie in a chair, realizing it has been what feels like eons since we were close.

She sticks her fingers into a jar of Vaseline and pauses before rubbing it on my face. Other pairs are happily chatting and laughing all over the room.

"So," I say, "how's life?"

She says nothing, methodically wiping the cream across my forehead, which is so disarmingly intimate after months of not speaking that I feel all the tiny hairs on my body stand on end.

"Well," I continue, "I finally have friends again, after a brush with complete and utter exile and isolation that sunk me into a depression so deep I thought I'd never get out. So, you know, that's nice."

"Good for you," Lottie says, flatly. "Um, can you please stay still?"

"Yes, good for me. Good for me. And gosh, I would hate to be rude, so let me ask: are things good for you? You and the Pink Ladies still the reining queens of cool?"

"The what?"

"God, watch a movie."

I hate this, this bickering. I sigh. "So," I say, making eye contact and trying to connect with Lottie, my BFF for years, my sister from another mister. "I heard that Pete's moving out. Which, by the way, my *mother* told me."

Lottie says nothing, but her mouth becomes a tight line, which I know is a sign of fury.

I soften just a small bit. "Lottie. Jesus. You could have told me."

She looks at me levelly. Her shoulders drop.

"It's okay. I understand, I guess. Where is he going?" I continue, quietly, "I mean, I get that he needs his own life, but why is he leaving?"

Lottie takes a breath like she's going to respond, but just shakes her head.

"Well. You have two amazing parents. You're pretty, you're popular. You've got it all. I mean, my mom is a selfish and oblivious asshat, and her boyfriend is a . . . Well, anyway. My dad forgot about me because he's so focused on fair-trade coffee and his perky, hipster girlfriend. But you have these two interesting, amazing parents. You know what I'm saying, here? Hello?"

"Whatever. Stop obsessing over my family. The bigger question is, what about *you*?" she asks, her voice sounding close to tears. "You are suddenly a different person!"

"What? No, I'm—"

"You *are*! I feel like I don't even know you!"

"I had to, Lottie." I am almost crying myself. "Things were—"

"Well, things are bad for me, too. I wish—" She stops herself, then starts slapping the soggy strips on my face, not caring where they go, or if she covered that part of my face in Vaseline.

"Hey, go easy!"

"Stevie," she says finally, holding one in her hand, "shut your mouth."

"I just want to say something!"

Mr. DiFranco calls over, "Stevie, you need to keep your mouth still so your partner can apply the strips to the lower portion of your face. Tempting as it may be to speak."

Lottie smirks, and I feel my plastered face burn.

* * *

I take a bathroom break during Geography and decide to go to the downstairs one, dragging out my break to wander the quiet halls. On my way back, wiping my mouth after drinking from a fountain, I pull open one of the stairwell doors and see Aiden, leaning over to pick up a book he dropped. I freeze, and the door clangs shut behind me. He starts and turns around, surprised; then his face relaxes into a scoff. He picks up his book and turns to start up the stairs. I take a deep breath, my body thrumming. It's now or never, I think. Something in my new-found confidence, having Dee in my corner, gives me the strength in this moment to try to get to the bottom of part of what started it all.

"Why'd you do it, Aidan?" I call to him.

He stops and slowly turns back, hopping off the stair and taking a step toward me. My body stiffens.

"What?" he says, moving closer. I don't mean to but I stumble back, bumping against the old red-brick wall beside the doors.

"Why'd you tell everyone that shit about me? Nothing happened between us. Why did you do that?" My voice sounds so small. My body feels so small. I shrink, but don't disappear.

Aidan shrugs, getting closer. I can smell him. Sweat. Body spray. Detergent. Confidence. "I dunno. Something to do."

"What?" I whisper.

"I mean, it might as well have happened. You wanted it to. We both know that."

Closer.

My mouth quivers, and I am shaking my head no. *Never. I never.* I want to send out a burn, I want to insult him, but there's a sob in my throat.

I blink and say, "Oh fucking great," and try to move around him, but he reaches his arm out and stops me in that same moment, almost like it's an accident, almost like I walked into him, and grabs me in the crotch. He squeezes, hard, painfully, and I gasp, and he squeezes again, leaning in, his breath on my face, and then lets go. Like it didn't happen. Like it didn't matter.

"Better get back to class, Stevie. I'm late myself. See ya up there." And he turns and bounds casually up the stairs, leaving me in the stairwell, my palms against the cool of the brick, my heart pounding in my throat.

I don't tell Dee. I don't tell anyone. I don't even know if it happened.

16

Episode 71 00:15
So many classic movies are, I'm sad to say, full-on rape
culture offenders. I mean, look at Sixteen Candles, *one*
of the biggest culprits, and so are so many of the beloved
John Hughes movies. Or Back to the Future, Nerds, Say
Anything. *They turn rape and rape culture into a joke, a*
punch line.

A few days later, Saturday, Dee meets me outside my house. I've been sitting on the front step, staring into space. I don't know what's wrong with me, but I haven't felt like doing anything, not even eating, since I saw Aidan in the stairwell. Since he— Well, anyway. I look down the street at nothing while Dee sits beside me.

Our garage is open and Reg is hammering on a piece of metal, making a god-awful racket. He waves at us, asks us if we want to come check out the old railway ties he's turning into a table for my mom. I say nothing but heave a sigh for years.

Dee looks at me, and I can see that she sees something there. Something hurting. "Hey," she says softly, putting her arm around me, "I have an idea."

"Oh yeah? What?"

"Why don't we get out of here. Like, out of town," she says, smiling.

I look at her. "Okay," I say, morosely, "but where do you want to go?"

"I myself would like to see something wonderful, Stevie. Something enormous, dazzling, spectacular."

I roll my eyes. "We don't have any of that here, sorry. Do you even know where you are? There is nothing."

She spreads her hands out as though she's reading a name in lights, and pausing for effect first, she says in an awestruck voice, "Niagara. Falls."

I laugh hollowly but agree to go down, deep down toward one of the wonders of the world because there is literally nothing wonderful here.

Maybe it's not the seventh wonder. Maybe Niagara Falls is on a list of the top fifteen, or the top two hundred, but it pulls us in some reversed tidal force, and the idea appeals to me, and soon I forget myself. I am sucked into the promise of its tacky, drooling mouth, full of gum wrappers and chewed-up garbage and tinfoil, the sun glinting off its trashy gob like the best kind of star. We park our bikes at the bus station, and I feel my heart lift. We ready ourselves for our voyage, prepare to ride the waves on a Greyhound bus.

There are a lot of people going to Niagara Falls. Tourists and locals. Some kids, some teenagers, a woman who wears lots of perfume and a man who tells everyone that he worked on a movie with Tom Cruise. Right before we get on, I see a young woman empty a cloth sack full of brown and bruised bananas into the garbage. One after another after another, like a beat-up magic trick.

"Imagine all the banana bread she could have made," Dee says in my ear.

It isn't a long ride to Niagara Falls from our town. We watch the outlets and parking lots rise and fall from the window. Dee is on the other side of the aisle from me, snapping her gum and jiggling her leg. She looks like a little girl, and I'm reminded that it wasn't that long ago that she was, that any of us were. When we were innocent and didn't know that people would zero in on us, make it their mission to ruin us. But we know now: there are so many assholes looking to put cracks in the windows of our lives. I feel that burn that started when I first met Dee, that feeling that we can take our fate into our hands and change the landscape.

We pass signs for helicopter rides and stores that specialize in sex toys, giant realtor billboards and theme restaurants trying to outdo one another's crazy names and characters. People look small, wandering between these deliciously crazy eyesores. The whole dirty, cheesy town is trying too hard and kind of failing, but that makes it even better.

"This is awesome," Dee says, turning to me, eyes glittering. We are going to have the best day. Something to push away the worst ones.

The bus stops in the Niagara Falls bus station, and I can feel it before we even get off the bus, while we're waiting to get out. The doors open and it slides in, slick and smooth, up the stairs, up my shirt, behind my ears, licking every crevice: a warm breeze. It's warmer here, sunnier, stickier, trashier. We stand in the street and a big fat fly buzzes lazily around my head, drunk on decadence, and the bus pulls away again, its engine revving and its wheels shaking off sweat.

We laugh and head in the same direction as though pulled by a magnet.

Where we go, naturally, is the wax museum. It's on Clifton Hill, an area that is chockablock with noise, where giant billboards carry the strained smiles of tired strippers. The Great Canadian Midway is calling us in its hoarse voice, and the restaurants shake their hips and tempt us to feed our weary bodies, but it is the wax museum that nods quietly and knows what we really need.

We want Niagara Falls in all its finest, waxiest, untouchable fakery.

We go past impressive wax celebrities, like Taylor Swift and Katie Perry, who seem to be getting on just fine, and then head in, Dee leading the way with a fat grin on her face, like she just broke into the barn and ate all the chickens. There are groups of teenagers and couples and friends and families, all jostling and laughing and posing with these people, these waxy larger-than-life people. Indiana Jones and Marilyn Monroe and Freddy Krueger. The peeling paint is trying to hold itself up— tummy in, tits out—and the audio system is coughing out its scratchy, hungover voice. Our Lady of Frozen Beauty, Our Church of Celebrity and Eternal Youth. Give us a taste. We could be born again: dedicated parishioners, junkies of the camp faith. Maybe this place could save us.

We spend the day there, and if this were a movie, it would be the part where the fun music is playing, the montage, where we laugh and scream and pull faces. It is where we see Johnny

Cash all mournful, and Prince, that smooth fox who whispers something so dirty and poetic that I will never forget it. Dolly Parton looks right at us, and we are starstruck, and she tips her head back and laughs and it feels like we're drinking the best southern lemonade. Dee says Justin Bieber looks like her aunt after a stroke. Jack Sparrow is terrific. Indiana Jones is missing an ear, and then, his whip. I know it's in Dee's backpack, coiled like a snake, promising to come out later.

It gets quieter as time goes on, and then we are the only ones here. We stand in silence in front of James Franco. We both notice the same thing. He looks like Reg: he looks eager and full of shit, like an opportunist and a homewrecker and a homemaker. Like he has bad ideas and bad breath and terrible impulses. He looks like he slept in those clothes but loves how it looks.

Dee puts her hand in her pocket, and I look over my shoulder. She has a lighter in her palm and holds it up.

"It's your turn, Stevie."

"My turn for what?"

"Do it," she whispers. "Now."

I stand up on the platform and reach up, the lighter under his nose, the flame tickling him like a feather. And it takes forever, but then suddenly his face is distorted, caving in, and it feels great. We watch him. He has no nose; his moustache is covered in beige wax, like he just drank the head off a pint of acid. He looks defeated. He's everyone: a stand-in for all the hurt. It feels so good, and I want more.

"Much better," Dee says, and I nod, feeling strong.

We immediately get the hell out of there, hitting the sidewalk at a run once we're out of the museum, laughing and gasping for air when at a safe distance. We lean against a building painted a bright yellow. I stand back to look at it: an old wall mural ad for the Marlboro Man, standing in a field of wheat.

"Look at that cool bastard," Dee says, and I nod. He's twenty feet of I-don't-give-a-shit.

"Unflappable."

"He doesn't care about anything."

"Nope."

We start walking down toward the falls, and a fine mist fills the air the closer we get. We reach the fence and put our hands on it, looking down at the wonder itself.

"Wow," Dee says. "Pretty amazing."

I shrug. "If you like that kind of thing. It's a little over the top for me."

She laughs, and then we are quiet as we watch for a while.

Dee turns and looks at me, considering something.

"What?"

"I'm just thinking . . ."

"About what? Spit it out."

"Well, okay. I'm thinking about Lottie."

"What about her?" I ask, closing my eyes against the spray.

"Don't you think maybe she needs a wake-up call, too?"

I look at Dee, suddenly feeling protective, defensive. "What? Why?"

Dee scoffs. "Seriously, Stevie? *Why?* Did you forget that she's the reason this all happened in the first place? I mean, at the very least she was a silent party to what they did to you. She never stood up for you."

I look away, my eyes stinging now, from either the beauty or the misery. I wipe them and watch a small family taking pictures. The mother holds up the little girl while the father takes the pic; they switch, then take a selfie of the three of them. The girl starts to wriggle, and they put her down and move away.

"Whatever. It doesn't even matter. I don't even know if she hangs out with them anymore, so who cares. There are worse people."

"Okay, suit yourself." Dee leans into her cupped hands and lights a cigarette. She stares out over the fence at the falls. "I mean, one of the 'worse people' is definitely Aidan . . ." She looks at me, and I stare ahead.

"No," I say, firmly, quietly.

"Why?" she asks, throwing up her hands in exasperation.

Because I'm afraid of him. Because I'm afraid he'll hurt me again, worse this time.

"I just don't want to. No, I said. Just leave it."

Dee rolls her eyes and takes a drag of her cigarette, then passes it to me. I take it, inhaling, and it gives me a dizzy feeling. I close my eyes to the mist of the falls, which spray around us lightly.

A moment passes between us. I think of Lottie and Aidan, and a small shock of fury inside me flares up bright and sharp. Lottie has no idea what my life is like. There was a time that maybe I could have told her what Aidan did, but not now. The feeling of that moment with him is almost palpable again, and I shake my head. It disappears for now.

* * *

On our way back to town on the bus, it feels like we're pulling the cover over something behind us, protecting and preserving where we've been. Dee dozes against the window in a seat across the aisle from me. Her body relaxes. I lean against the window in its rattling motion, my eyes open and alert.

17

My shift is almost over at the Dairy Queen. It's been quiet. Dee, Antar, Jesse, and Ava are sitting at a corner table, playing cards and sharing fries. I have pulled up a chair and am hanging with them when the door chimes, and Paige walks in with Breanne and three of her other friends, all lip gloss and boobs, people I partied with two short months ago but who hate me now. My heart takes a nose dive and my hand goes to my hair, tucked into a hairnet, in some primal protection instinct. They march up to the counter, and Paige gazes around impatiently, pretty and bored. She sees me, and something passes for a second between us. *We were almost friends*, I think. Things could have gone differently.

"Um, hello?" she chirps at me. Breanne says something I don't catch. They cackle together like witches.

I don't rush to get up, not like I once might have. I try to hold Paige's stare as I walk slowly around, behind the counter. Dee and the others are watching, their cards still in their hands.

"Yes?" I say, matching her bitch for bitch.

Breanne gives me a cool smile and orders a chocolate dip. I say nothing and turn around to make it.

"Nice hairnet," I hear Paige mutter, my back to her. Breanne snickers. My shoulders tense, but I keep moving the soft serve into a spiral. There is a lump in my throat, and I blink a few times. *Keep it together.* When I'm done, the chocolate dip drying, swirled to perfection, I turn and hand it to Breanne. Paige stares at me, challenging. Something hard in her expression. It hits me right in the gut.

Breanne looks at her cone. She turns it back and forth, evaluating the swirly top. Then she looks over her shoulder at Dee, Michelle, Antar, and Ava, and says, "Hey! This looks familiar! It's *you,* Antar!"

There is a shocked silence. Paige looks at me, her face faltering for a moment.

"Seriously?" I say to her. "Why are you friends with her?" I point at Breanne, feeling bold and furious, fearless outrage coursing through my veins.

Breanne looks at Paige, and there is a moment, and then Paige laughs, a hard bark of a laugh, like she's forcing it. Then she takes Breanne's cone and shakes it back and forth like it's talking. She puts on a voice like Apu from *The Simpsons* and says, "Thank you, come again."

Breanne covers her mouth in that way of hers, all shocked laughter. Paige shrugs. Breanne tosses a few coins on the counter, and they walk to the door. Getting into the spirit, she looks at Antar as she takes a bite out of the ice cream, grinning savagely. The door chimes.

"Bitches," says Dee immediately.

Jesse puts his hand on Antar's shoulder and asks if he's okay.

"Yeah, I'm fine. They're idiots, whatever." His mouth is set in a straight line, and he's looking out the window. "Hey," he calls to me, "can we get some more fries? I am starving all of a sudden."

Later, Dee and I walk toward my house.

"I can't *believe* them," I say, clenching my fists.

"I told you. Paige is no better. She is completely evil," Dee agrees.

"But no, see, she didn't used to be. Like, I felt like there was some good in her, even after everything. I always thought she just got swept along by Breanne. But now? I cannot." I pause, shaking my head. "We should do something, you know?"

"Well, sure." Dee smiles.

"People should know that she's, like, a racist bitch. Just as bad as Breanne."

Dee glances at me and smiles. "Yeah."

"What should we do?"

"I think you've got this one," she says, looking straight ahead.

I pause, thinking. "Yeah." We walk in silence for a bit, passing my old elementary school. It looks so different to me now. So small.

We get to my house, and Dee gives me a squeeze and keeps going. As she saunters away, whistling, hands in her pockets, I think about what I can do. And like a bolt, I remember the Makers' Space, that artists' clubhouse I have the key for. I feel a shiver of excitement and almost call out to Dee, but then just leave it. The shadows of the trees are long, but nothing touches her as she strolls down the road; she seems to just float away like some kind of ghost. She knows I'm watching her and raises a hand in a salute to me.

I look up at my house. The front porch light is broken, but there are lights, and lives, inside—without me. I can see them walking around in silhouette. I think of Lottie's house down the street, that house that used to be like my own, better even. There's a second then that I feel something soft, warm, for Lottie, like an old worn blanket. Then I remember what Dee said, and wonder if she would ever do something to Lottie without telling me. *No.*

I shake my head and return to the present. Paige. I look back toward where Dee was, but she's gone. *You've got this one,* she said. It's not too late, I think. I can get this done quickly. My heart is beating and pumping out that feeling I've come to recognize when I'm doing something, when I'm not taking it lying down.

My handlebars are a little cold and the seat is damp, but as I get closer to the school, I am sweating. I have used the Space on and off since Pete gave me the key. I'm usually a little nervous with the older students, but I'll be damned if they don't have some cool equipment: great software and a soundproof audio suite, and even a darkroom if I feel like getting extra moody and arty. Sometimes I work there alongside the upper-years, and I love that no one really knows what anyone else is working on. Everyone ignores everyone else, and it gives me a thrill to think that I can get up to all manner of justice and mischief, that I can scheme and plan and execute right under everyone's noses.

I swipe the card through the reader, just as a dog in a nearby yard starts barking like mad, jangling my nerves. I slip inside. The bright lights surprise me, coming on with a hum. The Makers' Space is empty. I throw my backpack on a table and slide into a chair at a computer, scooting it forward while it warms up. This shouldn't take long, what I have planned. I putter around for a bit, scanning, working with Photoshop, digging up pictures, and I am feeling stronger and stronger. This is the right thing to do. My body thrums with justice and the knowledge that I am so balls-out in my actions, my fingers flying across the keyboard. Before long, the printer is booted up, buzzing with dangerous vengeance, and soon it's spitting out copy after copy of our next job. Dee calls them "jobs," what has been happening, what we've been doing, these vigilante acts of revenge, like she's in *Oceans 11* or something. It's over the top, but I love it.

I lay all the printouts in front of me and get started.

18

There seem to be hundreds of posters, all with the same image: Paige, grinning and cute and pretty as a stock photo of a cheerleader, her face glowing in the Polaroid we took together months ago—except there is a KKK hood drawn over her face and RACIST written across the top of the poster, all in red lipstick. In another, I cut her out and put her in the middle of a group of hillbillies I found online, blacking out her front teeth. They are plastered on the doors to the bathrooms, on bulletin boards, and all across the hallway of ninth-grade lockers.

People take pics with their phones before the teachers and janitors can tear them down, so the fire shoots across social media, moving from person to person, from page to group to message until everyone's phone is burning hot. A video appears on YouTube within an hour, a shaky, amateur pan of the posters, people laughing, Paige herself turning from the camera with tears in her eyes. The title of the video is "Racist Girl Gets Schooled" and it's seen hundreds of times by lunch, comments ranging from questions about what she did to emojis of brown hands clapping to suggestions that this is bullying.

Dee slides into our table with her lunch tray, joining me and Ava. She's grinning. I hide behind my sandwich, hardly tasting it. My heart is beating hard.

"This is amazing!" she says. "That bitch will think twice about saying any of that shit now!" She reaches for my hand and gives me a little squeeze.

Ava looks sideways, and I see that Antar is sitting a bit further down the table with a few other kids. I follow her gaze. "Why's he over there?" I ask.

"I don't think he's as happy about this as you thought he'd be," Ava says, looking at me. "But, I mean, I think it's pretty sick," she says, smiling.

"What's his problem?" I ask, worried.

He sees us looking and says something to the other kids, then stands up and comes over to us.

"Hey, Antar," I say. "Did you—"

"I do not need you fighting my battles for me," he says. "I mean, I'm all in for fucking shit up, you know I am, but let us do it ourselves, you know?"

"What?" I say, looking for support around the table. "This is not just for you, Antar, this is—"

"Seriously," he cuts in, "I will pay back who I want to pay back. Trust me." He walks back and sits down again, his friends looking over curiously.

"Whoa," I say, shaking my head. I look at Ava, who shrugs, biting on a fry and rooting around for another. "I mean, I kinda see what he's saying," she says, her mouth full.

Dee raises her eyebrows, and I follow her gaze. Breanne, with her arm around Paige, walking toward the exit.

She passes our table and leans in. "You are *such* a loser,

Stevie. Just because you have no friends doesn't mean you have to take it out on everyone else."

Dee laughs loudly and puts her hands in the air in mock surrender. "Okay, sheriff, take it easy. Don't you guys have some books to burn or something?" I laugh, and so do a few other kids around us. Someone yells at the girls to *get out*, and a French fry comes flying at them from somewhere. Paige bursts into a sob. I almost go after her but swallow it down.

Dee stands up. She opens her arms. "Justice!"

I look across the room and see Lottie. She shakes her head.

* * *

The next day in homeroom, Pete addresses what he calls "the recent stream of immature and potentially dangerous acts of mischief."

Dee scoffs and rolls her eyes, smiling at me. Urging me.

I raise my hand. "But couldn't you argue that they are just responding to the school administration's failure to act on the real issues of bullying that take place in our school community?"

Everyone is silent, watching me. It feels great.

Pete raises his eyebrows and sighs. "Okay. I get it. Sure, stuff happens in a high school that goes under the radar of the teachers and administrators. And I'm all for activism. But vandalizing, causing real harm, and bullying in retaliation is not the solution. The solution is to talk to someone. Come to us. Tell us your concerns. Let us handle it."

Right. The teachers could never know or get a handle on the wide range of crap happening here every day, happening online, outside these walls, inside our homes, everywhere, everywhere. And everyone else seems to feel the same way, because they are all looking anywhere but at Pete. They are looking at me. No one will tell. They can't prove anything, they don't want to snitch, they're not 100 percent sure; they just want to mind their own business, they don't want to be next. All the reasons to say nothing. To look away.

"Okay? Okay. Moving on."

* * *

I deflate when I leave school. It used to be the opposite, but now I get my energy from the action, the attention. It's like a literal charge into my body, whereas being home gives me nothing. I want to keep the feeling going, the rush of the eyes on me, the feeling of people by my side. Because when it's gone, I am completely alone.

I push open the door and smell something cooking.

Mom calls from the kitchen, "Hi, honey!"

I slump in, throwing my bag on a chair. "What are you doing?"

"Making spaghetti and meatballs for us! I thought you and me could hang out together tonight."

I look around. "Where's Reg?"

"Oh, he's out with his buddies tonight, so it's just us girls!"

I walk over to the stove, where she's standing, her hair sweaty against her forehead, and stick my finger in the sauce, then taste it.

Mom puts her hand around my waist and smiles at me. "What do you want to watch?"

I smile in spite of myself because I can't help it. She is flighty and sweet and innocent, and she just wants to be loved, and I miss her.

* * *

Totally stuffed but still sharing popcorn, we stretch out on the couch to watch *Ferris Bueller's Day Off* for the 100th time. It's still light out, so we've pulled the curtains shut and are hunkered in together. It is so good. Just like old times. But then, just as Ferris is serenading the city of New York, Reg walks in.

"You started without me?" He laughs, and Mom jumps up and hugs him.

"I thought you were going out with the guys?" she gushes.

"Couldn't stay away, could I?" he says, her hero, and the next thing I know he's telling me to scooch to make room on the couch for him.

I get up. "Never mind. You two go ahead."

Mom *tsks* and protests. "Stevie, come *on*, don't do this."

"Don't do this, Mom? Seriously? I don't know why I ever believed you. You never have time for me anymore. Only your boyfriend."

"What? No, honey! I thought he was— Hon, we can all watch a movie together, for God sakes."

"Stevie," Reg says, "don't be mad at your mom. It's my fault." He shares a look with Mom like *eek, sorry!* but she dismisses it with a slight shake of her head. "I'll just go, girls, seriously."

"No! No, Reg. She's fine. She's just acting spoiled," Mom says, and that is it.

I walk right out of the family room, pulling a stupid print of a girl on a swing off the wall as I go. It crashes to the carpet, and I hear the glass break.

"What the—? Stevie!" Mom yells.

I slam the front door behind me.

There are bees in my ears, and they are buzzing around, and I'm afraid they're going to take over my brain. I am out of the house and walking down the street now, feeling like I'm dreaming. My face is wet, and I realize I'm crying. When I snap out of it, I see that I have walked to school, through the smokers' alley, which is covered in graffiti, and am standing outside the football field, hanging on to the chain-link fence, the metal making red grooves in my skin. The only thing that calms me down is planning. The only thing that makes me feel a pulse is action. Everything that we've been doing here, in this gladiator stadium of learning, is making me feel alive, seen, when everything else makes me disappear.

19

Antar still isn't really talking to me, but even if he is mad, other people have been inspired. Suddenly lots of others are in on the revenge action. It has caught on, the vengeance bug. There are more people, more acts of—as the administration calls them—"mischief," over the next two weeks. It's surprising and unsettling and I'm not even sure what to make of it, because we didn't plan this, me and Dee, and don't even know who's doing what now. Things are happening outside our control and the Love, Heather stunts have taken on a life of their own. Random acts of retribution by people we don't know. I'm watching; things at Woepine High have taken a turn. The stakes have been raised. It's a movement. It's a revolution. It's verging on chaos.

A senior, who is a known MRA misogynist, has eyes—real eyes, like from a cow or something—left in his bag, with Women are watching you. Love, Heather written in red on a note inside. One of his friends pulls it out and reads it out loud while he keeps screaming, "What the fuck? What the fuck?" over and over and shaking his hands. It's a real *Godfather* horse-head-in-the-bed moment.

"Where'd they get the eyes?" I ask Dee on the way to class, and she shakes her head in gleeful disbelief while the boy's screams echo down the hallway.

The photo of a handsy Biology teacher's children is removed from his desk, returned later with the addition of paper speech bubbles that say, I AM WATCHING YOU, DADDY and DON'T BE A PERV. LOVE, HEATHER.

A bunch of homophobic guys on the basketball team have their lockers painted pink and NO HOMOPHOBES written across them. LOVE, HEATHER.

The captain of the soccer team, who made the position, people say, because her dad is the coach, is blatantly tripped in a crowd and twists her knee, incapacitating her, Tonya Harding style. No one saw who did it. No one fesses up. I don't even know why anyone would do that. But someone wrote on her locker, too, just a sloppy, red heart and SUCK IT, CUNT. No artistry at all.

A guy who keeps a "slay list" of girls he's slept with is found to have shoplifted from the store where he works in the mall. A T-shirt in his backpack sets off the alarm, and he's fired.

The student council freshman rep, a tall and skinny kid who everyone seems to think is a "totally nice guy," is swarmed and beaten up in smokers' alley, but later won't snitch on his attackers. He was spray-painted red and staggered, crying, into the front foyer of the school, looking terrified with snot and spit and tears running down his face. I am shocked by this. There is no way he deserved that, I think, but then realize that I don't know who is doing what, who has what coming, or why.

Up and up and up. More and more and more. All grades,

not just freshmen; all the people, not just those I know. Like everyone gave permission, got permission, to take what they want, give shit to the rest, to knock people down. Maybe we are behind some of these, but maybe not, not all of them, anyway. At this point, it's so hard for anyone to tell. Dee never admits to anything, and neither do I. No one does.

At lunch, Antar and Marta, and even Ava sometimes, have started sitting a little further away from us, but the table where we sit is full of other kids. We are not alone, even if our friends are spreading out, away. People talk excitedly about all the pranks, and about whether they were warranted or not. Sometimes people fantasize about getting even with those who tormented them and others over the course of their lives.

People scrawl calls for vengeance and condemnations in red lipstick in bathrooms. There are sloppy notes left behind on chalkboards:

Rob is an asshole, someone Heather him.
Heather can suck my dick.
Heather help me

Suddenly LoveHeather Instagram and Snapchat accounts have cropped up. People talk about Heather on the student-only Facebook group, everyone tirelessly ranting about how the pranks are great or they suck or WHAT THE HELL IS ALL THIS or FUCK OFF or LOSERS or HEATHER CLAPS BACK or WE ARE ALL HEATHER. It is more than one thing; it's so many things. Dee wanted to turn the tables on the power dynamic at the school, and at first, I thought this was working, but I don't know what to think anymore. We have no control over any of it. Who are the bullies, and who is bullied; who is right, what is true.

People steal and humiliate and scream for justice. There is a paranoid whisper gaining volume in the halls and online. It gathers strength, becoming a furious wind of retribution. It howls through the corridors and bangs all the lockers shut. People are called hypocrites and snowflakes and bullies and social justice warriors. No one is safe. No one knows what it is, or how it started, or what it means. If it's the victims fighting back or a new many-headed bully-monster.

Letters go home to parents, and posts show up on the school's social media accounts.

WOEPINE HIGH SCHOOL HAS A ZERO-TOLERANCE POLICY FOR BULLYING OF ANY KIND. ANY STUDENT FOUND TO BE PER-PETRATING ACTS OF VIOLENCE OR HARASSMENT TO THE STU-DENT BODY OR STAFF WILL BE DEALT WITH IMMEDIATELY.

Zero tolerance for bullying. Where were they when I was afraid to go to school?

My mom asks me about it while we're getting groceries. She is looking at her phone in the middle of the pasta aisle, her cart blocking the way for anyone else.

"What is all this stuff about bullying at the school? Do you know anyone doing that?"

I examine the back of a box of macaroni and throw it in the cart, shifting it so an old lady can get by. "Not really. The school is just being paranoid. They're probably afraid of getting sued or something."

"Well, I hope everyone is okay," she says, doubtfully, "No one is bothering you, are they?" She puts a hand on my back and rubs it in quick little circles.

"I'm good, Mom," I say, giving her a small smile.

"I know you are, honey," she says. "You've never been a troublemaker. Just make sure that you stand up for yourself, right?" She puts on a tough face and clenches her fist, then laughs, "Or you just call on your old mom."

"Haha. Okay, tough guy."

She lifts one of my hands as I put some sauce in the cart and says, "I like your new nail polish, by the way."

I look at my nails: a bright fire-engine red.

"Thanks."

* * *

Pete talks to our class again, about how this is getting out of control.

"This might seem like harmless fun to some of you," he says gravely while Dee and I exchange looks, "but people are getting hurt. Physically and emotionally. I will not name names, but this should be a safe space for every single student. I do not take this lightly."

"There's blood in the water," Dee says to me, quietly.

The thing is, though, even though it's unsettling, it's so great to see people rise up. Pete doesn't get it. He doesn't know what it's like down here in the trenches. It's different than when he was young, and even when Lottie and I were young. I don't think he really could possibly understand. People need to play dirty sometimes, and yes, maybe it's a little out of control, but I kind of love that.

Pete asks me to stay after class.

I saunter up to his desk, which still has a sign on it that says MRS. SHERMAN. I jut my chin out and try to effect some attitude, but this is a person who cleaned up my Brownie tights when I peed in them in kindergarten, so it's a little hard to pull off.

"How long are you going to keep that name tag?" I ask, pointing to it.

"I'll ask the questions, thanks." Pete sighs, gesturing for me to sit down on the chair in front of the desk, the one reserved for kids in shit. I sit and lean way back, lifting up the front legs of the chair. He raises his eyebrows.

"What's going on with you?"

"What do you mean?"

"Are you behind any of these, I dunno, pranks?" He leans forward, folding his hands. I notice that his face has broken out in a rash of tiny pimples, and I remember what he said about how transitioning would be kind of like going through puberty again. I briefly wonder how he's doing with it, then push that out of my mind.

"I don't know what you're talking about."

"You don't."

"Nope." I let the chair fall forward with a bang.

"I revert to my original question: what is going on with you? You seem kind of out of control lately. Things okay at home?"

I don't know why grown-ups always ask this. They think it's the kind of question we have to answer, the secret key that is going to get kids to open up. *Man! If someone would just ask me if things were okay at home!* I mean, for Pete standards, this is pretty weak.

"Sure, things are okay. Things okay at your home?" I pick up one of his pens and start to fiddle with it, spinning it over my knuckles in a way Dee taught me.

"Watch yourself, kiddo. We have a relationship outside of school, but part of the condition of my being your homeroom teacher, as you know, is that you don't cross the line."

He's referring to the fact that I begged for Pete to be my teacher and agreed to any conditions, not that my mom cared either way—namely that I would not be overly familiar or informal with Pete, and that I would accept his authority as my teacher. And until now, I always abided by these. But things are different now. Everything is different. But something bubbles up inside me and it comes out like a mumbled apology. I'm looking in my lap and noticing there is a long pen smudge on my jeans.

"Stevie, look at me."

I do. He looks tired. There are bags under his eyes, and he needs a haircut.

"I don't want you lashing out or getting into trouble for attention. Are the other kids bothering you? If there is anything wrong, I want you to know that I'm always here, okay?"

"Yeah, except you're not."

"Pardon?"

"Nothing," I grumble.

"No, what do you mean?"

"Fine. You act like you're all clued in, like you know what's going on with young people, but you are so out of touch, you have no idea. I mean, do you even know me? Do you even know Lottie?"

"I like to think I do, yes, although sure, I'll grant you that sometimes teenagers are a bit of a mystery to everyone."

"Well, she's totally different. *I'm* totally different. And you never even noticed."

"That is not true, Stevie." He puts his hand on my arm briefly. "Hey," he says gently, "you don't need to be tough, okay?"

I feel my lip quivering. No. I will not let him get in my head only to give me some pat on the head and then leave me to the wolves. I need to shut him out and be strong on my own. I look out the window, lift my eyes to the blue sky so the tears won't gather in my eyes.

"I wanted to talk to you *because* you seem different. I'm concerned about you."

I say nothing, but return his gaze with a hard stare. He sighs, seeing that I'm not giving him an inch.

"Try and stay out of trouble. It's not worth it. I don't want to have to call your mom in here," he says.

I scoff.

"She loves you. And so do I."

I nod and look away again. Pete stands and comes around the table, and I stand up, too. And in a moment of total weakness or forgetting, I hug him. His body tenses in surprise, there is a pause, and then he gives me a quick squeeze. I almost lose it, in that moment. I feel eleven again, like I'm going to dissolve right into his arms, which are like the best sweater, the comfiest couch, like the home I wish was mine. *Pull it together, Stevie.* I wipe my eyes and pull away, and as I do, I see that Breanne is just outside the room, watching us. I sniff, mutter a thanks, and leave without saying another word.

I pretend not to see Breanne as I move through the doorway but feel her eyes on me. She follows me down the hallway, then grabs my arm. I spin around like I might punch her out. She sees it in my face and steps back.

"What?" I demand.

She quickly regains herself. "Wow, that was kinky. I mean, I knew you were a slut, but I didn't know how far you'd go to get good grades." She smirks.

"Shut up," I say, turning around again.

"Does Lottie know you are having after-school cuddles with her mom?"

Before I know it, I am back, inches from her face.

"Do not make me hurt you, Breanne," I hiss, surprising

180

both of us. Her eyes widen and her mouth clamps shut. My chest is heaving. There's a beat, a moment between us, when neither folds, but then she looks away and mumbles "Whatever" and walks away, her hair swinging at her back. I watch her go and head for the doors, my eyes squinting in the sun.

20

There is a trip today to the recycling plant for the Environmental Science Club, or frankly, anyone who realized the trip was an option. I heard about it on the announcements yesterday and need to get out. I cannot sit in class right now. I feel a rumble of anger bubbling inside me as I start my day with Pete, who teaches things that used to matter to me but seem unrelated to real life anymore. I remembered how Ava was always trying to get me to join the club, and Mr. Wilson is so desperate to get students involved that he agreed to all the last-minute slackers who provided him with a permission form.

It is sticky and warm, and if you're the kind of person who cares about environmental science, a little alarming, even for May. Most everyone is on their phones, even those who are pretending to listen to their friends. Dee isn't there. I stand alone, watching two squirrels chase each other around a nearby tree, one of them finally catching the other, pinning it down and humping it like a squirrel robot. Then he scoots off and the first squirrel just lies there. You never really see a squirrel lying on the ground unless it's dead, but I guess she needs some time to collect herself. We file onto the bus while our teacher checks our names off a list.

I sit close to the front on the left-hand side. I grapple with the window for a while, trying to jimmy it down a couple of inches, but I can't do it. I slump down in the seat, which lets out a defeated wheeze. Someone sits down beside me and I turn to see that it's Lottie. I look around and see there are no other seats, and so that's why she's sitting here with me.

"Oh, hi," I say.

She smiles a little, and says, "Hey."

"I didn't know you were in this club," I say.

"I am very concerned about the environment."

I let out a low laugh as she takes a book out of her bag and begins to read.

The bus comes alive and starts moving, and right away we are jiggled about like a train in an old-timey cartoon. People are laughing and goofing off because being in a school bus is like getting into a time machine, and you just can't help but turn nine again. Lottie is reading, and I look out the window and it feels like nothing and everything has changed. Our bodies bump into each other as the bus hits potholes. I miss being next to her and wish we could just hook arms, feel that closeness again.

"Sorry," she says, as she is knocked into me.

"It's okay," I say, and my heart feels like it's cracking.

We move out onto the main drag and pass the No Frills, and the hair salon where my mom used to work before she decided to open one in our house. I used to hang out in the basement salon with her, reading old *Cosmo*s and trying out the curling irons and straighteners. I loved the smell of it down there. The hair sprays and permanents and dyes, and how the smells were always on her, even after she showered and changed. It's different now. Ever since Reg. Now he hangs out down there. He reads the magazines and sits in the hair-washing chair with the footrest and makes comments on all the women in the pictures. He flirts with Mom's clients and they all laugh at his jokes. They think he is charming and that she is lucky, but they don't know that he stole my mother from under my nose, just leaving me with one more hole in my life.

We are on the highway now, going fast, Lottie reading beside me as scraps of songs float like pieces of garbage in a wind up from the back of the bus. We drive past a long, low building with a sign for a company called Earth Boring, past offices and plazas and car dealerships and warehouses. I look down at the people in the cars driving beside us and wonder about their lives. Is she going to eat that sandwich later? Why do they have so many blankets in the back seat? How can he stand smoking in the car like that? There is a woman singing along to the radio, and I smile just watching her because she is so into it; she is on stage and not in a little Hyundai Sonata. She shakes her hair about and pounds her palms on the steering wheel.

We reach the recycling plant. It doesn't look that big from the outside, but I realize later that it is, and that the entrance is almost like the doorway to Bilbo Baggins's hobbit hole.

A man in safety goggles ushers us into an empty room with tables and chairs and two pop machines. "Okay, now listen up here, because it's really loud on the tour, so it will be hard to hear me all the time. You're each going to wear a safety vest and glasses," he says, while another man walks around with a bin of gear for us to put on. We follow them into the factory, single file. Lottie is in front of me, her messy, crazy hair in all directions, her hands at her sides, in fists.

As soon as we go through the door into an enormous, endless warehouse, it is impossibly loud: a racket of noise and garbage, tiny pieces of paper flying around like dirty magic dust. The tour guide leads us down some metal stairs and along a pathway that cuts through the middle of it all, on one side forklifts raking and lifting piles of junk mail three stories high—a pyramid of paper—and enormous bound cubes of crushed cans like metal haystacks are being somehow organized on the other side. The tour guide shouts at us from the front of the line, but I hear nothing. I look at a woman working a switchboard of machinery in a cagelike contraption to my right. She wears her hair back in a ponytail and has on the same glasses we all do. She smiles at me and returns to her work, pulling switches and dials in the world's filthiest video game.

We continue up more clanky metal stairs and across a metal bridge that oversees the whole operation. Below us, conveyor belts covered in trash move at a remarkable clip while workers pick off the occasional piece and throw it into a bin behind them without looking. Juice boxes and bags and broken toys and cans and long tangled jumbles of ribbon and plastic rings for pop and twisted pieces of metal and more, more, more. We clump down the stairs and file in behind the sorting line, which is what it is called, to watch. I catch a snatch of information shouted from our tour guide about how their job is to pull anything that isn't plastic from the line. I watch as employees, bored from hours and days and years of this job, methodically pick through the wave of crap that whizzes in front of them. They are missing so much, so many pieces that aren't plastic, and some small obsessive-compulsive part of me is seizing up. *There, there, there, that piece, what about that, quick.* But they are accustomed to the job, I suspect, and so they move at a measured pace. Each person has a large bin behind them, and some of these are decorated with mascots and treasures that must have been pulled from the line. On one, there is a Barbie horse—a white one, with silvery hair. It's scuffed and the hair is tangled, but I could totally see why it was saved, and it makes me kind of sad. We keep walking.

Lottie's head is down, and she's covering her ears. I see the scar on her arm from where she fell off her bike when we were eleven. I remember how bad the cut was, full of gravel and dirt, but she was so tough. Pete cleaned it and put a bandage on it and gave us ice cream with cookie crumbs on it, and I remember that we said that it looked like the dirt from her arm. It tugs at me, seeing that scar, and her with her hands over her ears. She stumbles as we finally walk through a closed door and into an area where we can hear again. We gather in a crowd while the man who works there tells us the stats about how they recycle up to ninety-seven percent of the material that goes in there, and how the recycling plant we are in is a charity that transforms so much of what goes in into something else. He opens a bag he's holding and holds up a piece of crown molding.

"This," he says, "used to be a Styrofoam takeout box. It was crown molding trapped in the body of Styrofoam, and we helped it become what it wanted to be." He chuckles and so do a few other people. The man gestures for the group to follow him into another room, and the crowd starts to move.

Most of the group have gone through the doorway when

Justin, a guy standing beside me, nudges Lottie in the back. "Like your mom," he says.

His friends snicker and act like they are shocked and offended between giggles. I look at her, her lower jaw sticking out, and feel a rush of old loyalty burst up, surprising me.

I turn to him. "Shut the fuck up," I hiss, loudly.

He raises his eyebrows and makes a face of mock concern, clutching his chest. "Oh, sorry. Did I offend your girlfriend?"

I glance at Lottie.

"Stevie, don't," she says.

I ignore her. I look back at Justin. "You are such an asshole, and let me tell you: guys like you? Your time is up,"

"Oh really?" He smirks. "Lemme guess. You're part of that Heather shit. We all know about you and that tranny teacher."

"*What* did you say, you transphobic dick?" I shout, thrusting my body forward like I'm going to start a fight, like I'm going to beat this guy up who could flatten me. Because he's still Pete, after all, even if I can't count on him like I once could; he's part of me, somewhere deep inside. I won't stand for anyone trying to take shots at him.

Justin laughs, but nervously, because i notice there are a bunch of other students who have turned around and are snapping their fingers and smiling at me. "Preach," someone murmurs, and someone puts their hand on my shoulder.

Justin shakes his head, laughing. The noise of that place rattles around in my brain like we're inside a machine. It's echoing all over.

I am still staring at him angrily when I feel another knock on my shoulder. I look up and see that Lottie has shoved me.

"Hey—"

"Seriously? What is *wrong* with you?" she shouts over the din.

"Wrong with me? *Me?*"

"Why do you have such an ax to grind about everything?"

"An ax? What?"

She looks at me for a long time, and then says, "You know, you don't need to make everything about you." And she starts to walk away.

"Fuck you, Lottie!" I yell. "You are not the only one struggling."

She turns around, lifts her hands, and yells back, "Who said I was struggling?" I start to respond, but she continues, "You know, Stevie, everything doesn't have to be a battle. Everything isn't a chance for you to have the spotlight."

"What the—"

"Join the drama club or something. Get an outlet for your, I dunno *what* this is. Look, we get it: you're pissed at the world. Just—stay the fuck out of my life!"

A bunch of the guys are shaking their fingers and saying "Ooh, burn" as they turn to leave, and I could kill them, honestly. But my fury is for Lottie right now. Lottie, leaving again. She turns, moving through the door with the others, and I am here, in an empty room with wisps of recycled paper drifting around me.

21

When I get home that day, Reg is watching TV in our family room. I walk in, eating an apple.

"Where's my mom," I ask him, stone cold.

"She's on her way." He looks at me. "How you feeling?"

"What? Fine."

He mutes the TV and turns around, all serious. "Listen, kid. Your mom told me what's happening at your school lately. And, you know, it makes sense why you've been acting so agro."

Aggressive. Jesus H. Christ, this guy.

"And I gotta say, I get it. I'm not proud of it, but I used to give some guys at my school a hard time when I was your age." Big surprise there. "Bullying is serious stuff, man. I hope you know that you can come to me and talk about it if anything happens to you or one of your girlfriends or something."

"Talk to you."

"Yeah." He leans in and opens his hands, all welcoming. "I get it if you can't tell your mom stuff all the time, but you can confide in me if you need to. Maybe it's because I never grew up"—he snickers—"but I understand kids." He raises his eyebrows. "It's hard to get any shit past me, let me tell you."

"Right . . ." I close my eyes, and when I open them, he's changing the channels again. "Tell my mom I went out."

I turn on my heel and get the hell out of the house. I get on my bike, gripping the handlebars so hard my knuckles hurt. I am riding through my neighborhood. Faster, faster, faster. As I'm zipping down the road, pumping my pedals like mad, I turn down Lottie's street and see a truck in front of her house. It's not a huge moving truck, but it is a pretty big one, and I know what it's for. I'm not even thinking about seeing Lottie. I just see Pete and can't stop pedaling.

Pete, who for my whole life was there for me, who made me lunches and cuddled me when I cried, who was Snowy Owl in Brownies and caroled with us at Christmas, and is now mopping his brow with a handkerchief. Since when does he have a handkerchief? And why the hell is he moving out? What the hell is wrong with our parents?

The closer I get to the house, the madder I get, and I stand up on my pedals, yelling, "Hey! Hey, Pete!" as I careen crazily down the hill toward the house, my hair whizzing around. He looks up, focusing on me, and starts to wave, but it turns into a *whoa, whoa* motion since I am not really slowing down. I know I'm going to crash. If you've been riding a bike as long as I have, if it's like a loyal old horse to you, you know when she's going to toss you, ass over teakettle, but quite frankly, I couldn't give a shit. Good, I think, as I half-assedly try to stop but slam right into the side of the truck. The pain feels good.

And it hurts like a bitch.

Pete is gathering me up, returning my head to my neck, putting my arms back onto my shoulders, snapping my feet

into my ankles and wiping my bleeding elbow with that goddamn handkerchief.

"When did you get that thing?" I mumble, sounding like a
drunk baby.

"What's that, honey?"

"That thing. That handkerchief. I've never seen you use a
handkerchief before."

"What?" He looks at it, then back at me. "I don't know. A
while ago, I guess."

"Why?" And I'm crying. "Why did you get a handkerchief?"

"Why did I get this handkerchief?" He lifts me up, and I
move all my joints to make sure they're working. He's looking
in my eyes, and they are full of love and I miss them.

"Yeah, why?"

"Well, I liked it," he says, softly. "Why did you get that shirt
you're wearing?"

"Like, is that part of your big transformation?" I wipe my
eyes.

"What do you mean, hon?"

"Next thing you know you're gonna be living somewhere
else and buying fair-trade coffee with your new girlfriend. Or
boyfriend. Or whatever."

He takes a breath and looks back at the house, and I know
he's wishing that someone would rescue him. "Ah," he says. "So
this isn't about my transitioning but about my leaving."

"Yes, about 'your' leaving, Mr. Grammar Cop. Why the hell
are you leaving? Why does everybody leave?" I hear myself,
blubbering, snot running into my mouth.

He touches my shoulders with both hands. "I'm not really
going anywhere, Stevie. I'll still be here. Just not in this house."

"Right. Not here. Just like Lottie's never here, and my

mom's mentally not 'here' anymore, and Dad has Eleanor, and there's always that goddamn douchebag in my house—"

"Sorry, what douchebag?"

"Where is Lottie, anyway?"

"Lottie's not here, I'm afraid." He tries to wipe my face with the handkerchief, and I swat him away.

"Oh? She's not here? Well! No shit, Sherman. What a surprise."

"Listen, Stevie, is this about all that Heather stuff? Did you want to talk about anything?"

"No, Pete, I do *not* want to talk. I'm done talking." I pick up my bike, which is definitely on the wobbly side now, and steer her off the driveway, spitting a little blood on the road as I go.

"Well, that was just awesome," I hear Pete mutter, and my ears go red because that's what happens when I act like a dick.

I am riding again, a little lopsidedly, with no set destination, but I hit the main drag and pull in at Tim Hortons. Through the window I can see the outline of Dee. Well, actually, specifically, the outline of her hair. Her hair has more presence than I do. I drop my bike against the brick facade and push open the door.

"Wow. You look like shit," she says, calmly sipping a coffee. "What happened?"

"One vanilla-dip doughnut with sprinkles, please," I tell the kid working at the cash. We know each other from school but pretend not to. He hands it to me; I pay and head to Dee's table, sitting heavily on the plastic chair, which swivels around beneath me. I can feel all the life whiz out of me like a balloon with no knot to hold the air, flying around the room, getting smaller and smaller. I realize I haven't eaten in a really long time, and this doughnut is amazing. But I still feel like something isn't working, like the bike chain of my brain fell off and no one knows how to put it on right.

"Nobody sticks around, nobody's good," I mutter.

"'Nobody's good'?"

"I can't think of anyone. I mean, everyone's making the wrong choices, everyone's copping out, or not being here. No one is ever around, no one is a friend, no one is good!" I am still eating the doughnut, but I'm crying now, again, which would have struck me as high irony at another time, since the vanilla dip with sprinkles is the happiest of all the doughnuts. But I'm really having a go at crying, blubbering away with sprinkles all over my bloody lips. Dee hands me a napkin and I wipe my face, and that just makes me think of Pete and his handkerchief and what a jerk I was to him.

"And Reg, that asshole. He's, like, brainwashed my mom. And it's not even like I can leave. I mean, I am so fucking stuck."

"Jesus." She looks out the window.

"Yeah. And also there's Pete. I cannot believe that he is leaving. When he was a mom, he never left." I sniff and wipe my nose, knowing how stupid I sound, but I don't care. "And Lottie. I don't even know what happened with us. It's just, like"—I make a *poof* gesture with my hands—"gone."

"Her loss."

"Yeah. Maybe." I pause. "I mean, it's not like she's actually gone. She just doesn't want me anymore."

"Wanna go for a walk?"

I nod. She leads, which is what she does now, and I follow, which feels so much better than doing nothing.

We walk behind the Tim Hortons, where there is a path that leads to the Bruce Trail beside the creek. The water moves around a whole bunch of crap in the bed of the creek, like a grocery cart lying sideways, and Tim Hortons cups that look like they're trying to swim upstream. The path leads to a small bridge, and we stand in the middle looking down at the water, which is rushing like crazy. We don't say anything for a while, and I start thinking about why no matter what I do, I fuck things up, and the only thing that makes me feel better is pushing back.

Dee is looking at her phone. She chuckles and holds it up for me to see: a new Twitter account called @We_Are_All_Heather claims to be POSTING ON THE PAYBACKS AT WHS. There are a ton of posts already, blurry pics of fights after pranks happened, of lockers that were defaced, of some of the early LOVE, HEATHER pranks and some I didn't know about until now.

"The power of the people," Dee muses. She links arms with me, and her strength pulses through me. Then I let go of her and bend down and pick up a rock that's wedged between the metal rungs that make up the bridge. And I heave it into the water, throwing it as far and as hard as I can. It makes a tiny, impotent splash.

"We can't stop, Dee."

22

Episode 72 00:00
Hello, film nerds. Today we are going deep. Payback.
Vengeance. Revenge. Those films that make you put your
fist in the air and yell at the top of your lungs, "Yes! Take
that!" Those movies that take us on a journey of justice,
that give a voice to the voiceless and show how they can
raise their weapons and take what's theirs.

A few days later, I lie in bed listening to music. An album
Lottie turned me onto. Lottie. She's still part of me, part
of the inside-out of me. Half of me would love to get even
for the way she tripped the wire that brought the school down
on me, for the way she abandoned me; the other half just wants
to lie around listening to records and make up. Last year, we
gave each other necklaces, each with half a broken heart, that
say BEST FRIENDS when you put them together and make a
whole. My half, the part that says ST and ENDS, is in a tangle
of knots at the bottom of my jewelry box along with all
the things I know about her: that she used to be so scared of

the dark that she slept with all the lights on, that when she first got her period she didn't know how to use a tampon so I had to teach her, that she has back acne, that she took forever to learn to ride a bike, that she is smart and solitary, that she is secretive and quiet. Dee says Lottie started it all, that none of it would have happened and none of them would have turned on me if she hadn't, and maybe she's right. She says that Lottie has more than she deserves.

She has a loving home, a family, even if it's changing. I miss that. I miss playing checkers with my dad, years ago, or watching an entire movie with my mom.

I don't have a comfy home anymore, not like Lottie, not like stupid Paige and Breanne. I wish I could move in with Pete, move to his new house, help him decorate his place, become his daughter. I think of all the other people doing the jobs or pranks or whatever; I wonder what they are trying to protect and stand up for. About how many of us lie in bed and feel absolutely, desperately, alone.

A movie is playing on my TV on mute. I've seen it a hundred times. *Kids*. It's so disturbing and true and tough that tonight I'm watching it, while listening to something else or I may feel so much I'll explode. Everything is so close to the surface now, every emotion and experience just under the ice.

Today, someone broke into a girl's locker and put red paint all over the crotch of her gym shorts. Yesterday, someone wrote RAPIST in red on the lockers of every guy on the basketball team. The day before, someone shoved a boy's head in the toilet between classes. I saw him, blotchy and wet, coming out of the bathroom. I don't know now: was he the bully or the victim? But part of me doesn't care. I think of Aidan grabbing me and my face reddens, even in the privacy of my room, in the quiet of my thoughts. So many people go unchecked. Do what they want to anyone, and they are getting a taste of it now— some of them, anyway. If there are some unintended conse- quences, I chock that up to collateral damage, but something creeps into my mind, knowing that the revenge game can go both ways.

I reach for my phone and text Dee. My life preserver, my buoy in the storm.

Hey girl what's up? she says.

Nothing. Just hanging out

You ok?

Yeah, I'm good. Question

Shoot

Do you worry that someone will come for us? Like, do something big?

. . .

I wait, biting my lip.

No.

No?

No one's coming for you. I gotchu.

And she does, I know. She eases the pain, whenever it comes. Lots of kiss and hug emojis coming my way, my phone buzzing with love. I lie back and close my eyes, letting the echo of those little cartoons of love float behind my eyes.

23

On Monday and Tuesday, we sat awkwardly in Health class, because apparently this tiny school, in this itty-bitty old town, is going to be the place where progressive sex ed takes a wobbly first step. They decided to keep us all together, they said, for now. I think they were afraid of the students who are enlightened enough to claim that splitting us up is adhering to a gender binary, and that some people may not be comfortable being told or being pressured to choose a group. The Safe Spaces group was likely consulted, which probably made them feel extra important.

Mr. Cavalier, our Phys Ed teacher, doubled as our Health teacher. He was mortified but made up for it with volume, as though he was trying to communicate his lack of knowledge through sheer force of will. I wished he wouldn't keep rambling, stomping over terms like a water buffalo, leaving words like *orientation* and *identity* and *binary* rubbing their heads woozily while he waved his arms about, correcting his own blunders, blushing. He showed a lot of videos and TED Talks because otherwise someone would have had to tell him that the word is transgender, not transgendered, and he would massage his chin and nod *yes, yes, that's right*.

Not everyone was awkward, I guess, at least about the topic of sex. The kids who are in the Safe Spaces club have been waiting all year to watch a teacher try to fumble through the terms that are the feature of hundreds of Tumblr accounts, AMAs on Reddit, even shows on Netflix, YouTube, articles and reviews. Some people are very well versed in everything to do with sex and health and gender identity and like talking about it all the time. That doesn't necessarily mean they're experienced in the fine art of actual sex.

But, I mean, a lot of people are having *it*.

A lot of people are getting whatever they can: blow jobs, hand jobs, full-on sex, too. I don't think girls are getting many jobs done for them, to be honest, but they're participating, they're the worker bees, from what I can hear. It's happening all over: in bathrooms and parties, in bathrooms *at* parties, under the stairs, behind the bleachers, in cars. In this way, we are no different than teenagers of the past hundred years. The Industrial Revolution probably just inspired more places for teenagers to have sex.

Some people here also show no interest in sex, and in the new age of everyone having an identity, some of these kids self-identify as "asexual." Others are so into "healthy sex lives" that they make it their mission to embarrass everyone with their extreme comfort with their sexuality. And some kids get totally turned on by something else altogether: social justice. The social justice warriors, who naturally hate being called that, learn every term, every way in which privilege reveals its ugliness, and will be the first people to tell you to check yourself. Woke AF.

I am a late bloomer, I guess. I've never had a boyfriend, but that doesn't make me a nun. I mean, I have danced close enough to feel someone's dick. Guys used to like me, but I usually dodged and deflected. The next thing I knew I was the school slut, so go figure.

Look, I'm no hero; I know I fall right in here with the insufferably smug and self-righteous. I know all about checking privilege even when my self-pity seeps out of my pores like grease. I read articles online about cultural appropriation and transphobia and I consider myself pretty woke. The only thing that educating yourself doesn't inoculate you against, though, is becoming a know-it-all, and as thick in the trees as I am, I know I am that. And yet. *STFD, Mr. Cavalier,* is what we're saying with our rolling eyes.

At the doorway, there is a basket of condoms. On the way in, and on the way out, the Aidans and Lukes of the class stock up because *God knows they are getting just a* shit-ton *of action.*

On Monday, Aidan held one up for me. "Stevie, it's important that you don't procreate, so make sure you pay attention," he muttered, just loud enough for his cronies to hear, and Paige, whose ass he'd grabbed as she leaned up against him and smiled at me. She let out a little yelp and swatted him. My eyes prickled and I squeezed them shut furiously. When I opened them, I saw Dee staring after him, her face a mask of rage.

On Monday and Tuesday, we were taught the terms. We learned, some of us, the idea that gender is a construct. That biology, genitalia—the things that open wide or hang and pulse and quicken—are separate, sometimes, from how we identify. From who we crush on. From who we are. We learned that gender is a performance. And this made me perk up a bit. It was a throwaway mumble from the teacher, who was reading off something, but it snaked its way toward me and looped under my arms and threw me into the air.

A performance. I looked down at myself and remembered Pete asking me where I got the shirt I was wearing. And then all I could think about was that goddamn handkerchief, and man, if that didn't blow my mind. All the performances around me ran through my head, including Reg-who-looks-like-James-Franko (without the melted face), with his belts and scarves and god-awful V-neck T-shirts. And this idea propelled me from Monday right through to Wednesday, where I am now, alert and listening, while Mr. Cavalier sweats and stutters and is performing brilliantly as Teacher Who Wished He Was Anywhere Else. But something is different. There is someone else here today. Today, Mr. Cavalier gets a lucky break.

He tells us, "Today, we have a special guest. Pablo Estavez, of the White Ribbon Campaign, is here to talk to you all about consent."

Consent. I feel nervous, like everyone can see my face going red. I don't risk a look at Aidan, who I'm sure isn't giving a thought to me or to what he did in the stairwell.

Dee is leaning back in her chair with a look of amused curiosity on her face, which quite frankly is the badge of those of us Who Know More Than You.

And that's when a young, super-sexy man with rolled-up sleeves and arms covered in sleeve tattoos enters our classroom, rocking back and forth on his heels, biting his lower lip and smiling. It's like he's trying to seduce the entire class, and it's working. Dee's chair falls forward with a thump. There is applause.

Pablo Estavez waves and steps forward, with a loud and

hearty, "Hi, there!" while Mr. Cavalier grins all the way to the front row seat that he takes with visible gratitude. No one in the history of the world has ever been so grateful not to have to talk sex with a grade nine class. He is nodding enthusiastically like Pablo is telling his favorite story.

"I'm here to talk to you folks about when someone really, really, *really*"—here he bends his knees and groans a little—"wants to hook up with you."

Everyone giggles. Man, he's got them wrapped around his finger.

"But"—he puts up a hand—"I'm also here to talk to you about when they don't. Or when they change their mind, even in the last, last minute. And how it's your job to make sure they are A-okay at all times. And I'm here to talk about how it is okay for you also to say, in any way you're comfortable with, at *any point*, that you don't want to hook up, or that you don't want to touch, or that you don't like how someone is touching you, or that nope, you're done, even if you already said yes. Even if you said yes, yes, yes, yes—you can then say no. We're talking about touching, and rubbing, and hooking up, but more importantly, consent."

I am listening. Watching. The conversation is very one-sided for the first while. And then, slowly, people start scoffing to themselves. Mostly the dude-bros who sit with their legs spread wide apart. Those guys. But Pablo is waiting for this, and he cocks his head and says, *What are you thinking?* Like a gentle challenge. And the jocks with the spread legs start saying, *Well, sometimes it's really clear that they want it and you don't need to ask.* And then some of the class loses it and rolls their eyes and throws their arms in the air and groans, and others cheer and clap. And Pablo grins. *Sure, sure, I get it. But you can find some hot way of checking in. Can't you?*

Man, say the jocks, *I don't know.*

"I do know. I know you gotta. Check in often, and be sure you have enthusiastic consent. That is your goal."

That is not their goal. I look over at Dee. Her face is rapt with attention. Some of the girls are quiet.

"Sorry, man," says Aidan, and heads turn his way. He is slouched way down in his seat, like the act of sitting up is boring and exhausting. He shakes his head and says, "But how do *you* know that's what girls want?"

Pablo smiles. He says, "No one wants to be assaulted. No one wants to be attacked. No one likes to do something they're not comfortable doing. It's universal. Our bodies are our own. End of story."

My body is still, blood pumping loudly in my ears. His hand was so strong and he so easily hurt me. In that squeeze he told me that he could take anything, that he could do worse. He leapt up the stairs and back to class like it was nothing.

Pablo continues, "But also—and with permission, Mr. Cavalier, I'm gonna go off script here for a minute, but it feels right." Everyone sits up. And Pablo says, "I used to be a woman. And while that doesn't mean I know what 'girls want' as you say, I do have the unique experience of being in both gendered worlds. I do have experience with being touched without my consent, and also experience with the entitlement—and, I'll grant you, sometimes pressure—guys feel to ignore consent. My experiences have informed how I live my life, and what I do." He opens his arms and stands with his feet wide, completely comfortable in his skin.

I see Breanne cover her mouth to keep a laugh inside, and I hate her.

"So—that's the short story: I'm trans. I hear you folks learned what that means already."

I can see Mr. Cavalier's brain fizzling into a fine dust while the murmurs in the class rumble around like rocks going downhill. I think about Lottie, who is not in this class, and about Pete, who is probably teaching right now. Some students are snapping their fingers appreciatively and grinning; others are looking at each other like they've been the victims of a major heist. Pablo keeps talking, regaining control, and discussing safety and consent and our basic rights to enjoy sex. He takes questions, his voice wafts over me.

Safety.

I watch Aidan laughing and can almost feel his hand on my body, on my crotch, the unprovable, shameful shock of it. Maybe I'm making too big a deal of it. Maybe it wasn't that bad. I feel my face getting hot like it does before I cry. I clench my teeth and hold it in, polishing it, turning it into anger. I let that burn more deeply. I like the anger. I want to start fresh, to get a new chance. I want to burn everything to the ground and emerge brand new: a strong, happy, funny, confident Phoenix.

Chairs are pushed back and the class is over.

24

'm going to a party. I don't go to a lot of parties, but (a) I will take any opportunity to get out of the house that I can, and (b) I was invited, and since am not usually invited, I am game.

The party is at Sienna Martin's house, tomorrow, Thursday night. It's some end-of-the-year thing since we're headed into summer vacation. I hardly know Sienna Martin, but I mean, she seems pretty nice. We went to elementary school together. She used to chew her braids. Now she's kind of a pothead, her eyes always sleepy, her hair in a tangled bun on top of her head. Lately I've been looking at people like Sienna and thinking, "Is everything okay at home?" like Pete said to me. Is everything okay at this person's home? Or that person's? It looks like it, but who the hell knows. No one knows at all. But we will pack ourselves into Sienna's home and ignore all our own personal realities, our own home lives. People will drink and gossip and laugh so hard that they're sick.

There is a buzz in school. About the party, about the end of the year, but also about HEATHER, and how anyone could be next. Every day now, the talk is about whether anything new has happened, and what it was. The teachers seem on extra-high alert, carefully entering classrooms, opening desk drawers, making sure their cars are locked. The students are acting like it's Christmas every day. They are always waiting for the next incident but really hoping it's not about them. It's like waiting to see if you get coal in your stocking, except that the coal might be a ten-foot banner in the gym that says you've got a small dick. That happened to Josh, who is rumored to have been slut-shaming his girlfriend. Since then, the gym has been locked outside of classes.

At lunch, Dee and I see Ava and the others at a different table. I push away the thought that they're distancing themselves, trying to get away from us, and join them anyway.

Marta looks surprised as we clatter our trays down. Almost afraid. Ava and Jesse exchange looks, then scoot over to make room.

"Did you see that banner in the gym?" I ask.

"How did they even get that thing up there?" Marta whispers.

"No idea, but you should have seen Josh's face," says Dee, shaking her head. She sips her drink, then: "Are you guys going to Sienna's party?"

"I dunno, probably," Marta says, tracing her cafeteria tray with a finger and exchanging a look with Ava. "You guys?"

Ava looks at Antar. "Yeah, we're going." Antar is largely ignoring us, his earbuds in, music on while he eats.

He pulls one earbud out and says, "Just leave us out of anything you're planning. It's getting out of control."

"I'm going, for sure," says Jesse, before we can respond. "Shit always goes down at big parties."

"Preach," says Dee.

At that moment, a few guys come toward us with trays of slushies. Aidan is one of them.

It happens so quickly.

He deliberately crashes into Dee's chair, dumping a Slurpee down her back. She jumps up, her chair screeching and toppling over.

"Oops. Sorry. Must have tripped."

"What the fuck, man?" she howls, turning on the guys. Their eyes widen in exaggeration, like they're afraid.

"It was an accident," Aidan says. "Oh shit. Don't go psycho on me now." He pretends to look scared. "Chill out. Literally." They laugh and move on, while the teacher in charge calls out across the room, asking what's going on, without actually moving from his post. Dee steps over her chair and storms out of the caf to the sounds of people catcalling and laughing. I see Paige watching, her hand on the shoulder of her bag, before she leaves the room.

I follow Dee into the bathroom. She has her shirt off and is drying it in the hand dryer.

"This is some *bullshit*," she says, her lips a straight line of fury. A girl comes in, looks furtively at Dee in her bra, and darts into a stall. "He's going to be sorry for this," she mutters.

"Maybe it was an accident?"

Maybe she asked for it. Maybe she got in the way. Maybe she brought it on herself. My eyes sting with tears trying to get out. This keeps happening, coming out of nowhere and surprising me, ever since the stairwell. I look up and wipe under my eyes.

"No fucking way. He's one of those assholes who has been posting all over social media about us. I believe his latest was"—she cocks her head as though trying to remember—"ah yes: 'Die, feminazi cunts.'"

"Charming," I say, inspecting myself in the mirror.

"What are you doing?" Dee asks my reflection. She puts her shirt back on.

"Nothing. Are you ready?"

*　*　*

Later, I tell my mom that I'm going out tomorrow night. She is pouring a can of mushroom soup over a bunch of ingredients in a casserole dish.

"Good for you, Stevie. You need to get out more."

Reg is sitting at the table, scrolling through his phone. "Oh, I remember those summer parties in high school," he says, smiling but not looking up. "Do I ever. Good times, *good* times."

I wonder if his "good times" involved him bullying other kids, making them feel small in so many ways. I can picture him: cokehead, music guy, long hair—he was probably pretty good-looking, I hate to say. But undoubtedly a complete douchebag. I shudder at the thought of all the girls he must have cornered in some smoke-filled basement or manhandled in the high grass of a field party, talking about Nirvana.

"I still hang out with most of those guys. One of them got me my first job. Talked the manager into giving me a chance, and I bailed another guy out when . . . well, anyway." He grins, impishly. "All of us, we were like this—" He crosses his first two fingers.

"I remember those parties, too," Mom chimes in, smiling at Reg. "So many memories. Those were the days." She turns to me. "Whose party is it?"

"Uh, Sienna Martin."

"Oh, I remember her."

"Yeah."

"Is Lottie going?"

"I have no idea."

Lately I've seen Lottie hanging out with a group of kids other than Paige and Breanne. Kind of the nerdy science kids: they are always near the labs, and whenever there are partner assignments in Biology, Lottie chooses one of them. I don't know if something happened between her and the others, but I have to say I'm glad she's not hanging out with them, or at least doesn't seem to be. But we haven't been paired up for anything since our doomed papier-mâché project. Lottie's sculpture of my face looks like a giant potato. It doesn't help that she decided to run with it and painted it like Mrs. Potato Head, complete with "eyes" all over and some cartoon facial features stuck in random places.

"You two fighting or something?"

"No, Mom." I roll my eyes. *I don't know. Yes. No.*

I ran into Lottie in the bathroom the other day. She asked me if I was going to the party while she was drying her hands.

"Yeah, I think so. You?"

"Probably. See you there?"

"For sure," I said, feeling lighter as she left the door swinging behind her.

"Are there gonna be guys there?" Reg asks, grinning like he and I are in on something.

I think about Aidan, and all the comments online. There is a hatred burning in my chest. It's like Dee is standing behind me, whispering in my ear.

"Are you a feminist, Mom?" I ask, leaning in the doorway, on my way out of the room.

"Oh, please, honey. I'm a realist. I *love* men." She winks at Reg, who kisses the air.

And I'm out.

*   *   *

That night, hundreds of kids in our school get a message from Aidan from his Insta account. It's not that hard to hack Instagram. There are even tutorials online that can show you how to do it. I guess Dee found out how. I mean, I can only assume she did. Nothing else really explains this:

HEY THERE. I THOUGHT IT'D BE A GOOD IDEA IF I LET YOU KNOW: I HAVE HERPES. IT'S CONTAGIOUS AND DISGUSTING, BUT IMPORTANT FOR PEOPLE TO KNOW. KNOWLEDGE IS POWER.

*   *   *

I get a text from Ava with a screenshot of the message.

Is that even true??? she asks.

Does she think I'd know? Does it matter?

But that breathing, pulsing online world never sleeps if we don't, and so of course there is more. People reacting, other posts, Aiden's own fury whiplashing back, saying he'd been hacked and that whoever did that would not get away with it.

Dee and I get texts from the others. Michelle, whose attention from Breanne was part of the beginning.

Did you see that thing on insta

Yeah

Do you think it's going too far

Dee writes back: *No, man, not at all. Not far enough. Think about who he is, who they all are! I can't believe you are doubting, now, after everything!*

Ok Ok I'm sorry you're right.

Goddamn right I'm right. Don't look back. Eyes forward.

She makes me nervous when she's like this. So unshakable in her beliefs, so committed to letting things unravel, to watching to see what will happen, to nudging it, or pushing it along if necessary. I watch through my phone as everyone is commenting, laughing, furious. Everyone feels different; everyone feels the same.

And then, late in the night, there is an Insta story from Breanne.

She flips her hair and talks to the camera: "I feel the need to speak out about something I've been worrying about for a long time, and that I think puts our safety and comfort at school in jeopardy.

"One of my teachers is changing her sex. I don't think that's appropriate for a teacher. I know maybe that's not politically correct, but I'm just saying what lots of us are thinking. School is crazy enough right now, what with the bullying and stuff, it's confusing, and now we don't even know *what* our teachers are!

"But even worse than that is that I have a feeling she/he has a thing going on with one of the girls who I think is part of all the bullying. I saw them together and there's no denying they have a relationship. A physical relationship. This person is very unstable anyway, if any of you have seen her videos. This makes me feel uncomfortable, so I thought I should speak out."

I feel sick. It was the hug I gave Pete. She saw him and turned it into this. I put my hands to my face and close my eyes. There is no peace.

I go into the kitchen. The house is in darkness; Mom and Reg are asleep. The light in the fridge blazes out at me when I open it. My body is thumping, my breath fast. I take out one of Reg's beers and open it. I sit at the table and look out the glass door at the darkness. The shape of my reflection looks back at me. I stare at her, at myself, and take a long haul off the beer, wiping my mouth with the back of my hand. I finish quickly and am ready. I open my phone.

Breanne, I see, also put a pic on her Instagram of a fist, like a social justice "Fight the Power" fist that she is totally using the wrong way. It's innocuous if you haven't seen the story that will soon be erased.

There is a storm of responses, like rolling thunder, one after another after another. She is brave. She is transphobic. She's ignorant. She's right. That is disgusting. It's PC bullshit. She's the one who makes people uncomfortable. She's a bitch. She's got guts to speak out. LOVE YOU GIRL. U R BRAVE! THANKS FOR SHARING, BRII! STFD YOU IDIOT. STEVIE AND PETE KNOW EACH OTHER FROM OUTSIDE SCHOOL, YOU MORON. SHE'S FRIENDS WITH HIS KID. THAT GIRL IS FUCKING NUTS SHE FREAKED OUT ON A FIELD TRIP. SHE'S DOING ALL THOSE PRANKS. SHE'S A SLUT. YOU'RE A SLUT . . . On and on. I watch this unfurl before my eyes, my face burning up like it's on fire.

Lottie. I need to talk to Lottie. I text her, not knowing if anything will come back. My heart is beating fast.

Hey I don't know if you've seen that bs online but I'm sorry your family is getting caught up in this.

A few minutes pass. I stare at my phone, willing it to respond. There are ellipses. She's thinking. Or maybe checking to see what I'm talking about. I wait. I wait.

Yeah I saw it.

Are you ok?

I'm fine

Maybe things are getting out of hand; maybe that's why even my new friends have been keeping a distance. It's like I'm peddling downhill, but it is good and scary and fast, and sometimes there are consequences, and maybe this is one of them. I wonder if I should reach out to Pete. Should I tell him? Warn him? But then I think about Lottie, and how she would hate for me to get more involved. Her tactic is always to lay low—not my strong suit.

I text Dee.

Hey did you see that shit

Yeah. She's an idiot. It'll come back to her. It'll bite her in the ass. Go to sleep.

I turn my phone off. I lie in bed and finally fall asleep, but each time I wake during the night, I check my phone. More responses, more and more, and eventually, by morning, the story is gone and Breanne has removed the pic. There is momentary quiet.

25

walk alone to school. Nobody is at our rock on the grounds when I arrive, so I walk right in, focused on my locker like a heat-seeking missile. I try to ignore the looks coming my way. Occasionally someone pats me on the back, like a gesture of solidarity. But there is also snickering and muttering, whispering and giggling.

Everyone is talking about all the stuff happening online. It's not just Breanne's posts, or the Insta message sent through Aidan's account, but everywhere we can go and talk and shout, everywhere the teachers can't reach us. People are whispering and arguing, conspiring, gossiping. There are side group messages and public declarations, trash talking and threats. There are peacemakers, and those trying to diffuse with GIFs and memes. Some people can't wait to get away from the school for the summer, from the drama; others are sad the first year of high school is almost over.

I sit through Pete's class watching him for a sign that he caught wind of anything Breanne wrote. He acts the same as always, but it's hard to tell if he's just rising above it. I leave quickly after class, my head down.

At lunch, it's just me and Dee at our table. Antar looks our way and shakes his head, choosing to sit at a different table and listen to music. Michelle, Ava, and Marta shrug and follow him, looking at their phones. Lottie isn't there. I am guessing she's in some far corner of the school, maybe eating her lunch in Pete's classroom. I bet they're together. They are family, after all. I watch my friends and consider going to join them, to talk it through, to tell them that I know it's all too much.

"What're you thinking?" Dee asks, looking at me over her sandwich.

"I dunno. Just want the whole thing to end."

"I hear that."

But I don't know that she does, or that she would want things to end the same way.

By the time the bell rings, gossip has reached a fever pitch, and on top of that, everyone is talking about the party tonight.

"I don't know about you, but I am *not* going," I scoff, opening my locker.

Dee is looking at herself in the mirror, applying bright-red lipstick. "Like hell you're not," she says.

"I'm sorry?"

"Don't give them the satisfaction, Stevie. Jesus, hold your head high. Otherwise they'll think it's true. I'm going. Fuck them."

* * *

I relent. I'll go. But I'm not sure what to wear. I am nervous, trying on a bunch of different things before settling finally on jeans and a baggy shirt—casual and not trying too hard, despite my efforts. Dee is here, sitting on the bed, eating a bag of chips. There's a nervous energy pulsing through my body, making me jumpy, irritated.

"Try and stay out of trouble tonight, Dee." I say, looking hard at her. It's her fault if anything happens, and I am not going to take the fall.

She smiles. "Yeah? Why?"

I sigh, exasperated. "Just—maybe let's, I dunno, just lay low for once. Everything doesn't have to be a spectacle, does it?"

Dee pops a chip in her mouth. "I'm just saying. Tension is high. Something's gonna blow. You can feel it. We just need to control what happens. We don't want to be at their mercy."

"When have you ever been at anybody's mercy?"

She locks eyes with me and shrugs, the moment over, and I wonder, not for the first time, who Dee is, and how much I've changed since she arrived on the scene. Who I am.

"It's getting carried away, Dee."

"What? No way. We're standing on a land mine, Stevie. It's a powder keg about to blow. We just hafta be ready to run."

"It's just a party, not a revolution," I say, trying not to care.

"If you say so."

*   *   *

We get to the house, and it is already packed. It's not quite a *Superbad* house party situation yet, but it is a regular suburban house that is already in full swing: pulsing from the inside out, people starting to spill outside like an overfilled bathtub that smells like body spray. People stare at us as we arrive, like we're in an old-timey movie where the music stops when the cowboy walks in the saloon.

I scan the room. Looking over some heads just inside the house, I see Ava, Marta, and Antar. I wave, and they look at one another and turn away. Dee gives me a shove, and I make my way in their direction. Ava's hair is piled on her head like a black bird's nest, Marta looks like a tiny doll in a flowered dress, and Antar is in a suit that he is wearing the shit out of.

"Hey," I shout over the music. Ava nods; Antar takes a sip of a drink and looks across the crowd. Marta smiles weakly.

Dee snorts at this. "Really, guys? That all you got?"

Ava takes a breath and gives her a hard stare. "What do you mean?"

"I mean what's with you guys?"

Someone bumps into Dee and she knocks into Ava, whose drink gets on them both.

"Watch it!" I say to the girl shouldering her way through the room. I realize it's Breanne, and she lifts her middle finger at me as she moves away.

Antar and Marta exchange looks, before Antar says to Dee, "I'm not afraid of you, you know."

"Why would you be?" I ask, surprised.

"I know you have this, like, 'If you're not with us, you're against us' bullshit, and, like, some kind of rage problem. I don't care. Just leave us out of your weird club."

Dee laughs and says, "What's your damage?" She looks at the three of them. Ava looks away.

"Ah, fuck you guys," Dee says. "You're fucking weak."

We turn and Dee says, "Let's get a drink, sister soldier." I feel their stares but don't care because there's something else pulsing through me with the music.

I'm not really a big drinker. I've been drunk a couple of times, but I wouldn't say it's something I do often, although maybe that's changing. When Dee hands me a red cup filled with heady draft, I take a swig and have to choke it down. I wipe my upper lip and grin, and she's taken a healthy gulp of hers, also. She moves her head to the music and looks around the room, pointedly ignoring the corner where our former friends are in a tight circle. There is a pretty good cross-section of the school here, a range from the gorgeous to the geeky, all pressed up against each other and staring over shoulders and at their phones, hardly paying any attention to who they're with. Within a few sips of my beer, I sense a buzz coming on. I sway my hips to the music and enjoy the fact that none of us can hear each other, not really.

I see Lottie across the room and feel the sudden need to talk to her. I push and weave through people to get through. Dee tugs my shirt, but I shrug her off.

"Lottie!" I call out, but my voice is swallowed up. "Lottie!"

I finally reach her and grab her arm, relieved. She turns and looks at me, and for a tiny minute we are twelve, not fifteen, and a world lies between those years. She's standing with a few kids from our elementary school, kids I've known my whole life. They say hi to me, ask me what's up, smiling kindly at me, but keeping their distance.

"Lottie," I say, "can I talk to you?"

She takes a drink and says, "I dunno, okay."

"I, um," I say, and suddenly my voice is cracking. But I can't tell her that I need her, that I miss her.

She looks in my eyes and I know that she knows. That she can read me, because we've always had each other's back.

"What's going on with you?" she says in a low voice.

"Nothing! Nothing," I say, wiping my upper lip. "I don't

know." Someone bumps me, and Lottie and I stumble and sway together, jarred out of any moment we might have been having.

Lottie eyes me, her voice hardening. "You've been so different," she says. "I—I feel like I don't know you anymore."

I look over my shoulder and see Dee checking in from across the room. *You okay?* she mouths. I ignore her and return to Lottie.

"I know. I just—" I start to say, but she hasn't heard me. Some guy is talking to her. She smiles shyly at him and looks back at me to say, "Look, I'll talk to you later." And she's gone, moving through the party like a small lost thing on a wave, lost to me. Her friends exchange looks and shrug at me, sipping their drinks innocently as people have been doing since the dawn of the awkward conversation. I drop my hands at my side and put my head back, letting out a sigh of mounting frustration that could probably have been heard over the music if anyone was listening.

And then it hits me that I've been here before. A birthday party, maybe? Or for Brownies? A childhood memory washes over me, something familiar but also maybe embarrassing, and just out of reach. I move into the kitchen, sideways-dancing between people; the memory slips away. Someone grabs me, but when I turn around, the crowd has closed again, and Dee puts her arm around me and steers me through the people in front of us.

The house is thumping. The pictures on the shelves are swaying gently, and the fake flowers in the vases are bending forward and back, to and fro, and the couches are just asking to be squeezed onto. It's a friendly house. People are loud, laughing in our ears as we go by. Dee's energy is contagious, and I start to loosen up. People we don't know say hi to us, and we fist-bump and side-hug and high-five them.

In the kitchen, the fluorescent light makes everyone just a little uglier. There are a bunch of dude-bros near the sink, laughing loudly and pushing into each other because God knows they don't know how to touch each other otherwise.

One of them turns around and I see that it's Aidan, and he raises his arms wide when he sees us and yells out, "Oh, look who's here! Don't you have some social justice warrior bullshit crimes to fight?"

I blink and freeze, but Dee takes a breath beside me and holds up her cup. "Nice to see your genital itching isn't slowing you down, buddy."

"Fuck you, you weird bitch."

"Touché. There really is no way to come back from that. What will I do?" Dee is laughing with a bunch of other kids standing nearby.

I cannot believe that asshole, they are saying. I sneak a look at Aidan, and his face is a dark cloud. But he recovers, laughing at something a friend says, tipping back his cup, and going to the fridge to get another beer.

*   *   *

We spend the next hour or so in the kitchen, bumping into people, swaying to the music, laughing and looking around, seeing and being seen. Everyone's on their phone, taking selfies and snaps. People keep asking us about the Insta hack, if it was us, asking me about what Breanne said. Dee is having a great time: singing loudly, twirling around with her drink held high. People get caught up in her energy, they are crowding around, laughing and dancing. The drinks keep coming. Every time I pick up my cup from wherever I leave it, it's full again. People bumping, moving, grinding, twerking, rubbing, singing, sweating. The music gets louder and louder, and my head is feeling thicker. I see someone puke in the kitchen sink. Some sounds are coming through a cloud, but others are right inside my ear.

I'm being held up by the bodies around me. A ship in a storm.

I see Paige across the house, feel her looking. I lift my arm and wave at her, and she looks confused; she nods and turns away. I am giggling about something, my mind rocking around in my head, my body crashing into other bodies. My eyes blink slowly and someone laughs nearby.

Dee and I find our way outside. The backyard deck, where we are now, with a whole new set of people who went outside to smoke up, make out, and get out, has a wraparound banister looking down on the backyard below. The yard slopes down, and there are more people there, milling about, lying down, laughing and yelling. The bass is throbbing and I feel strange. I know I am drunk, and I hold fast to the rail, and see that Dee is doing the same.

Suddenly I'm aware that Paige is there, talking to us.

"You need to watch your back."

"What?" I say, because I'm honestly not sure what she's saying.

Dee giggles in my ear.

"Right, it's so funny." Paige rolls her eyes. "You know, people are getting hurt."

"You started it," I slur, looking over the banister.

"What? No, I didn't—"

And then Aidan is there, and he's shoved himself between us, squeezes up against Paige.

"Why are you talking to *her*?" he asks Paige, putting his face on her neck, not looking at me, and she pushes him a little. We all seem to sway back and forth and back again.

"Shut up," she mumbles.

"Make me," Aidan growls into her hair.

Dee makes a grab for his arm but just ends up swatting him. "Leave her alone," she says, barely audible.

He turns his head and laughs in my face. Paige looks at me over his shoulder and sighs. She takes Aidan's hand—"come on"—and they walk back into the house. He puts his hand on her ass as they go.

We turn back and look at the people below, watching them silently for a while.

"These people," Dee mumbles finally, gesturing over the banister. "They are all such . . . assholes."

"Yeah," I say.

"We could jump off this thing, and no one would care."

"Not Lottie, not Pete, not my mom," I slur.

"They'd dance on our bodies."

"Use us as a mattress."

"A blanket."

"Firewood."

I laugh sourly and put my head down on the railing.

Times passes, and it could be minutes or hours. It's nice here. I smile.

"You okay?" It's a different voice. I look up.

Someone has their arm around Dee. I see through the buzzing fog that it is one of the dude-bros from the kitchen. He has a nice face. Her head is nodding, but no words are coming out. Or I can't hear them. He's saying something, and they are moving back into the house. My feet have come off the floor, and I am floating behind them, trying to catch up but just letting things happen now, letting things happen because it feels so relaxing and I could just sleep like this, moving.

There is a basement, and there are couches. I watch as she lays down on one of them. There is laughing from somewhere. There is talking nearby. Someone brushes her hair out of her face. My eyes are closing because I am comfortable.

Someone says my name and I say *yes*.

26

I dream about a lot of things. But first, nothing at all. First, I
am empty.

*Then, it is like there's a white screen behind my eyes. It
is thick, and almost sticky, as if I am swimming through glue. And
then I am pushing through, slowly, trying to move, trying to speak.
I am gliding on top of ice, but I am warm, hot almost, just moving
forward, but again, slowly; as though someone is holding on to my
boots and pulling me back, or I am dragging them with me. I am
making such an effort for so little. For so long. I am left behind.*

*   *   *

It is very early morning. Not even light out. Birds are chirping
somewhere.

My eyes open slowly, like there's gum in them, and I see
through a fog of smoke and crowd of bodies. It is Friday. We
are still at Sienna's house. I feel so sick. I feel like I'm in a cloud.
And I remember, then, that I had been here for a birthday
party, when I was a kid. We played duck, duck, goose, and
when the birthday cake came out, I hid under the table because

I was afraid of fire. And when they put on *Bambi*, they had to call my mom to come pick me up, because of the forest fire scene. I remember all that in a slow, sloshy wave.

I am on the couch, cold. I shift and feel why. My shirt. My shirt is pulled up, almost off. My pants pulled down. I am wet, cold. I focus on my torso as I try to pull my shirt down and see.

Red marker. Like lipstick. Capital letters.

CRAZY BITCH

I cry out, a small sound.

Dee?

Dee?

I am pulling at my clothes, trying to see through the fog inside my head. I hear someone weeping, and then realize it is me.

Dee where are you?

Dee!

I am stumbling, on my knees, finding carpeted stairs, chips ground into the fabric. She is gone, she's not here. I need to find her, I need her. I find my way outside, around the side of the house. I remember that I don't have my bike, that I walked here. I put my face against the cold brick.

Dee.

I lean over suddenly and throw up like a shout.

DEE! I cry.

There is nothing.

* * *

I am at home.

I climbed right into bed as soon as I got home, before Mom woke up. I was shaking while I put my pajamas on. They usually make me feel so cozy, but nothing feels right.

I open my phone, ignoring texts from anyone but Dee.

There's so much there, but I can't look at it now. I try to call and text her. No answer. No response. Where is she? What happened to her? My fingers are trembling. There are tears racing down my cheeks. *Dee. Dee.* I want to go find her but feel helpless, immobile. Moving takes so much effort.

I try to remember last night. Is this what it means when someone drinks too much and blacks out? Is this what they mean? Did something else happen? I'm dizzy and I finally scramble out of bed, stumbling to the bathroom. I throw up, over and over again. No one holds my hair, no one rubs my back. I moan, and the puke comes through my nose and burns. I am sobbing now, but no one comes. Mom can sleep through anything. I lean against the wall and wipe my face with some toilet paper, and it tears and sticks to my face. There is a part of the ceiling that is peeling off, and it makes me so sad, and I start to cry quietly again. Finally, I get up and go back to bed. I am exhausted, but sleep doesn't come. Eventually I hear Mom crashing around in her room. She's calling out to me, *Stevie, Stevie.* But my mouth won't work. The door opens.

"Stevie! Get up, girl."

"Okay," I mumble.

She squints at me. She needs glasses, but she's too cheap and too vain.

"What's wrong with you?"

"I don't know. I don't feel well."

She comes in and sits on my bed. I can smell her shampoo, and it turns my stomach. She puts her hand on my forehead, and for a second, I am so grateful to be looked after, like a kid.

"Did you get drunk last night, Stevie?"

And I'm crying again.

"Jesus," she says, sighing. "Okay, okay." She rubs my back.

She doesn't say anything for a while. Finally, she inhales and gives my back a pat. "Well. It was a stupid thing to do, but I was doing way worse at your age."

"I'm sorry," I blubber.

"Yeah, yeah." She blows out her cheeks and looks at her watch. "Look, I have a client coming soon, so I gotta get downstairs." She stares hard at me. "I know I should probably force you to go to school as punishment, but you seem like you're really suffering here. You wanna stay home today? I mean, school's almost done; it's not like they're gonna fail you, right?"

I sniff and nod.

She shakes her head and ruffles my hair, and it's really nice.

"You dummy," she says, and gets up.

After she shuts the door, my phone starts going off. It's buzzing and buzzing, over and over again. I'm afraid to pick it up. I am lying on my side, watching it on my bedside table, vibrating so much it's threatening to explode. I turn it off, and it feels like the silence might strangle me. I close my eyes, but it's no use. I am wide awake now. And my mouth feels like I ate a sweater.

I pick up my phone again to try Dee, but I can't ignore the other texts anymore. It's like in *Harry Potter* when they destroy that locket Horcrux and all the bad shit comes flying out. I am face-to-face with an onslaught, a downpour of texts, complete with photos. From lots of people: unknown numbers and people who maybe were once my friends.

Holy shit look at this

omg I can't believe what they did

are you ok are you ok are you ok

have you called the police

what are you going to do

are you going to school

the pic is on Instagram

they hacked that heather account

do you think its Aidan

are you ok are you ok where are you where are you are you ok

they posted it everywhere

call me are you ok

There are many people in the photos, but I can't tell who's who. A prone body. Shirt lifted off, fingers pointing, grabbing, the body limp, blurred. I turn it off and know that this is it. I won't turn it back on. There is sadness like a building pressure storm, but then something else happens. It flips on itself.

I throw the covers off me and stand in front of my mirror. I take off my pajama shirt.

I look at the smeared red marker all over my body.

CRAZY BITCH

I touch the letters, then clench my hands into fists.

I look at my reflection, and suddenly, finally, she is there.

Dee.

"Where were you? I needed you."

I'm here now, she says, my dry lips moving. *I know what they did. Everything. And nothing.*

She wipes the tears away.

27

I do not cry again, although I do throw up two more times.

I scrub myself in the shower until my body is red and raw, but it's having a hard time forgetting. It looks basically the same, but I know that it's not. I get out and dry myself roughly with a towel. I can still see some of the marks on my body, but I get dressed, I cover it up.

I am not going to school. Mom called and told them I'm sick. My phone is off. Off forever. The curtains are closed. But I have lots of work to do.

Dee started the fire of vengeance that took over the school. She did it because I had no control. Because the hate, the cruelty, the violations left me without options. She gave power to the powerless. She inspired people. She taught us how to fight back. Most importantly, she's the reason that the assholes, the thieves, will not get away with anything.

I need her, she tells me. *Now more than ever. We can make them understand. We can start fresh.*

I am not a violent person; I never have been. I love animals. I feel sorry for everything. I don't collect firearms or gun paraphernalia; I don't play violent games or get a rush from aggression. I am a film nerd, that's all. I am a social justice warrior, simple. I support March for Our Lives. I believe in gun reform and gun control and protecting kids. I mean, shootings are not an epidemic here, they hardly ever happen, but I pay attention, I know what's going on, and I'm not the type. It's not me.

And yet. Maybe I've changed. I've been changed. All the confidence and self-worth and anger and sense of justice that Dee gave me—that I found deep inside her and me—it came at a heavy price. They took so much from me and left me scrabbling, scratching, and clawing, backed into a corner, trying to stay alive. All those passive parts of me that lay docile as lambs are now jumping around screaming with a bloodthirsty growl and a desire to show them what it felt like, what it feels like to be constantly under threat—in class, in stairwells, at hockey games, online.

But mine is a revenge of my own design, of my own making. I will build my vengeance from found objects that don't look like trouble, don't look dangerous, until they are together. Like me and Dee.

I put on loud and furious music and start doing research. Google provides me with everything I need to know. All the freaks out there who like to experiment, who love spectacle, who have their own peacemakers: they have laid out for me step-by-step directions for my big show, my poetic finale, my final assignment.

Something really creative, isn't that what you said, Pete? That's my plan.

I have such a clear-eyed focus that the morning slips by without me even noticing. I am propped up on pillows in bed, my laptop on my knees. Eventually I hear my mom come upstairs for her break and lunch. She comes down the hall and knocks while opening my door.

"Hey, kid. How you feeling?" she asks. I close my laptop and pull up the covers. She looks at me thoughtfully.

"Okay, I guess."

"Yeah? You hungry? I can make grilled cheese."

"Sure. Thanks."

She smiles at me and closes the door, and I miss her so much it hurts.

Soon I hear Reg's car pulling into the driveway. People like him: they start off in high school, the giant petri dish, and everything is handed to them. They are cool. Life is easy. The Aidans and the Breannes and the Paiges of the world—I can see the future laid out for them like a movie in my head. No one ever tells them they *can't*. They grow up to become the kind of person who makes jokes about your body when you aren't even ready to give away your stuffed animals.

There is a hot lump in my throat and tears trying to get out, but I push them away. I hear Reg laughing with my mom when she tells him why I'm home. They are murmuring and giggling.

Another car arrives, and Mom yells, "Stevie, we'll be in the salon; I've got appointments all afternoon. Your lunch is on the table!"

"Stay out of the liquor cabinet, ya lush!" Reg shouts, snickering.

Soon I hear him guffawing from below me in the salon. His laugh coming through the vent, my mom chuckling along with him. And suddenly I think of last night: someone laughing, a foggy mirage of a couch. Someone saying *don't, don't*. Was it me? I briefly wonder what is happening in the Pandora's Box that is my phone. What will happen if I open it?

*　*　*

There is knocking at the door while I'm sitting in the kitchen. I figure it is one of Mom's clients who forgot that the entrance to the salon is through the side door, leading to the basement. I sigh, tossing my grilled-cheese plate in the sink and wiping my face with the back of my hand.

It's Lottie.

I stand aside and let her come in.

"Are you okay?" she asks.

"Yes."

She nods.

"Why aren't you at school?" I ask.

"It's almost the end of term. I think I'll survive without going to Math."

"Right. So, you wanna—" I gesture up the stairs to the kitchen. She shrugs, yes.

I open two pops and put them on the table. We sit down and it feels stupid and formal. But I am on a tight schedule now. I have things I need to get done.

"Were you there last night, when—?"

She shakes her head. "No. I'd already left. I saw all the stuff about it later, though. Pictures . . ."

"Right. Well." My stomach tightens and turns over. "Fuck that."

"Yeah," says Lottie. "I'm so sorry. I wanted to, I don't know, see if you were okay." She sips her drink and looks away. "I was so afraid something like this would happen."

"What do you mean?"

"Nothing. Just that I was worried someone would do something to you, you know, to get even or whatever."

"What, this is my fault?" I can't go there now. Not anymore. I cannot let anyone tell me I had a hand in this, not even Lottie.

"What? No, that's not what I mean, Stevie, of course not."

"Because I don't like watching people get away with things? Because I care?"

"No!" She opens and closes her mouth. "Just—sometimes you took it too far. That shit you were doing was crazy. I just—I was so worried about you getting hurt."

I am standing but don't remember getting up.

"What was I supposed to do? And where were you, Lottie?" I am crying. "I needed you!"

She backs her chair up and stumbles a little.

"Will you just get the hell out of here?"

Her eyes are welling up, and part of me feels bad but it's just a small part, and the rest of me is charging forward. The rest of me is Dee, taking control.

"Just go!"

And she does, and the door closes quietly behind her.

My anger is strong, energetic. There is a part of me, the Stevie part, that wants to crawl into a ball and cry so much I'll puke. There is part of me that wants to stay in bed forever. But I push it down. I let Dee out.

I grab my canvas purse and book it out the front door. I see my bike, busted and bent, leaning against the garage like a dead thing, and I start to run.

I run to the other end of town, to the top, up the escarpment, to the Ridge. I can't run once it gets steep, but I am hiking now, huffing and puffing, my legs aching and moving up, up, up. Up the Bruce Trail, up over rocks and fallen trees, further up, crunching branches underfoot. I get to the lookout point where I leaned over and sang the song from *Heathers*. Me, Stevie. All those conversations with Dee. I made her, she made me. But now I need her more than ever.

I look for the school, find it from up high, like a pin in the map of our town. I see a group of students doing high-knees and other exercises. I watch them until they are told to stop by cheerful Ms. Kwan, and they gather, hands on their knees, panting, and I can feel their relief from here.

I feel Dee. *They're all down there, waiting for you to do something. They're talking about you. They're going to suck you in. And before they eat you up and spit you out, they will move you around their sharp teeth, feel you with their tongues, taste your fear. Play with you. Then they'll watch you dissolve. They'll cover their mouths while they snicker and look the other way while you cry. Then they'll abandon you. They'll feign ignorance to your pain. They have their own lives, you know. They are very busy. Too busy for you. Too busy to notice you planning, scheming, designing the perfect final project. The perfect final scene before the credits roll. They have their classes and their jobs and their own shit to figure out; they have the big game coming up or cheerleading practice, or a moving van to pack, someone's hair to color. They have their Tumblr to update, their Insta to check, they have friends to like and enemies to unfollow, they have other friends to punish and other enemies to manipulate. And so they won't notice while you plan and plot and organize. They won't see you as you stick to shadows and get ready to surprise them. They underestimate you. Make them notice and remember and realize who you are.*

She's right.

I keep looking online for help with my research. It's all out there. You can find anything you put your mind to, any strange, rage-filled fantasy. Instructions, videos, plans, designs. I need them, and they are there for me. There are, I guess, a lot of reasons why people might need these kinds of how-to tutorials. I, for one, have never been as keen on learning as I am right now. *A+ for research, Stevie.* I just need a place to put my plan together.

And I already have a key. I'm halfway there.

28

I wake early Saturday morning and creep into the kitchen. I throw a bunch of bread and a jar of jam into my bag, some apples, and a water bottle. I haven't checked my phone since yesterday morning.

Instead, I spent the rest of the day walking around, from one end of town to the other, which doesn't take long. My mind was buzzing like it was full of Pop Rocks. Got a slice of pizza and sat by the lake. Some middle-aged ladies were paddle-boarding, the sun making their hair shine. It looked really peaceful, and I felt my anger lift for a moment, felt the sads dilute. Then I looked around me at all the trash left on the shore, and it was back in a flash. Damn place. I walked back into town.

I went to the local bookstore, Ex Libris, and had a chat with the owner, who everyone calls Big Al. No joke. This town.

"Hey there," he said.

I didn't answer but just kept walking.

"Can I help you with something in particular?"

I turned and asked, "Do you have, like, a DIY section?"

"Sure thing. You making slime? I have about a hundred books on making slime."

"Maybe, yeah," I mumbled, wishing life was still just as complicated as making slime and getting in trouble for leaving it on tables.

"Thataway." He gestured to the back, returning to his own book, open in front of him on the counter.

I lost myself in there for a while, reading up on woodworking and welding projects, looking for anything that might help me. Hunting and the outdoors, just in case. Eventually I emerged with my head full of ideas, and I thanked Big Al, who I think had forgotten I was there. He waved at me as I left, never lifting his head from his book. The door jangled on my way out.

I stopped at the hardware store, where I got my supplies: some plumbers' pipe and other odds and ends that looked so innocent in my cart. I swung them in a bag from my hand, and it felt like they were radiating justice.

I went home, where Mom and Reg were eating spaghetti at the kitchen table. Reg was sitting in my spot.

"Where the hell have you been?" Mom asked, her mouth full.

"Out."

"You feeling better?"

I shrugged.

Reg shook his finger at me all buddy-buddy. "You might have called your mom, you know. She was worried." He winked, and I looked at Mom scrolling through her Instagram.

"I left my phone here, so couldn't," I grumbled.

I helped myself to some food and sat in what used to be my dad's spot. Mom started talking about her clients. I tuned her out, my mind already way ahead of her. I cleared my plate, glanced at Reg, who had sauce on his moustache, and headed to my room.

"You're welcome for dinner!" Mom called after me.

Now I write a note telling Mom I'm working at the library all day on a project. The excuse is so weak that I can hardly believe I'm writing it, but she will barely glance at it. She and Reg have a "mini-break" planned for this weekend. A mini-break, like she's in a Bridget Jones movie. They are just going to Sherkston Shores campground with her friend Holly's trailer, but Mom has been acting as though they're going off to Europe. Point is, she isn't exactly paying attention.

I leave my phone on my dresser. I know what awaits me if I turn it on. They can all go to hell. And with that, I pack my supplies, and I am out the door into the warm summery morning.

People with dogs are all out walking them at this hour. And joggers. I get into the groove of nodding and saying "good morning." Sometimes I lean over and scratch the ears of a dog as it goes by. It is a hopeful, happy morning for everyone else, I can see that. People are enjoying the season, the weather, the hour.

But as I get closer to the school, my stomach starts to tighten. My mouth has gone dry, and I'm taking deep breaths. The only thing this school has ever made me feel is different. Weird. A freak. I tried to fit in, and then I tried to change that place, and neither worked. And so, I'll do things my way. I am an artist. A maker. I'm not like anyone else. I am different.

My shoulders square, my chin high, I head behind the school to the Makers' Space door. I take a big breath and press the card against the reader and set it all in motion.

Everything is dark and quiet. No one's here at this hour. I flick the light switch and the room hums to life, and I can't help but smile. I love this place; I have missed it.

Be sure to make plans, outlines, prototypes, Pete says sometimes, when he comes in here to check out what people are up to. And I have; I have made plans. Up late last night working out exactly what I needed to do, taking measurements, doing math, drawing all kinds of sketches. I am ready. I am emboldened.

I could easily get my hands on a gun, a real one. I've heard Reg brag enough times about how people would have to take his out of his cold dead hands to know that there is probably one in my house now. It's probably not even well hidden. He probably stuck it in what used to be dad's bedside table drawer. But I don't want that.

I sit at one of the tables and run my palms over the smooth wooden surface. I open my bag, rooting around my provisions for the day, and pull out my materials and my laptop. The window is open to my DIY project plans, and I send a silent prayer of thanks up to the goddess of vengeance. Sure, she is worshipped by disgruntled boys and men, because it's always boys and men who do this: make homemade peacemakers and deliverers of justice out of a few pipes, some wood, 3-D printing, and the power of their convictions. They are the ones who post videos and blogs, blueprints, terrible websites and forums and Reddit posts with how-tos about this stuff. The great unloved, the mass of ignored. They would want nothing to do with me, a girl.

But the fire, the power and passion behind revenge and pain, would surely be a woman.

I spend the entire morning working. Cutting, soldering. I make a bunch of mistakes and get angry at myself for sloppiness, throwing pieces of pipe into the recycling and reveling in the solid noises they make on impact. *Keep trying, Stevie.* I have my earbuds in, and I'm listening to anything that moves me forward: anything fast and furious, pieces of metal and wood flying at my safety goggles in a blur. And soon, my plan starts coming together. I've done something right, it looks the way it should, and I hope to God it works. My instrument of change is ready. It lies on the worktable like some kind of homage to steampunk and Unabomber survivalism. Plumbers' pipe, welded together with messy globs, but ready to light up with power. Now I need atmosphere. Now I need to call upon the patron saints of female revenge flicks. They are going to cheer me on, stand behind me and be my backdrop, my stage. They've always been there for me, and I'm going to ask for their support one more time. For the assignment, Pete: the final assignment.

I move to the editing computers and call them up, those mavens of movies, and spend the next few hours casting spells to bring them all to the same place. Their faces wretched, bloody, and dead set on revenge. Carrie, Veronica, Ms .45, Lady Snowblood, The Bride. The queens of vengeance. The time skates by me, and before I know it, it is late in the day. I am ready.

Saturday near the end of the school year. It is dark and cool, and there is evidence of a mass cleaning effort from the janitorial staff. Bulletin boards are cleared off; election posters that have been hanging all year are gone. It looks like the LOVE, HEATHER incidents, the acts of red revenge, never took place. It's like the party never happened, couldn't happen, in a town with a school as clean as this. I put my hand to my midsection, and my throat feels tight.

I walk through the halls, my footsteps loud in the silence. I feel Dee, steering me toward the girls' change room and the entrance to the pool. I push the heavy door and go in, the smell of the chlorine almost overwhelming. The change room is spotless, although the lost and found—a large garbage can with no lid—is overflowing with water bottles and T-shirts and the occasional pair of shoes. The wooden benches are wiped clean, and the lockers are empty and open. I bang the doors with my hands as I walk into the pool area. It's dark, and I flick the light switches and the room wakes up, fluorescent lights one by one bathing the still water in its stark brightness.

I know she's here. I can tell she wants to make sure I don't change my mind, go off course. I can feel her energy pulsing in the room. *Dee.*

I take off my socks and shoes and put my foot in the water, then sit on the edge and submerge my legs, splashing and kicking like a kid.

Remember that first time we went to the lake? Dee asks, and there she is, sitting up on the high diving board, her own legs dangling over me.

"Sure. You turned me into a nudist."

You needed someone to tell you to take a risk.

I smile. Then peel off my shirt, and shiver.

Now we're talking! Look how easy it is now! You're not afraid anymore, says Dee, laughing, and she stands, the diving board firm and unmoving under her weight. She teeters on one leg, pulling off socks, pants, then all the rest. She jumps lightly, up and down, watching me, everything out in the open, jiggling. She is free and fearless. *Come on, Stevie. Be bold. Take back what they stole.*

I stand and take off the rest of my clothes, throwing them in the corner, and I dive in. The water is cold against my bare skin, it bubbles around my face as I expel all the air in my cheeks, and I emerge, with energy to spare, laughing loudly and joyfully in that moment, my voice echoing off the walls.

I look around, gasping, but Dee is gone.

* * *

Rows and rows of lockers, and I'm heading toward mine on a kind of autopilot, my hair wet and my clothes sticking to my body from the pool.

There it is. I stand in front of it.

Black marker in small, childlike writing. My stomach lurches.

SUCK MY DICK BITCH

I laugh once, a bark like a dog in the empty hallway, and kick the locker, hard. It is so satisfying, that hard bang into the still air. I do it again, and a dent appears. Again, again, wailing on the thing, letting it all out. It becomes a sorry, battered thing, shrinking against my fury. I put my forehead against the cold metal, tears running down my flushed cheeks.

Last year I was still in elementary school. Last year I was a pirate for Halloween and Lottie was a parrot. Last year Mom didn't have a boyfriend, and she and I went on a camping trip, and even though she complained and whined and said she'd never do it again, we did it. Last year I danced at the grad formal with Matthew, and we had knocked knees and laughed about how we couldn't believe we were leaving that school where we'd grown up. But I'm not grown up. High school broke me. Lottie broke me. Aidan broke me. Paige and Breanne and the rest of the school broke me. Pete broke me. And so Dee came, and she turned me into a force, and here I am. One last, feeble kick to the locker, and I am done. I leave the school the way I came, my bag slung over my shoulder, a plan in place.

29

t is Sunday.

Is this my last day? I don't see it that way. Maybe it's a new start. I am rattling with nervous energy. Like it's the day before my birthday party, Christmas Eve, the first or the last day of school.

I got home to a dark and empty house last night. Mom had left me this note:

Stevie hon
Have a great weekend! We love you!
Mom and Reg xoxo

I took a pen and changed the "We" to "I" and scratched out Reg's name.

This morning I have to do some digging around the garage.

This place is like the *Stranger Things'* Upside Down version of the Makers' Space: it is dark and disorganized, and it makes me nostalgic for my dad, because most of this shit is left over from him. It is like the treasure trove of a sloppy pirate, a general dumping ground for paint cans, buckets, gasoline, nails, screws, clamps, hand tools, electrical tools, paintbrushes, tires, grimy old canisters and toolboxes, pieces of cars, mysterious jars of metal objects, and firecrackers. And it's the firecrackers I want. Those childlike dynamos of power are the perfect choice. I find an old paper bag of them. Varying sizes. I hold them in my hands, reading the names of them: Black Cat, Thunder King, Forced Entry, Happy Nut, Scarface. I choose a handful that will fit perfectly into my piece.

I find gunpowder, too, in a coffee can. I stir my finger into it and my stomach jumps. I put a little in an old baby food jar full of nails that I dump out. I might need it. To make a bigger bang.

I go to my room and pace, energy pumping through me. It's Dee. She's whispering, elbowing her way in, pushing me to be bolder. Every time I get images in my head from the party, whenever I think of all the assholes, all the bitches, the people who said they were friends, the liars and lions and wolves, whenever I just want to stay home, whenever I doubt, she boosts me up: *Think of tomorrow. You can do this.*

I'm ready.

The last thing I need to do, before I go to bed, is test it. I leave the house and walk quietly in the dark to the woods and the creek nearby. It's so silent here, so peaceful. It will help to set me free. I consider how different I am from everyone. I hang my head. But she's here: Dee pushes me to see through the detritus and sadness, to recognize opportunities for real justice and change, or at the very least have the balls to do something. I know, deep in my heart, that this is necessary, that everyone else is just too scared to take a stand.

I set up the perfect target—my phone. But before I destroy

it, I open it one last time. Notifications adding up, more and more and more. So many texts, so many images of me, of my body.

No. Enough.

I lay it against a tree and walk back a small distance. I can barely see it, that tiny little pocket bomb that has haunted me for so long. It's there, though. Shiny pink case glinting in the moonlight. I can almost see its beating heart. I can nearly hear it. Pulsing, throbbing. Trying, dying to draw me in. I know who's in there, who's out there.

I stand firm. I place a firecracker inside it. I light the wick. I take aim.

My shoulder kicks, something small hits me in the face, but it works. It works! I quickly put in another one, and do it again, ready for the power this time. My heart racing, and ears ringing with the noise, the thrill of this cold, shocking, real deliverance from evil, the bold potential I have created *out of nothing*, I take the charred and tiny pieces that are left of that little phone bomb and throw them in my bag. No one can contact me now. No one can follow or comment on me anymore. And for that, I give myself a million likes.

30

Monday morning.

I'm not like those other guys. I'm not going to get decked out in camo and wear a bullet belt and do a YouTube video proclaiming that this is the Reckoning and everyone is going to pay for my misfortune.

I am nothing like them. I am like no one. I am Stevie. I am Dee. She is me. Any doubts I have are pushed down. She stomps on them, and I feel her eagerness. We are one.

I put on the shirt I have planned just for the occasion. I put my jacket over top. I pick up my bag and relish in the weight of it. I have prepped the gun: added some gunpowder for extra power. Filled the bag with my colorful, celebratory ammo, ready to light up the world.

I leave something for Mom. Nothing big. It's just a bag of popcorn and a poster of that mom-and-daughter flick she loves, *Terms of Endearment*. I MISS YOU. It's lame, maybe, but true. There really isn't more to say than that.

Everything is in hyper focus. I am aware of my every move. I look outside and see that the neighborhood has come alive; it looks so colorful. It is sunny and warm, and kids are chatting as they walk to school, parents are leaving for work, and joggers weave around everyone, their feet pounding *slap, slap, slap*. I close and lock the door, and I am thinking of only one thing. Nothing about what will happen after, or what has gone on before. I am the present. I am focused. I put my earbuds in and look straight ahead, the songs of my vengeance in my ears.

As I get closer to the school, other students start to look at me. They are staring, but I am immune. My blood is pumping through my body like a beat. Someone jogs up beside me, grabs me, and I start, whipping around to see Ava, her hand on my arm. She is talking, but I can't hear her. I shake her off and keep going. *Stay focused, Stevie.*

The bell rings; I can hear it dimly over the music. I am a magnet, and people are watching me, waiting, and trying to get my attention. I walk past my locker and straight into homeroom, finally taking off my earbuds.

Pete sees me, and I know he doesn't know exactly what's different or why, but his Spidey sense is tingling.

"Feeling better, Stevie?" he asks.

There is murmuring from the people around me.

"Feeling great," I say, meeting his eyes. He nods and returns to the tasks at hand, shuffling paper, calling attendance. I turn and look at Aidan, unblinking, waiting. He smirks and looks away, fiddling with the pencil on his desk.

I know there are eyes on me, and people are tapping away at their phones to friends in other classes. My body is buzzing.

"Okay, folks!" Pete announces to the class. "Settle down, settle down. Okay, so I know you're all excited about presenting your media assignments to the class, and so am I!" There is more whispering and some nervous chatter.

"Now, where shall we begin?"

They are all watching me, my classmates. I can feel them zeroing in, talking, wondering.

"Wow, you're a lively bunch today." He waits. "Who wants to go first?"

He scans the room. A couple of tentative hands go up. Those people who want to get it over first, who might be more nervous than anyone about speaking in public, and also those who are proud of the work they did.

I put my hand straight in the air. This is my moment. This is my time. My ears are roaring as Pete's eyes meet mine. He raises his eyebrows and I see his mouth is saying *Stevie?*

I stand up. The room falls silent.

It is now.

I shirk off my jacket, and some people gasp.

I am wearing a white T-shirt. It's the best kind to show off the red marker, the big, capital letters I scrawled on the front.

CRAZY BITCH

I look straight at Aidan. He stares back, his chin up, his face betraying nothing, but I see his Adam's apple jump as he swallows. I walk to the computer on Pete's desk to call up my presentation video. People are whispering and holy-shitting. I see a phone in my peripheral as someone takes a picture of me. Pete tries to regain control. The projector light is in his eyes. He raises a hand to shield them.

A picture of a face is frozen on the screen. It's me, passed out. From one of the pics taken of me at the party. It's blurry, but it's me. My mouth lolls open; I look like a little girl dozing. There are more gasps, exchanged looks.

Pete glances at it, too, but is focused on my shirt right now. "Stevie, that's not an appropriate T-shirt, even if you're wearing it as part of your presentation. I mean," he says, "I'm all for edgy commentary, but let's please be mindful of offending or triggering anyone."

I smile, then, thinking about my secret, my special thing, lying in my bag, ready to pounce. Pete doesn't know. He knows nothing of what's been going on. Like every other grown-up around here, he's the last one to know about the burbling under-current of activity outside his radar. He was always there for me, but now he's so far away that he might as well be a stranger.

He's leaving me like everyone else.

I laugh, and it sounds strange in my ears.

And then I say, looking at my peers, my classmates, my friends: "Want me to take it off? I have the same thing written on my body, and it seems permanent."

Everyone is still. You could hear a pin drop. No one will tell. No one says anything.

I didn't do anything, they're thinking.

They did everything.

They did nothing.

"Stevie? Is this part of a character? Is this a theme?

I don't answer.

He pauses. "Okay, you know what? Go ahead." He sighs, sitting on the edge of his desk. "Push the theatrical envelope. It's the end of the year, thank God."

There is a long pause, during which I could change my mind, and I almost do. My chest tightens. I feel a rush of sad-ness, of fear, regret. I am so nervous.

I wait a moment. Then I walk, trembling, to the light switches and flick them down, casting us into darkness. Our classroom door, like all of them, has a small lock. Whenever we have lockdowns, teachers push the button in, locking us inside.

I stand with my back to it, reach back and quietly lock it. And with a tiny click that only I can hear, with that small noise, she's back. Dee. Giving me courage, helping me find my voice.

People look at each other; someone laughs nervously.

I stroll over to the computer and press play. My face on the screen slowly changes to a still from *Carrie*. Her anguish is splashed across the screen, in all her bloody, holy glory.

I look out at them.

There is music, while the faces of heroines of on-screen vengeance flicker in the darkness on the screen. It is loud, pounding.

Say it, says Dee.

I open my mouth and pull the tie that has been holding me together. My voice is loud and clear. I look at these people in front of me. They are all still. They are listening. Dee is speaking through me.

"I hid from you, but you found me."

I am moving around the room.

"I cried, and you laughed."

I walk between the rows of desks, speaking loudly, heads swiveling to watch me.

"I stood up, and you pushed me down."

Breanne, her eyebrows raised in the universal sign for *what the hell is happening?*

"I lay down, and you walked on me."

Paige is trying to exchange looks with her friends, but their eyes are all on me. I walk to the front of the room. Behind me, a flickering montage of the damned.

"I slept, and you robbed me."

I see Aidan's face, a mask of phony indifference, a small smirk on his face, refusing now to look me in the eye, but his leg is jiggling, I know he's scared. *But not scared enough*, Dee tells me.

The room is completely silent.

Pete is looking around. He's onto me now. He knows there is something more to this than art.

I stand in front of the door. I am reconsidering. I am scared. I reach into my bag and touch that perfect thing to remind myself. Its weight, its power. The thing that I made in the Makers' Space, with help from a gang of rebels and loners and losers and winners online. People who would hate me also. I am afraid. I swallow. I retract my fingers. I doubt. I can't.

But Dee can. Her fingers wrap around it. She pulls it out. She holds it high. And from here on out, she is in control.

They recognize it, even in its homemade glory: it is a gun.

There is a riot of screams and screeching chairs. All the lockdown drills come to life. They are on the floor, hiding behind chairs, under desks.

"Stevie," Pete shouts above it, but in a firm, calm voice. He is moving.

Dee holds the lighter up and points it at them.

"Who knew what was going on, but did nothing? Who knew the truth but didn't set it straight? Who saw my pain but didn't reach out to me?"

There is silence, a shaking, tearful, panicked silence. I can smell it on them. It is terror.

My voice is cracking and I ask again, "Who. Knew."

Sniffling and silent sobbing.

"You all did. You all knew, and you looked away. You left me all alone! You left me to disappear!" I scream, my voice breaking. "My friends. My enemies."

I whisper now. "I tried to teach you. I tried to tell you." There are tears pouring down my face. I can't see anything, hardly, anything at all, through them. "There is no justice. No one wins." I begin to drop the gun; I don't want this. But Dee lifts it back up.

She turns it now to Aidan, Paige, Breanne, all of them, swiveling it to and fro.

"You all," she barks, her voice firm and low, "on your knees."

Pete is now moving toward me so slowly that he thinks I don't notice. I hesitate, but Dee urges me on. *Don't fail me now,* she says. *Finish it.*

I flick the lighter, my hands shaking, and in one smooth motion point the gun at the ceiling. The fire ignites the gunpowder, sending an explosion into the water-stained white boards above us. A blast, a boom, dust everywhere, and now they are listening. Now they are paying attention. I am covered in white, and I shake it from my hair. I quickly refill the gun with another firecracker while the smoke clears.

"On. Your. Knees."

"Holy shit, holy shit!" People scramble.

"Oh God," someone sobs.

I hear footsteps in the hallway, in the adjoining room.

There is crying.

I feel a panicked urge to run, to stop this, but Dee pushes back, holds me firm.

I am fighting her. I am losing.

Pete's voice is quavering and he walks slowly forward with his hands out gently, like he's lost his sight and is finding his way, like he doesn't want to trip and fall.

"Let's think about this, okay?" he says. "Let's not do something that we'll regret. It's not too late to change our minds, okay? I'm here for you."

"I don't believe you," I say. "You weren't there. You left, Pete!" I cry out, my voice hysterical in my ears. "So stay, now,

Pete. On your knees." There are tears, or maybe it's blood running down my face.

He falls where he is, his hands still out, trying to placate me.

Aidan's large frame is crouching near the front of the room between two desks, close to Paige, who is shaking with sobs. He looks up at me and shuts his eyes tightly, shaking his head in fear. He gags, then, and vomit trickles from his mouth. There is rattling at the doorknob; someone is yelling and trying to get in. I hear sirens in the distance.

"You act like you care about things, but you can't see what's right in front of you. You never get to know anyone." I look up at the hole above me, lift the lighter again. I close my eyes and whisper, "Who knows Dee? Who knows me?"

The gun feels light, but I suddenly feel tired, weak. It is exhausting, this loneliness. This solitude. It is a burden. *I don't want this, Dee. Please. Just let it go. Let me go.*

There is someone at the door, screaming, "Get off me; that's my dad's class! Pete! Pete!"

It's Lottie. I pause, turning my head to the sound of her voice.

Something reaches me as if from a distance. I can't . . . It's a fog, a ringing in my ears. But. All the pain. All the hurt.

Stevie.

I just want a release. Relief. I don't want to hurt anyone.

You've gone this far. Come ON.

No. I want to stop, Dee.

The lighter is flicked. The wick is lit.

I take charge. I push her away.

I am Stevie, I say.

Pete lunges. There is screaming. There is an explosion. There is nothing.

* * *

PAIGE: I knew there was something that wasn't right about her. She thought she was better than everyone. I tried to include her and make friends with her, but she [indecipherable] away.

MATTHEW: She had been acting different over the last few months. I've known Stevie for a long time, but I think all the bullying really got to her. I just wish she'd talked to someone about it.

MARTA: No, I never could have predicted this. That's all I can say, sorry.

ANTAR: Please. Just leave us alone. This is too upsetting. Just [indecipherable] please.

LOTTIE: No comment. Get out of my way.

AVA: Yes, we were friends. Look, she's not a monster. Not at all. They all had it out for her for so long. It wasn't right. For a while she was trying to defend people, trying to put the shoe on the other foot, I guess, trying to make a difference. It got out of hand. And then . . . what they did to her . . . I'm so disgusted with the people at this school. The pictures they were sharing around, too. Those are the real monsters. I'm not forgiving or justifying what she did; I'm just saying that's not all she is. She is more than this.

JULY

31

From Salon.com:

Rape Culture made a girl school shooter, plain and simple. In last week's attack at Woepine High School in a small town in Ontario, students witnessed what is a rarity of its kind: not a gunman but a gunwoman, using a handmade gun. And while shootings are few and far between in Canada, there has been such a rash of school shootings and attacks in as many years in the United States that we've become desensitized to them. What they have in common is that the accused are overwhelmingly young, white men. So much so that there have been books, articles and movies about angry white men, a disenfranchised and misunderstood group, and what is troubling them as a generation, about toxic masculinity and its impact. Now we have a new problem on our hands, and it may well be thanks to the same guys. The shooter was bullied, harassed, and possibly assaulted. She took to violence—whether for the purpose of self-harm or harm against others might never be clear—as a means of pushing back.

We are accustomed to rape culture, that normalizing of violence and harassment against women. We are also accustomed to angry young people taking their furious revenge out on their peers. What we weren't ready for was the intersection of these two things, and for the attacker to be female, for her rage to be gender-based. But here we are: at a moment when the pressure cooker blows and young women are finally releasing the tension of years of abuse. We are post-Weinstein, post-#MeToo, post-Women's March, and now we are here.

We created an environment that left little choice and few options. We must shoulder some of the blame. (cont'd)

From CBC:

Following the violent attack by a student shooting a homemade weapon at Woepine High School last week, an inquiry has begun into one of the teachers who had associations with the alleged student attacker. The young woman remains in hospital. Peter Sherman (formerly Rhonda Sherman, following a recent public transition), who was injured in the attack while attempting to prevent the homemade firearm from being activated, also remains in serious condition at hospital and yet has come under fire by the school board for allowing students—including the student in question—after-hours access to an art studio where police suspect the weapon that was used in the attack was made.

A spokesperson for the school board explained that this access was not in the best interests of the students or their safety and that the policy around student access to dangerous equipment will be reexamined.

"We are all still healing from the shock of this tragedy in our small school and are trying to find out how something like this happened," she stated in an interview with CBC.

While administration and parents were aware of a culture of pranking at the school and were taking steps to change it, neither seemed to be fully aware of the scope of it, nor the specific actions perpetuated on anyone's or any group's behalf. (cont'd)

From Reddit:

TOrOntO1987: Big shock: a girl attacks other kids and goes fucking nuts and now she's the SJW's new feminazi hero claiming rape culture bullshit is the reason. If she was a guy they'd have cut off his balls.

URMOMStit: Rape culture is feminist for "Oops I drank too much." She couldn't fire the gun properly surprise surprise

Y3sIsaidiT50: Here she is in all her ugly glory (jpg) after passing out like a lightweight.

Ch3rrypOp: She's fucked up. And now there's a tranny teacher involved in the whole thing. I call bullshit.

* * *

I am everywhere online. I am a hero, a slut, a troll, a waste of space; people feel pity and anger and fascination with me. People hope I die. People wish I'd shot myself. People want whoever assaulted me to die, the privileged bros to die. People say it's about time a girl did this, that they aren't surprised a girl did this. People can't believe a girl did this. People say of *course* a girl did this. I couldn't even do it right. DIY gun guys mansplain the hell out of why my weapon blew up. People write think pieces on marginalized people seeking revenge. People talk about race and rape and shootings. People call me a terrorist and a feminist; people say they are the same word.

People analyze the role of transphobia in the discussion. People say this is what happens when freaks teach our kids. They post pictures of Mrs. Sherman and Pete, side by side. People think Pete is a deviant. People think Pete is a hero.

People don't blame me for what I did. Others do. People think our generation is spoiled and entitled. People are all obsessed with online bullying and gangs and how little parents know these days. There are charts and screenshots of all of the online behavior leading up to the "attack." There are pictures of all my revenge screen sirens with articles about violence in the media and its impact on young minds. Students at our school are shown tearfully holding each other in photos. They are interviewed as experts on me, on the school, on what happened. People have poured over my video channel looking for some secret evidence of mental illness, sadness, depression, aggression, plans for violence. They say I am crazy. They tell me in the comments that I should try again, but this time kill myself. They say I am the product of rape culture. They say rape culture is bullshit. They say I am ugly. They say I am beautiful.

They say nothing about Dee. They never knew her. She never showed herself to anyone but me, and now she is gone. Disappeared like she never existed. She was a casualty. It's hard for me to even call her face to memory. What did she look like again? What did she sound like? Gone. Fractals of color, 24mm per second, on the cutting room floor. Parts of me, edited out.

* * *

School is over. All the lockers have been scrubbed clean. Notices taken down. The graffiti power-washed off the bricks. The counselors, who came to school for the last few days, have left. The Makers' Space is closed indefinitely.

I know all this because Matthew has been here with me. Quiet, strong Matthew. I don't ask why he comes. I don't push it. I accept his presence. Visiting me. Visiting Pete. He reads silently beside me. He teaches me how to play Magic: The Gathering. Sometimes he shows me what people are saying online, until he decides I've seen enough. He says there is nothing good on there and he is right.

When I'm alone, I lie in my bed and stare at the hospital ceiling. I count the little holes in the discolored squares and remember how it looked when the same ones blew apart at school. I lose count and start again. I look out the window. I feel so much, and then so little: shame, self-loathing, disgust, anger, frustration, then nothing: medicated boredom. The days pass, clouds flitting across the sky, and mostly my mind is empty. I think nothing. I am holding myself, floating above it, because if I look down, I'll feel everything. It is too deep, too far.

Mom, meanwhile, hasn't tired of telling the media to fuck off her property, away from the hospital, off the phone, telling them it's their fault this all happened, as though I'm Lady Diana and they're the paparazzi. She wants to start a group for parents who want to learn about digital literacy, and I just can't wait for her to tell me that I should really change my passwords regularly.

"I broke up with Reg, honey," she says one day, two weeks after, surprising me out of a nap.

"Oh yeah?" I say, sleepily, finding my voice out of the fog of painkillers.

"Yeah," she says, rubbing the fingers on my good hand. "Who needs the hassle." She waves a hand in forced carelessness.

And then I say the thing I say all the time. "I'm sorry. I'm sorry for making it hard for you."

"Oh, never mind. It's not the right time for dating!" she says, overly cheerfully. Then she pauses. "I want to spend all my time with you, Stevie." Her voice is breaking now, and her hand is squeezing mine. "I'm going to suffocate you with love until it drives you crazy. Well. Not *crazy* crazy, but, you know."

I laugh a little and nod.

I am protected because I'm a juvenile, or what they call a young offender. The press won't print my name because of this, but that doesn't matter. Everyone knows my name. Everyone knows that I have a mole beside my belly button. Everyone has seen the photos. But I am protected from worse, I guess. Not charged as an adult. Saved from prison. I will spend a month of days at a juvie center once I'm recovered from my injuries, plus what works out to about a year of community service. There they will work with me on my mental health, on my regret, on pain, I'm told. There will be other girls there who have committed crimes, and we will do group therapy together. It feels so far away from where I am now that I don't think about it.

I'm still in that criminal no-man's-land between childhood and adulthood, where kid games nod to sexual violence, where braided hair passes self-harm in the hallway. There won't be a trial, because I pled guilty. Guilty of mischief, assault, but not attempted murder, which no one charged me with. It was a botched teenage suicide, a girl whose mind was bent by trauma in a moment of desperation. Bent and mangled. Like my bike. It was an accident, they say. I won't be sent to jail but have been given a lifetime sentence of shame, or so it looks from here.

It wasn't quite how I'd imagined it going down. I didn't think that I'd end up losing most of my right hand and getting burns all over my arms, one leg, and part of my face, as though Dee was quite literally blasted away.

The homemade gun had only a couple of shots in it, if that, not that anyone really knows that. Who would I choose? Aidan was crying like a baby. Breanne was under her desk in a puddle of pee. Paige was praying. I see this all, over and over in my head, like a movie, my own, awful movie. And what was the plan? To choose one person, or to scare them all? I thought I'd decide in the moment, but the moment was too much for me. Too terrible and painful. I couldn't make any choices.

In those last seconds, before Pete grabbed me, I won out over Dee. I tipped the gun upward, toward my chin; I decided not to hurt anyone but myself and her. It wasn't the plan either, but in the end, when I heard Lottie's voice through the door, I saw no way out. The wick had already been lit; it was too late. I needed to end it, and Dee, end it all.

But then Pete had me, and the gun exploded in a way it hadn't the night before. The whole thing blew up. Pieces of shrapnel flew everywhere. There was blood on everything, mine and Pete's, and more. There was a dull noise. There was a lot of movement. My eardrums were temporarily blown by the noise. My senses were foggy and blurred. People rushed around. There were sirens. It went black.

I thought I would ride out of the school on a rocket fueled by my own outrage and pain, that justice would prevail and I would feel something different, something more, something less than pain and sadness. That it would go away. I thought that none of our acts of justice, none of the vengeance was big enough, and so I needed to go bigger, to blast it all away. To cleanse myself. Start fresh. But the pain didn't go anywhere. I know now that it will always be a part of me. Part of who I am. Scar tissue.

And now I have daily meetings with a psychologist and a physiotherapist, both of whom work in tiny increments on improving my worldview. I have nightmares. In them, there are a whole bunch of tiny kittens, and they are close to a busy road, and I keep running into it to save them, but they keep getting hit by cars, and so I have an armload of maimed kittens, I'm covered in blood, and there are people screaming all around me. I don't mention this to the doctors but avoid looking at the motivational poster of a kitten in my room.

"I don't understand it all, but I get some of it," Matthew says one day, into the silence of the room. He is not looking at me. He's fiddling with the corner of a magazine on his lap.

I say nothing for a bit, and then, "You don't owe me anything."

"I know," he says, looking at me. "But we've known each other since we were little, Stevie."

His eyes are so big and honest, and it's all I can do not to start bawling, and then he says, "I'm your friend." He looks away while I wipe my eyes, then opens the magazine and starts to read.

Ava comes, too. She's always gone against the current, so I guess it's not that big a surprise. She said, the first time she came, "I'm sorry. I'm sorry I didn't know how bad it was."

"I thought I had it under control," I said quietly.

"They expect us to keep quiet," she said, gripping my hand. "I get how you got there. God, I get so angry sometimes, too. I mean, I could never do that." She meets my eyes, and I burn with shame.

Me either, I think, not knowing how I got there.

She continues. "But the pain. The anger. You are not alone in that. Half the world feels hurt and angry and we just normalize it. Girls are expected to just . . . keep going."

She is more political than I am. She articulates things, wants to talk in solidarity, wants to defend me, or at least explain me. I let her, just so relieved that I have a friend who made it through. The best is when we just share a laugh, or play a game, when we don't dig deep. When we are just girls. Just friends; that is all, and that is enough.

No one else visits me except Ava, Matthew, and my mom, and these days, that's ok. Dad came at first, but I told him I wasn't up for the visits, and he looked relieved. He calls every day, though, and we talk, and it is good.

I've become friendly with one of the nurses who isn't giving me the freeze the way the others are. I know they've all read the news; they know why I'm here. They all have their own opinions; nurses are not a timid bunch. They're not sure if I was trying to kill myself or everyone else.

I've gotten letters to the hospital from weirdos and perverts and feminists and people who love me and hate me, from all over the world, but none of them know me. Mom has been opening my mail and mainly throwing it all away. I expect my inbox has overflowed, that my presence on social has turned inside out with overuse. I can't imagine what's happened to my channel and then I don't care. I will take it down, or at least make it private. I don't want a presence anymore.

32

I t is a day, but I don't know which one.

I lose track of the days. There have been many of them. The nurse who likes me has come in to change my dressing. She has her hair sensibly tied back in a long braid. Her name is Geeta. She has a nice smile and a singsongy voice.

"Want to go for a stroll?" she asks me, and I shake my head. "Dr. Yang thinks it's important for your mental health to get up and around." Dr. Yang's a really nice woman who specializes in cases like mine, whatever that means.

Geeta pauses and looks out the door of my room. "Someone else could use a visit. He asks about you every day."

She's talking about Pete. I start to weep, and she puts a steadying hand on my arm. I cry all the damn time these days. Mom says it must be all the painkillers they have me on because her hormone replacement therapy makes her cry.

Geeta says, "It might be good for both of you."

"Okay," I mutter through the tears. "Yes."

She helps me into a wheelchair, and even though she's gentle, I wince as a jolt of pain runs up the length of my body. She squeezes my good shoulder kindly, in a way that's supposed to mean *come on, champ, you got this*. I nod. She pushes me down the hall, where I know Pete is. I've been avoiding his end of the hallway, choosing always to head in the opposite direction whenever I can. I haven't seen him yet. Geeta wheels me into his room, and it feels like I'm going to be sick. It's a shock, seeing him in bandages.

Lottie is there with her dad, Jacob. Her family. Jacob whispers a small hello, his face inscrutable. Lottie looks up, and she looks surprised, and concerned. There is love on her face, and it makes a small bridge between us. She checks with Pete quickly. His face is bandaged up, and much of his body. There is an IV taped to his hand, for pain, I expect. Same as me. When he speaks, he slurs a little.

"Stevie," he says, his voice soft, and I am crying harder now. And then he tries to say more, but then stops. His eyes are watering also. What a pair, we are. Jacob hands him a cup of ice water with a straw, and he drinks some. I look at Lottie, and she gives me a small ghost of a smile.

"Give him a minute," she says.

My mouth is dry, and I swallow, over and over again. Geeta wheeled me close to his bed, then left. He reaches for my good hand with his. He squeezes it.

"I'm sorry," I say, my voice thick. They are the limpest words in the world. "I'm sorry, Pete. I'm sorry to all of you." I look at them, my favorite family. "I wasn't—"

I wasn't what? Thinking? Myself? Who I thought I was? I wasn't okay? I wasn't sure? I'm still not. There are tears running down Lottie's cheeks. Jacob puts his arm around her.

"I'm sorry, too, Stevie," says Pete. This is the voice that has been comforting me my whole life. I am hanging on to his hand so tightly I'm afraid I'm hurting him. "You needed me, and I wasn't there for you."

I am nodding. I would nod at anything; my head is pounding with the effort of not sobbing uncontrollably. "You were going through your own stuff," I say.

"I was," he says. "I am. But I always have room for you, Stevie. Not to excuse what you did."

"I know." I know. I will always know. I can never not know again.

"We're gonna be fine, Stevie. We're gonna be just fine."

I hear a sob come from Lottie, and it is almost too much to bear, but I will bear anything from now on.

"Okay," I say, and hold his hand forever.

EPILOGUE

I t is the fall.

So much time passes during those weeks and months. There are surgeries and recoveries. I have lost the last three fingers of my right hand and now am adapting to what amounts to a kind of claw. I can't flip anyone the bird on that hand anymore, which is a bit of a shame, and I am trying to relearn how to do so many things. I can still make a gun symbol using my thumb and forefinger, which no one will find funny. I will have scarring on my arms and face and legs for the rest of my life. I look like a proper survivor or criminal, a gangster or a freak, depending on your point of view.

By the time I moved home again, the media circus had slowed down a bit. I mean, I'm not a headline anymore. Other people have done terrible, embarrassing, shameful things, and they have moved on to them. Most have, anyway. I know I'm still out there as a favorite topic and target, as a mascot and prop. I'm a celebrity to some, a disgusting villain to others. I looked a few times, and there are long, opinionated think-pieces about me. Well, not about me, but about what it means, what I did.

How they can use it as a mirror, how it fits into a larger picture, you know. A zeitgeist. A paradigm shift. A tipping point. A moment. I look away.

I went to the Youth Custody Centre every day for a month. Mom drove me, and I stared out the window while she chattered away nervously. It went by quickly. I met other "troubled youth" and noticed that we are all different, all the same: some were tough and mean looking, others quiet and broken. We were all some version of lonely, defensive, sad, regretful, but then, miraculously, hopeful that maybe we could change. Some of us were shy and reluctant to talk, and then, over time, we did. We talked about how we got there, what we did; we cried; we hugged each other. I didn't tell anyone about Dee, but I was honest about the rest. It was exhausting, like something had been leeched out of me, and I usually slept on the way home. I don't know if I'll see any of them again, or if I want to, but my faith in restorative justice is actually the only political position I have anymore.

I am taking time off school. Mom and I hang out. She's not a friend the way Lottie was, or Dee, but she's my mom. And I have Ava and Matthew now, and they come over when they can, and maybe, one day, I can reach out and find Lottie there. Maybe. Meantime, Mom and I do quiet crafts and play board games. She makes lunch, dotes on me, and I feel young and safe again. We spent one afternoon playing the Game of Life that she got from the Woepine Benevolent Fund, and even though it was missing a lot of pieces, we had a good time. Pretending we were making life choices and stuff. Matthew comes over and we play cards, although it's slow for me to master maneuvering them with my new hand. Ava and I listen to music and watch home improvement shows on TV, and it is relaxing and meaningless and exactly what I need.

One day, Mom comes into the living room, where I am resting on a big La-Z-Boy chair she got me. She's carrying a stack of DVDs, and she dumps them on the carpet.

"What d'ya got there?" I ask.

"The works. What do you feel like?"

I think about it. "How about *9 to 5*? I could go for a little Dolly."

She roots around the tapes, then holds one up triumphantly, singing the opening verse to the title song, shaking her hips in the worst Dolly Parton impersonation I've ever seen. I can't help smiling. She pops it in the DVD player and tells me to move over. I scoot my bum so she can squeeze into the chair with me. We watch the credits roll as Jane Fonda, Lily Tomlin, and Dolly all wake up to the same song my mom was singing. We smile and nod our heads. It's the perfect fluff for me these days.

"How are you feeling?" she asks, not taking her eyes off the screen.

"Good," I say. "Better." She doesn't ask better than when or in what way.

*   *   *

And somewhere during that day or another day, somewhere in that time we spend together, just the two of us again, we agree that it's time to move. We pack up the movies and the curlers, shove everything into boxes and scrawl on the front of them. When we back out of the driveway, down our street and past Lottie's house—the treehouse, and Martha the tree, and the screen door that I will hear bang shut in my dreams—I swallow hard but am okay. Some things you just can't get back.

*   *   *

Mom found a townhouse in a nice neighborhood about forty-five minutes away. It's actually not all that far from Dad, and he sent me a bunch of random emojis the day we moved in, mostly of food and balloons, but none to do with houses, which cracked me up. Mom set my equipment up for me, and she did a pretty good job. But she put all the movies in the family room because, she said, that's where we'll have our family movie nights. We started the night we moved in. I suggested *Gremlins* and dill pickle popcorn.

I know that Mom will meet someone else, and that it can't always be the two of us forever, but for now it is, and it's good. We go on walks together, and she sometimes reads the same books as I do, and we'll talk about how much we liked them or didn't. She doesn't feel sorry for me or bring up what I did. We don't talk about it. I know that she's taken a break from social media, too; she said it was full of bitches, which I guess means she was getting some blowback. We are the same, but different. We try not to dig too deep; we just look ahead.

Our new neighborhood is all right. I know that everyone here knows who I am and why I'm here. We didn't go far enough to escape that. But people mostly just avoid me, and that's fine with me so far. And Ava and Matthew take the bus to visit, and that is good.

I am doing community service at the library. When I got the job, the librarian, Miss Dorothy, told me I'd be a page.

"A Paige?" I repeated, dumbfounded.

"Yes, a page." She smiled and told me the duties required.

There is a lot of work using hands: shelving the books, typing, sorting, so I mainly use my good one for that. I like the job. It's relaxing and quiet—two things I now want more than anything else. Since Dee left the picture, I feel like the girl from *The Exorcist*, post-exorcism, without the pea soup. Maybe it's the antidepressants, but the fire isn't in me anymore. Sometimes I'll get a little spark, a jolt of anger or sadness, but then it just fizzles out and I return to this life. A quiet life. I put aside books on the cart while I'm shelving them in case I want to sign them out later.

Once, a group of girls who had been huddled at a table whispered to me as I pushed by with a cart of books that needed reshelving.

"Are you that shooter girl?" one said, as her friend elbowed her, shushing her.

I stopped and looked at them. They were smiling nervously at me. They looked familiar, like so many kids I knew. Like me, like Lottie and Paige, like Marta and Ava. Like Dee.

"I used to be," I said, then pushed the cart past them and into the stacks.

People stare at me out in public. Once, when I was walking to the library, a bunch of kids threw a cold coffee at me out a car window and yelled a miserable stream of insults. They missed, and after they drove off, I watched the ice cubes and coffee snake into the cracks in the sidewalk.

School started, but I'm taking a year off to be home-schooled. Mom and Dad and the therapist had long conversations about my recovery, and they found a tutor who is in university and who seems perfectly normal. She is so nice to me that I think I'll look forward to my lessons, or at least won't dread them. Her name is Amanda. She wears glasses and is studying kinesiology.

I stopped making videos. I made my channel private. But it's there, an archive. It's hard to get away from your old self, I guess. Sometimes we just pile more on top, get new layers. I still like movies, but they don't mean as much as they used to. I can't remember feeling that passionate about them, about anything. I didn't put all my posters up in my new room. I've left it clean and plain for now. I'll see what fills it up as time goes on.

Pete called. He's recovered really well from his burns, he said. Has scarring, but said it gives him character. He offered for me to join him at his new school, when I'm ready. He didn't even make any conditions. He just said that I have to promise to keep going to my therapist. He even made a crack that he can take me, if I start getting ideas. I said that I'm happy to go to the high school closest to my new house, but it was really nice of him to call.

I wondered if Lottie was there when he did.

᛫ ᛫ ᛫

I know I did something terrible. Lots of terrible things, really. Felt terrible things. And terrible things were done to me, right? People argue about how bad: it wasn't *that* bad, or it was *really* bad. Or that there were many things, death by a thousand cuts. How bad does it have to be for us to do something? How much bad? How bad can we be in return? Can anything be evened out? They talk about mental health, they talk about guns. I slip away from all of it. When I am alone and feeling scared, everything that happened leading up to what I did fills up my head again like water, and I worry that the thoughts will trap me and I can't breathe or swim up to the top, where the fluorescent lights are shining down, like at the school pool. But I'm trying to find ways to get air. Ways to keep moving forward, if not moving on.

In the end, I didn't try to find out who had done what they did to me at the party. The police talked about the dissemination of child pornography, but the people in the pics are blurry and difficult to distinguish. It was hard for me to tell, too. I didn't press any charges. An investigation would be worse than the whole thing in the first place. The police weren't surprised. They shook their heads and said this happens all the time, and I thought, I bet it does. People are afraid. No one knows what is going on in anyone's home, in anyone's school, in anyone's heart. *Everything okay?* We pack our lunches and go to school and spend all our waking hours pretending that nothing is happening, to us or anyone else. And then, sometimes, we get a nice, cool afternoon, where we watch TV or hang out by the lake, and maybe it *is* all okay, just for then, just for that time.

The day I got home from the hospital, the first thing I saw was my bike, its frame and wheel bent at an odd angle. And then, a couple of weeks ago, Pete came by our new house, and he took the bike. He had it fixed for me, saying that it was his moving truck's fault it was busted up in the first place. He had it delivered back to me, repainted and everything. It took a long time before I could ride it, but now, finally, I can, my finger and thumb gripping the handle, the air cooling the healing scars on my face. It looks different, but good, the bike. It feels almost perfect some days. And even thought I know it's not, that it's the same broken bike inside, I keep pushing those pedals just like it's not.

Riding all over, around my new town, and home again.

Dear Reader,

There is pain in this book. It might be familiar to some and foreign to others. It is my hope that by shining a light on aspects of the world we share—on some of our pain—that we might see shades and variations rather than simply light and darkness.

My interest in writing this novel was to push back on the question often asked by individuals and the media when it comes to bullying and violence. Some of us have been asked the question ourselves: "Was it really that bad?"

We all have different bars set for how "bad" things need to be to justify the actions of others. I don't have the answer, and neither do the characters in this book. They do, however, ask you to consider that to suffer alone, and without the empathy of others, is "that bad". It is the worst of all.

To find people who will stand by us, come what may, they are worth everything.

As Stevie would say, they are all the heart emojis. And a couple of unicorns.

Yours,
Laurie Petrou

ACKNOWLEDGMENTS

Stevie took a piece of me; she became a piece of me. That's what writing is. Yes, she's fictional, but I'd like to thank her anyway, for helping me reconsider things I thought I knew or believed.

The first real person I'd like to thank is my dynamo agent, Martha Magor Webb, who is wise and kind and damn good at her job. I owe you such a debt, MMW.

Thank you to my editor at Crooked Lane Books, Chelsey Emmelhainz, who never once doubted this novel and to the whole Crooked Lane Books team: I am so happy we found each other. Thank you for all your tireless work.

To Helen Reeves, Plot Doctor, my continual thanks for asking frustrating questions that need answering.

Thanks to Elan Mastai, Duana Taha, Sandra Ingram, and as always, Nicole Bell, for reading early drafts that ranged from ramblings to ideas to half-formed concepts. Love and gratitude to Celeste Taylor and Carter Weston. Your insight was invaluable and means so much to me.

To my support system: my girlfriends and my family—immediate, extended, and chosen. To Mom and Dad and Mike and more. I thank my lucky stars that I have you all in my life.

And finally, first, and always: Eli, Leo, and Jay. Ours is a house full of books, stories, readers, and storytellers. Thank you for all of it. May it always be so.